The First Kiss

"We should go back, Roger. They will be wondering where we are."

Roger laughed. "Oh, I think they know where we are, love." He tucked her hand in the crook of his arm, bringing her so close that she felt the movement of his hip against her as they walked.

This was all highly improper, Jane thought, but the unexpected contact gave her so much dizzying pleasure that she would not protest for all the tea in China. This was Roger, after all. *Her* Roger, who would in a few short weeks be *her* husband.

Jane felt suddenly light-headed. She was walking on air. For a heady moment all her doubts about the man at her side disappeared, and she let herself soak up the sensual pleasure of his touch. When they reached the horses, she was intensely aware of his hands on her shoulders, turning her gently to face him, his fingers tilting up her face to his. She lost herself in the blue depths of his eyes, her pulse fluttering wildly, and abandoned herself to him with a tiny sigh of rapture. . . .

Coming next month

THE DUKE'S WAGER & LORD OF DISHONOR
by Edith Layton

For the first time, two Regency novels by acclaimed author
Edith Layton—together in one volume!

"One of the romance genre's greatest storytellers."
—*Romantic Times*

0-451-20139-6/$5 50

THE SELFLESS SISTER
by Shirley Kennedy

Lucinda Linley faces spinsterhood after putting her younger
sisters' marriage prospects ahead of her own. Then she finds
true love with the Lord of Ravensbrook—but will a long-
standing family feud impede their future happiness?

"Shirley Kennedy's Regencies are a delight."
—*Debbie Macomber*

0-451-20138-8/$4 99

THE MAJOR'S MISTAKE
by Andrea Pickens

Major Julian Miranda accepts a long-term army commission
after catching his wife in what appears to be a very compromising position. Seven years later the couple meets again. But
will it be pride—or passion—that wins the day?

0-451-20096-9/$4 99

To order call: 1-800-788-6262

Lady Jane's Nemesis

Patricia Oliver

A SIGNET BOOK

SIGNET
Published by New American Library, a division of
Penguin Putnam Inc., 375 Hudson Street,
New York, New York 10014, U.S.A.
Penguin Books Ltd, 27 Wrights Lane,
London W8 5TZ, England
Penguin Books Australia Ltd, Ringwood,
Victoria, Australia
Penguin Books Canada Ltd, 10 Alcorn Avenue,
Toronto, Ontario, Canada M4V 3B2
Penguin Books (N.Z.) Ltd, 182–190 Wairau Road,
Auckland 10, New Zealand

Penguin Books Ltd, Registered Offices:
Harmondsworth, Middlesex, England

First published by Signet, an imprint of New American Library,
a division of Penguin Putnam Inc.

First Printing, July 2000
10 9 8 7 6 5 4 3 2 1

Contents

Dedicated to Lynde Lakes—
a friend in a million.
Thanks, Lynde.

Chapter One

The Mistress

Penhallow, Devon, April 1816

The early spring sun felt pleasantly warm on Lady Jane Sinclair's face as she rode leisurely through the scattering of ash and horse chestnut trees bordering the small stream dividing Penhallow from the Trenton estate to the north. She had originally been drawn away from the monograph she was writing on native Devonshire wildflowers by the prospect of discovering early specimens for sketching. So far, however, she had been unsuccessful.

The woodland along the stream had yielded little besides primroses, the sweet-scented bluebells carpeting the woodland floor, and a few white oxalis, all of which she had already sketched. Lady Jane had hoped to find a fully blooming specimen of the exotic *arum*, known locally as Lord-and-Ladies, but the only plant she came across still had its greenish-white flower-hoods tightly furled. She made a mental note to return in two or three days to gather the mature flower.

She was about to turn back, for it was getting on towards tea-time, when a splash of bright purple beneath a scraggly elderberry caught her eye. Nudging her mare up beside the bush, which had not yet opened its clusters of tiny creamy flowers, Jane slid down and bent to examine the plant. Elated, she confirmed her suspicion that she had stumbled across an early purple orchid, the first of its kind to bloom in the spring. Gently separating the black-spotted leaves, she spent a moment admiring the beauty of the flower before breaking the tender stalk.

The orchid would take her some time to sketch, she mused, examining the cluster of purple flowerets on the single stem. She would do so directly after tea, eager to add another illustration to her collection.

Jane had remounted and turned Primrose's head towards home when she saw the mare's ears twitch nervously. A moment later, she heard a rich female laugh ring out from beyond the thicket of dogwood that hid the stream from view.

Curious and not a little apprehensive, Lady Jane urged Primrose through a gap in the thicket. The mare's ears swiveled forward, and she let out a soft snort as she stared at the opposite bank of the meandering stream. Jane's gaze froze, and her breath caught in her throat as she discovered the source of the laughter. One swift glance was sufficient to take in the indecorous scene playing out on the greensward beneath an ancient oak, whose spreading branches provided a natural bower for a secret rendezvous.

The cause of that wanton laughter was obvious.

A lady sat on a tartan rug spread beneath the oak, the bodice of her muslin gown bunched around her waist. Jane gazed in fascinated horror at the flawless white skin of her back, dappled by sunlight filtering through the branches. But it was the hand that mesmerized her, a big, tanned, unmistakably masculine hand that trailed tantalizingly down the length of the lady's back, causing her to squirm and giggle, and occasionally let out a delighted, seductive laugh that raised goose bumps all over Lady Jane's body.

Jane could not see the man's face, hidden as it was behind the lady's bare torso, but the lady herself was easily recognizable. No other female in or around Torrington had hair that precise shade of red. Jane had envied it the moment she laid eyes on Maud Danvers, the buxom widow who had been taken in by Sir Giles Horton after the death of Captain Danvers—Sir Giles's godson—on the Peninsula. Soon after—far too soon, according to the local gossips—the widow had become Lady Horton. This development had surprised nobody in the neighbourhood, for Sir Giles was reputed to be very plump in the pocket, and the widow must have seen her chance and taken it.

Few had faulted her for seizing the opportunity to better herself, since it was rumoured that Maud Danvers' father had been a butcher over in Appledore on the coast. Lady Jane had encountered enough male opposition in her own life to feel immediate sympathy for the widow's plight, but her enthusiasm soon dwindled when the new Lady Horton had confided one afternoon, over tea at the vicar's, her intentions of producing a child with the old man to ensure her position at Horton Hall.

Jane had been shocked at such an immodest confession. She had secretly wondered how one went about enticing an ancient, semi-bedridden gentleman, who never ventured anywhere without his Bath chair, into one's bed to consummate the act that, Jane had discovered when she was fifteen, was a prerequisite to becoming *enceinte*. Evidently Lady Horton had found the way, because she had made much of her happy condition over the past months and had seemed to take particular pleasure, much to Lady Jane's embarrassment, in keeping the latter *au courant* of every minute development of her increasing.

Watching the amorous antics of the couple under the oak, it suddenly dawned on Jane that perhaps poor Sir Giles had taken no hand in his young wife's condition. The thought shocked her sensibilities, and raised all sorts of questions for which she had no answers. It also brought her thoughts back to the gentleman whose hand had begun another leisurely trajectory down Lady Horton's back. Who was he? she wondered, mentally searching for a likely candidate from the lady's long list of admirers. Try as she might, however, Jane's thoughts returned time and time again to one gentleman.

With growing dismay, she let her gaze wander to

the male form reclining languidly on the rug behind
Lady Horton in hopes of finding something unfamiliar.
Although she could still not see his face, she could
certainly see his long legs, encased in pale buckskin
breeches, defining a narrow waist and a pair of strong,
shapely thighs. Jane remembered ruefully the many
occasions she had secretly admired those manly thighs.
She felt her face color at the immodesty of the
thought. What was the matter with her? After all,
many gentlemen wore pale buckskins with top-boots.
Her eyes focused on these particular boots, shining
black in the sunlight, and her heart stopped. How
many gentlemen of her acquaintance flaunted those
silver tassels? Only one whom she knew of. And she
had good reason to know him, Jane reminded herself doggedly.

She was betrothed to him.

Dragging her gaze from the scene across the stream,
Jane carefully pulled on the reins until Primrose sidled
backwards out of sight of the couple disporting themselves on the opposite bank. Resisting the urge to clap
her heels to the mare's flanks and race blindly towards
the sanctuary of Penhallow's halls, Jane held Primrose
down to a walk, fearful that the couple might realize
they had been observed at their illicit dalliance.

Another peal of laughter, tapering off into an unladylike giggle, assaulted Jane's ears and caused a glossy
blackbird to take flight from the elder bush with an
angry screech of protest. Jane cringed at the sound of
the woman's laughter, the scene under the oak all too
fresh in her mind. Even had she tried—and Jane *had,*
innumerable times in the privacy of her chamber—to
infuse those suggestive, seductive, inviting undertones
into her own laughter, she was not at all convinced
that she could bring herself to laugh that way in the
presence of a gentleman. The very thought of such
impropriety gave her palpitations. Not even with
Roger had she ever comported herself with such levity, although she had known him all her life.

The thought of Roger brought a lump to her throat,

and for a moment Jane struggled with the urge to weep. She had always despised females who were forever dabbing at their eyes with damp pieces of lace, and she could not bear the thought of turning into a watering-pot herself. Determined to resist the temptation, she flicked the reins, and a startled Primrose broke into a canter that soon became a headlong gallop, as though the mare sensed her rider's distress.

By the time she had raced through the wood, across the north meadow, and along the lane bordering the tenants' cottages, scattering hens and children in her wake, Lady Jane was able to face the under-groom in the stable-yard with relative composure.

"Give her an extra measure of oats tonight, Tom," she told the boy who ran forward to take Primrose's reins as Lady Jane dismounted. "She has had a good run today."

The boy touched his forelock but grinned impishly, spoiling the effect. Like so many of the Sinclair retainers, Tom had been born and raised on the estate and had served Lady Jane since her father put her on her first pony.

"Whatever ye say, milady," he responded, his grin widening, "but it ain't more oats that fat old Primrose be needing, but more exercise. Leastwise that is what me dad said only yesterday."

"Oh, he did, did he?" Jane said, glad of the distraction. "You may tell your father from me that Primrose is not fat, neither is she old. And she is to have her extra oats regardless of her size or age."

"Anything you say, milady," Tom said, unbuckling the mare's saddle. "But I warn ye, we shall have to get 'er a longer girth if she gets any fatter. This one hardly closes properly as it is."

"Well, by all means do so," Jane answered shortly. Tom's remark about exercising the mare had made her feel guilty. Her father had pointed out only that morning that she spent far too much time indoors with her scribblings—as he chose to call her scholarly pur-

suits—instead of out enjoying the fresh air and putting
a bloom in her cheeks.

" 'Tain't stylish to ride a fat 'orse," Tom continued.
"No wonder ye never join the 'unt, milady. Old Primrose ain't about to jump a 'edge to save 'er life. No,
sir."

"I have no taste for hunting, as you well know,
Tom, and as for jumping, I have no desire to break
my neck chasing after some poor fox."

"I daresay ye would change yer mind if ye was up
on that filly 'is lordship gave ye for yer birthday three
months ago, milady," Tom insisted with that familiar-
ity of old servants. "A prime piece she is and no mistake. Besides," the lad added with a sly twinkle in his
eyes, "Ginger is bound to take the shine out of that
flashy black gelding Lady 'orton rides around on. All
show and no bottom that black, me dad says."

Lady Jane paused, repressing the sharp rebuke that
rose to her lips. The disgraceful scene she had witnessed beside the stream must have addled her brains,
for she felt the odd and uncharacteristic urge to out-
shine Lady Horton on horseback, and the means were
well within her grasp. She could never hope to rival
her neighbour's way with gentlemen, nor was her figure in any way a match for Lady Horton's curvaceous
form. But Jane knew herself to be a more than compe-
tent horsewoman, although her first love was books
and writing. That could change, she mused, and Tom
was right, she did not cut a very dashing figure on
dear old Primrose.

Jane ran a hand over the mare's round rump and
had to admit that Tom was right about that, too. Primrose was indeed fat. On impulse, she smiled. "Very
well, Tom. You may saddle Ginger for me tomorrow,
and I will try out her paces in the pasture."

Tom grinned broadly. "Ye'll not regret it, milady."

Jane hoped that he was right again, for to tell the
truth, she was a little apprehensive about riding the
sleek young chestnut her father had surprised her with
last February. She had not yet ridden the mare, but

suddenly she felt eager to do so. Perhaps some of Ginger's elegance would brush off on her. Perhaps Roger would be impressed enough to ride with her as he used to do when they were children. Perhaps . . .

Jane pulled herself together abruptly. She must have windmills in her head to be daydreaming of Roger when she had only minutes ago witnessed the rogue in wanton dalliance with a married woman. He had no shame whatsoever, but Lady Jane Sinclair should have more respect for herself than to waste a single instant mooning over a blatant rogue and philanderer. What she should do, she told herself resolutely, was to insist that her father release her from that promise he had made years ago to his good friend, the Marquess of Trenton, to unite the two families through marriage.

The notion of dissolving her long-standing though unofficial betrothal to Roger Hastings aroused conflicting emotions in Lady Jane's heart. For as long as she could remember, she had harboured tender feelings for the dashing Viscount Summers, heir to the Marquess of Trenton. On the other hand, was she prepared to tolerate a husband who had no respect for marriage vows?

It was not until she reached her bedchamber and allowed her abigail to remove her riding habit and help her into an elegant afternoon gown of twilled sarcenet, embellished with yellow daisies, that Jane remembered the purple orchid she had gathered so carefully in the wood. It was nowhere to be found. Had it been lost during that wild gallop home? Or had she dropped it there in the dogwood grove as she stared, her emotions in a turmoil, at the man who filled her dreams shamelessly making love to another woman?

Twenty minutes later, her mind still unsettled, Lady Jane entered the drawing room to find her aunt Lady Octavia Sinclair seated on the blue damask settee, her favourite pug, Sunshine, on her lap.

"My dear Jane," Lady Octavia began as soon as her niece took her place before the tea-table and signaled the butler to arrange the tea-tray within reach, "I declare you look positively fatigued. I trust you have not worn yourself to a frazzle riding around in search of those flowers you are forever sketching. It is not natural to spend so much time alone, dear. Your father does not approve of all this scribbling you do, Jane, and I must admit that I agree with him in this. Your watercolours are charming, but you should be turning your mind to other ladylike occupations, like ordering your bride clothes and setting a date for your nuptials with Roger."

"Is Papa to join us for tea, Aunt?" Jane changed the subject hastily. She had been counting on her aunt's support in her attempt to convince her father to release her from the tenuous understanding he had agreed to when she was barely a child and unable to defend herself.

"Why must you always change the subject when I mention your marriage, Jane?" Lady Octavia wanted to know. "All the girls I know of your age are already settled and have started their nurseries. I cannot understand why you insist upon writing about silly flowers, and wild ones at that. Who could possibly care whether primroses bloom in June or July?"

"They bloom in April, Aunt," Jane corrected her automatically. "Sometimes earlier if the winter has been mild."

"Let them bloom whenever they will," her aunt responded with a snort of impatience. "I fail to see why you must spend so much time with your sketch-pad instead of at your embroidery as a well-bred young lady should. Or at your scales, dear, since your playing leaves much to be desired. And you know how important it is for a young wife to be prepared to entertain her guests after dinner."

"I should remind you, my dear Aunt, that I am not a wife," Jane said with no little asperity. "And with your support—which I confess I had counted on—

many a year will pass before I become one, if ever I do."

Lady Octavia stared at her niece, a startled expression on her pleasantly plump face. "Never say you intend to defy your father, dear," she gasped faintly. "It will not fadge, believe me. I know my brother too well to place any reliance on him changing his mind once it is made up. And it was made up years ago on the subject of your betrothal to young Hastings, in spite of your dear mother's protests."

"I have no intention of wedding Roger, if that is what you mean, Aunt," Jane stated with more bravado than conviction. "He is the world's worst libertine—"

"You must not listen to local gossip, my dear Jane," her aunt broke in gently. "I, too, have heard those malicious rumours of Roger's little peccadilloes. Believe me, there is probably not a grain of truth to them, and if there were, you can take it from me that it is natural for a young gentleman of his rank to indulge in a little innocent flirtation now and then. Nothing to put you in such a pucker, dear."

"Well, there you are mistaken, Aunt," Jane replied with alacrity. "There is nothing innocent about Roger's flirtation with Lady Horton. Have you not seen them together?"

Lady Octavia looked uncomfortable. "I confess I have always considered Lady Horton to be not quite the thing, dear. I cannot imagine what poor Sir Giles saw in her, and I can understand why your father has forbidden us to invite her to Penhallow. She comes from working-class stock, and it is a waste of time to expect her to comport herself like a lady. She always manages to offend my sensibilities."

"Then I am glad you did not have to witness her frankly scandalous behaviour down by the stream this afternoon," Jane said vehemently. "Your sensibilities would not have withstood the shock, Aunt."

"I trust you were not spying on poor Roger, dear,"

her aunt said reprovingly. "A lady should never lower herself to such tactics, you know. It is most improper."

"I was not spying on anyone, Aunt. I went into the woods down by the stream to see if I could find an *arum maculatum,* or Lords-and-Ladies as they are called around here."

"There is no need to pour all that Latin gibberish into my ears, child," Lady Octavia protested crossly. "I know very well what Lords-and-Ladies are. Horrid-looking things, I always thought. Witches' baskets, we used to call them as children, I recall. You did not find one, I take it?"

"No, I found something far more shocking." Jane paused, Lady Horton's seductive peal of laughter still ringing in her ears. "I heard the laugh first. Oh, Aunt, you have no idea how tantalizing that laugh was."

"Oh, yes I do," her aunt shot back sternly. "I had the dubious pleasure of listening to her ladyship laugh at Mrs. Greenley's garden party last Saturday. She was amusing herself flirting with the two Downing boys, barely out of shortcoats, and beguiling that silly old fool Colonel Mason, who should know better than to ogle a woman forty years younger. Margaret Greenley should have more sense than to receive that woman. She is quite beyond the pale. Now, tell me what you saw in the woods, dear."

"She was sitting under one of those big oak trees on the Trenton side of the stream, laughing and giggling like a scullery maid. Quite disgusting she was, Aunt."

"I gather she was not alone, dear?"

Aunt Octavia's voice had become gentle, and Jane fought the tears that gathered in her eyes. She refused to weep over a worthless rogue like Roger, who obviously cared not a fig for her or any unspoken understanding that might exist between them.

"No, she was not alone," she said finally.

"I suppose Roger was there with her."

"Yes, he certainly was, but that is not the worst part." Jane felt her anger at Roger's perfidy stirring again, but far worse was her impotent rage at the female who all too plainly had Jane's betrothed so besotted with her person that he was behaving recklessly, with no concern for the scandalous rumours flying round the village. With no concern for her, either, Jane thought bleakly.

"Well?" her aunt interrupted impatiently. "Do not keep me in suspense, Jane. What was that wanton creature doing?"

"She was sitting there, bold as brass, her bodice down around her waist." Jane could not bring herself to describe the hand trailing down Lady Horton's back. As it was her colour rose at the mention of that lady's shameful state of undress.

Lady Octavia's eyebrows shot up in surprise, and her blue eyes bulged as though she had a fishbone lodged in her throat.

"Are you telling me that she was naked, child?" she croaked.

Lady Jane flinched at this plain speaking, and her blush became more pronounced. "Yes, Aunt, Lady Horton was definitely uncovered from the waist up. I saw her very clearly."

"And Roger?" her aunt queried, a salacious gleam in her eyes. "Was he naked, too?"

Lady Jane felt as though the air had been knocked out of her. The very notion of seeing Roger—or any other gentleman—unclothed gave her palpitations. She had, of course, wondered about such things when she was much younger, but more recently these improper speculations—particularly those concerning Roger—had caused her palms to grow damp and her heart to race with secret longings she refused to put a name to.

Fortunately, Featherburton chose that moment to enter the drawing room with a request from the earl, who wished to see his daughter in the library after tea.

Breathing a sigh of relief, Jane rose and followed the butler out of the room.

Chapter Two

The Betrothal

Lady Jane knew that her father was in one of his benign moods the moment she stepped into the library. Lord Penhallow was dressed for riding and had evidently just come in from the stables, for he still held his quirt in one hand. He turned to smile at his daughter as he poured himself a brandy at the sideboard.

"You missed your tea, Papa," she said brightly, returning his smile, "but I asked Featherburton to save some of Cook's raspberry tarts for you." She knew her father had a weakness for tarts and delighted in ordering them for him. Roger liked Cook's tarts, too, she recalled with a pang, but it had been several months now since he had stopped in to take tea with the Penhallow ladies.

"Good girl," the earl responded jovially. "I would have been home earlier, my dear, but Challenger threw a shoe up in the north meadow, and I had to walk him back."

Jane wondered whether her father had been in the woods, which lay beyond the north meadow. It was highly unlikely that he would say anything to her even if he had seen Lady Horton with Roger under the oak. Perversity made her remark with feigned casualness as she took a seat in one of her father's green leather chairs, "I had half expected Roger to take his tea with us this afternoon, but he must have had more important things to do."

Was it her imagination, or did the earl give her one of his penetrating looks in response to this comment?

Perhaps her voice had betrayed her bitterness. He said nothing, however, and soon broached what was on his mind.

"Jones tells me that you have ordered the new mare saddled for your ride tomorrow, Jane. I am glad to hear it. You have outgrown old Primrose these many years. Perhaps now you will join me in the hunt, dear. Trenton is holding his annual meet next week, and I would like you to accompany me. You will cut rather a dash on that Ginger. Jones assures me she is a prime jumper."

"I plan to put her through her paces in the paddock tomorrow, Papa, and if I feel she is right for me, I will certainly consider venturing out with you."

"It is high time you put away those books of yours, my girl," the earl remarked, as he had so many times before. "Besides, it is only fitting that you attend the Trenton Hunt, since you will be mistress over there one of these days."

Lady Jane saw the opportunity to broach the subject of her future and took it. "I doubt that will ever happen, Papa," she said with a nonchalance she did not feel. "It has been obvious to everyone for some time now that Roger's interests lie elsewhere."

Lord Penhallow looked uneasy. "Nonsense, child," he blustered, as he always did whenever he felt his wishes challenged. "You have too much sense to pay attention to local gossip, Jane. Roger will come about when he is ready, never fear. But in the meantime, it behooves you to make a push to be agreeable and not prose on forever about those silly plants of yours. Gentlemen are not interested in such things."

"How well I know it, Papa!" Jane exclaimed. "But I cannot believe that you wish me to be tied to a man who lives in the pocket of another. It is most humiliating to be subjected to the ridicule of the whole neighbourhood while Roger indulges himself in a scandalous affair with a married woman right before my very nose. I cannot be expected to tolerate it, Papa, and

must beg you to tell Lord Trenton that his son is not
acceptable to me."

Lord Penhallow drew himself up to his full height,
his face an unhealthy shade of red. Jane knew she had
offended him, but she was glad she had dared to make
her feelings known.

"You will do as you are told, young lady," her father said harshly. "Trenton and I made this arrangement the day you were born, and you will honour it
if I have to drag you to the altar."

He glared at her, his bushy eyebrows meeting in a
frown over his aristocratic nose, but Lady Jane returned his stare calmly. She knew her father well
enough to see that he was on the defensive and noticeably uncomfortable. She also knew that he would welcome a way to save face over the issue, but would, if
pushed, become stubborn and intractable.

"I understand that perfectly, Papa," she said gently,
"and under normal circumstances I would be in alt at
the prospect of having my future secured in such an
eligible match."

"And so you should be, girl," her father growled.
"Not every female can become a marchioness, as you
well know."

"Indeed I do, Papa," she replied mildly. "And I am
more grateful than I can ever say for your efforts on
my behalf. Mama always impressed upon me how fortunate I was to have a father who had my interests at
heart from the very moment of my birth." She paused,
noting that the colour had receded from his face and
his brows had retreated to their natural position.

At least she had averted an explosion of temper,
Jane thought. Her mother, carried off by an outbreak
of dysentery five years ago, would have understood
the necessity of glossing over the fact that Lord Penhallow and his lifelong crony, the Marquess of Trenton, had both been in their cups the night Jane was
born. It had never been established which of them
came up with the brilliant notion of sealing their
friendship with a union between their respective first-

borns, but the agreement had been duly recorded and
signed by both parties.

Jane had grown up knowing that she was promised
to Roger Hastings. It was, as far as Lord Penhallow
was concerned, a *fait accompli*.

Not so for Roger, Jane had discovered to her dismay on her thirteenth birthday. He had laughed at
her—quite rudely, too—when she had dared to mention her role in his future. He had later apologized,
of course, but she had vowed that the cows would
come home before she would again mention any understanding between them.

"The thing is, Papa," she said hesitantly, "that
Roger has formed what appears to be a *grand passion*
for another woman."

"Fiddlesticks!" the earl exclaimed impatiently. "Have
you not sense enough to know that Roger is merely
sowing his wild oats, girl? I confess he might be more
discreet about it, but you must rise above this youthful
exuberance, Jane, and focus on your future as mistress
of Trenton Abbey."

Jane sighed. It would be unthinkable to ask her father when she might expect to sow her own wild oats,
of course, but recently she had begun to wonder what
would be her fate if she refused to marry Roger. Or
rather if Roger, infatuated with his inamorata, refused
to honour his father's agreement. Jane was wise
enough to see that she herself had little choice but to
obey her father's wishes.

"I understand that, too, Papa," she said meekly.
"But rather than wait around here while Roger comes
to his senses, I was wondering if I might spend a few
weeks in London with Aunt Honoria. She wrote again
only yesterday to ask me whether I intend to wait
until I am irredeemably on the shelf before paying her
that promised visit. I thought that now would be an
ideal time to—"

"On the shelf?" The earl's voice rose to a bellow.
"How dare that old harridan insult you, my dear.
Honoria may be your dear mother's sister, but believe

me, she is a busybody of the first stare. Besides, since when is a gal of one-and-twenty on the shelf can you tell me? You are no longer a schoolroom chit, that I cannot deny, but—"

"I am five-and-twenty, Papa," Jane interrupted ruthlessly. "By any standards I am definitely on the verge of becoming an ape-leader, if indeed I am not so already."

"Five-and-twenty?" Her father gaped at her as if she had grown two heads. "B-but t-that is im-impossible, child," he stammered, running a hand through his greying hair. "Quite impossible," he repeated adamantly, as though his word alone would make it so.

"I know it seems only yesterday that dear Mama was taken from us," Jane said softly, "but it was five years ago, when I was twenty. And I clearly remember her reminding you of your promise to allow me at least one London Season before I wed Roger. Remember?"

The earl blinked at her, and Jane saw that her father's thoughts had retreated once again to his wife's deathbed, reliving that dreadful day when the world had come to a halt for both of them.

The sun was sinking behind the low-lying hills to the west, and a cool evening breeze had sprung up as Roger Hastings rode slowly home to Trenton Abbey that spring evening. His mind was in turmoil, and for the first time in his life he felt swept along by forces beyond his control.

If what Maud had told him that afternoon down by the stream was true—and Roger saw no reason why she should lie—he was about to become a father. The notion paralyzed him.

His life had suddenly turned into a morass of complications. It was not meant to be this way; indeed, Roger had always eschewed complications, particularly with females. He had considered himself an expert at manipulating the fairer sex, in getting what he wanted from them with the least possible fuss. It had always worked like magic, and Roger had grown to believe himself immune from the endless amorous entanglements his friends seemed to encounter.

Of course, his father's long-standing agreement with the Earl of Penhallow had shielded him from the usual assault of marriage-minded mamas. Besides, none of the marriageable females of his acquaintance could hope to compete with the earl's daughter, an heiress of quite astronomical proportions. Roger had always taken it for granted that eventually he would honour his father's agreement and marry the Sinclair chit. It would be convenient and comfortable, too. He had known Jane since she was in the nursery; there would be no surprises there. He had been quite content with the future that lay before him.

That was before he had returned from London last spring to find Maud Danvers installed at Horton Hall as the new Lady Horton.

Maud had changed his outlook on a number of things.

Roger remembered Maud from years ago, first as the wife of Lieutenant Peter Danvers, Sir Giles's orphaned godson, who had served—and later died—on the Peninsula with Horton's son Captain Stephen Horton, and later as Peter's widow. She had always been rather saucy, but last spring he had discovered just how wanton she had become.

At first it had seemed like an idyllic arrangement. Maud was a married woman and Roger was spoken for. He had foreseen no complications whatsoever to the brief, passionate affair that had erupted between them.

He had not counted on the overwhelming infatuation that had grown stronger with each clandestine rendezvous. What started out as a pleasant summer diversion had become an obsession, and by the time Michaelmas Day rolled around, Roger found himself taking increasingly wild risks to enjoy Maud's charms.

Risks like the one they had taken this very afternoon, for example. It was true that the romantic bower beneath the oak tree had seemed fairly safe from prying eyes, but few places were entirely safe, Roger knew from experience, having been caught in compromising situations once or twice in his long career as a philanderer. The risks at the time had seemed minimal, absorbed as he was by the tantalizing vision of Maud's softly rounded breasts, which she liked to flaunt for his amusement. It was only later, after his passion had been satiated, that Roger had admitted that a company of Wellington's cavalry might have galloped past without his noticing anything but Maud's lush body and eager lips.

He was still deep in thought as he tossed Jason's reins to the stable-lad and strolled up through the extensive kitchen gardens to the impressive bulk of Trenton Abbey, which cast long shadows in the late afternoon. Roger felt a surge of pride as he glanced up at the towering battlements, dotted at regular intervals with narrow *meurtrières* through which archers of long ago had defended the fortress. As a boy he had always regretted not living in that era of doughty knights and languid maidens. He had dreamed of being armed *cap-à-pié*, fighting beside his ancestor on the fields of Agincourt in 1417, the same battlefield where that loyal follower of King Henry V was knighted as he lay dying. Many a time had Roger envisioned himself receiving even greater honours from his sovereign—without having to die, of course, which had always seemed an excessive price to pay for a title.

The Trenton standard in yellow and purple that fluttered from the highest stone tower had followed many of England's kings into battle and the family had benefited mightily as a result. Unfortunately, Roger mused as he climbed the shallow steps to the wide terrace and entered through the conservatory, most of those benefits had been frittered away by subsequent generations of Hastings intent on living like kings and not merely serving them.

How unlike their neighbours, he thought, taking the stairs two at a time up to his room to change for dinner. The Sinclairs had prospered, too, in service to the Crown, but not at the expense of their land. Although not as extensive as Trenton, Penhallow was twice as productive, and Roger occasionally wondered if his father had spent less time with his gaming cronies and more attending to his estate, their affairs might not be in better shape.

After a hot bath and a change of clothes, Roger felt better, and by the time he descended to join his father in the drawing room, his mood had lightened considerably. What if his father was occasionally short of the ready? He had demurred last Christmas at Roger's demands for a new curricle, but he had come through in the end, so the coffers could not be as empty as the marquess often claimed.

Roger brushed the disturbing thought aside and strode into the drawing room to greet his father's guests. He never knew for certain which of Lord Trenton's many gaming cronies would be present at the dinner table, but Roger sincerely hoped Sir Giles would not be one of them. His father and the aging baronet were longtime gamblers, and Sir Giles was a frequent party to the late-night sessions of deep basset or poker Lord Trenton was addicted to. The big difference between them was that while Sir Giles was a consistent winner, Lord Trenton's luck fluctuated wildly.

Roger glanced round the room, nodding at old acquaintances, shaking hands with others, and relaxed when he noted that Sir Giles was mercifully absent. He was not sure he could face the old man with any degree of equanimity after spending the afternoon tupping his neighbour's prize ewe.

Being indifferent to games of chance, Roger did not join any of the card games set up immediately after dinner. As head of an all-male household, Lord Trenton had long ago dispensed with the tea-tray, so Roger excused himself early and sought his bed.

But his dreams were troubled. It was not his budding fatherhood that disturbed his rest, but a casual remark of Maud's that had not seemed important at the time. Old Sir Giles could not last much longer, she had said in that flippant, teasing way of hers. And then she would be free again, she had added, with a slanting look at him from beneath her long lashes.

Free again? The words returned to haunt him and took on a significance they had not had in the dappled sunlight beneath the spreading oak tree. Could she have been referring to an eventual match between them once Sir Giles stuck his spoon in the wall? The notion was bizarre. Maud was the ideal mistress, the best he had ever enjoyed. She seemed to relish the role, and it had never occurred to him to imagine her in any other, particularly not that of the future Marchioness of Trenton. But perhaps he had underestimated her.

The uneasy feeling that perhaps the future might not be as serene as he had expected kept Roger awake for half the night.

Two days later Roger was called into his father's study, and one look at Lord Trenton's face warned him that all was not well.

"Sit down," the marquess ordered without preamble.

Gingerly, Roger sat in one of the leather armchairs beside his father's carved oak desk. The summons had come unexpectedly as he was about to ride over towards Torrington in the hopes of running into Lady Horton, who often rode her black gelding along the country lanes surrounding the village.

He sensed that the matter was serious, for Lord Trenton made none of his usual jovial comments about the vast sums of money he had won or lost at cards the night before. This morning there was no smile on his father's face, and a glimmer of apprehension drove all thoughts of Maud from Roger's mind.

Lord Trenton cleared his throat—an ominous sound that reminded Roger of the many times he had been called on the carpet in this very room and roundly chastised for youthful indiscretions. However, he was

fairly certain that his father had more than minor indiscretions on his mind this morning.

Lord Trenton sighed and rubbed his chin. "Penhal-
low was here yesterday," he said at last, glaring at
Roger from beneath heavy brows. "He tells me that
Jane is getting restless. She is demanding a Season in
London, and you know what that means." He paused,
and his frown deepened.

This information surprised Roger, for it seemed so
unlike Jane to demand anything, particularly a stay in
Town, which he knew she disliked; but he said nothing. He sensed where this was leading.

"I should not have to remind you of your obliga-
tions in that direction, Roger," Lord Trenton continued, "but Penhallow tells me that you are making
yourself conspicuous chasing after that Horton
woman. Jane is convinced that you have actually
formed a *grand passion* for this female and is demanding that she be released from the arrangement
her father and I made the very day she was born. Is
there any truth to this?"

Roger hesitated, debating whether to confess his infatuation with Maud, or assure his father that it was
only a passing fancy. He knew well enough which answer his father expected of him. A Hastings was supposed to know his duty and do it without hesitation.
Roger knew his duty, all right, but the vision of Maud
in all her womanly glory caused him a pang of regret,
and for a moment he toyed with the idea of telling
his father that for once he would follow his inclination
and not his conscience.

"Well!" Lord Trenton barked. "Cat got your
tongue, lad?"

"No, sir. I fear those rumours are vastly exagger-
ated. A little flirtation, that is all it amounted to."
Roger regretted the lie the moment it was uttered.
His liaison with Maud was much more than a light
flirtation, but he could not bring himself to say so to
his father. Nor could he dare mention the child Maud
was carrying, which she swore was his.

His father stared at him intently for a moment, then sighed. "You relieve my mind, lad," he said in a heavy voice. "Penhallow also tells me that it has been an age since you took tea with them. I want you to go over there this afternoon and remedy that oversight. And while you are there, see to it that Jane forgets about this nonsense of a London Season. She is no great beauty, of course, and is definitely past the age for such frippery, but her fortune would attract every buck in Town with pockets to let."

Roger was taken aback by the frankness of this speech. He had to agree with his father that Lady Jane was no beauty and no schoolroom chit either, but she was sweet-natured and biddable, if somewhat of a bluestocking. Roger had known her forever and was inordinately fond of her. They shared countless childhood memories, and Roger could not recall the number of times he had rescued her from disaster because she insisted on tagging along with him on his wildest escapades. That time she had fallen out of the boat on the Trenton pond, for example, and he had dragged her out like a half-drowned kitten. Or when she had insisted upon jumping that ditch against all reason and ended up, pony and all, in a clump of nettles.

His father's voice brought him back to the present with a jolt.

"Besides, there are more pressing reasons for you to hold Jane to the agreement I made with her father all those years ago." He paused, and his eyes wandered to the window through which Roger could see the wide expanse of Trenton Park dotted with huge oaks and untidy clumps of rhododrendrons along the driveway.

Roger glanced at his father's face, and was startled at the haggard expression on that granite countenance. The corners of Lord Trenton's generous mouth drooped, the lines around his eyes seemed to have deepened, and his shoulders sagged as though the weight of the world lay upon them. Roger felt a tremor of alarm. He had never thought of his father as old. Lord Trenton was not yet sixty, but this morning he looked twenty years older. Was there something his father was not telling him? Roger was keenly aware that this man he had always considered invincible seemed to be crumbling before his eyes.

"Is there something amiss, Father?"

Lord Trenton turned slowly and stared at him, and Roger noticed that his father's skin had an unhealthy pallor to it.

"You might call it that, lad," the marquess replied with a wry smile. After a moment his smile faded, and he rubbed his face with both hands. "I lost twenty thousand pounds last night—to Gardener, of all men. I should have known better than to bet against him."

"Not Sir Robert Gardener?" Roger exclaimed. "I thought that Captain Sharp only cast his net for the young bucks in Brighton's less savory gaming hells."

"He is a houseguest over at Rose Manor, and that fool Cheswick brought him as his guest last night. Gardener made everyone nervous, of course, what with his reputation as a confirmed gambler, but I could hardly exclude him from the game. And as Fate would have it, I had one of my bad days and lost heavily. Too heavily, I fear. We are rolled up, Roger. Quite run into the ground. Gardener took my vouchers, of course, but . . ."

Roger stared at his father blankly. Lord Trenton had always indulged in deep play, and he often lost substantial sums of money. But he had always come about, Roger reminded himself.

"Surely your luck will change, Father," he said bracingly. "It always has before. Gardener can wait for his blunt. Perhaps you will have more luck at the table tonight and fleece the wretch."

His father shook his head slowly, and Roger felt his insides congealing into a lump of ice. "No, lad, no chance of that. They are meeting at Horton's tonight, and I have already told Sir Giles I will not be there. I simply cannot raise the blunt. I am so far up the

River Tick, I may never find a way back again. I swore to my father I would never mortgage the Abbey, but I may have to, unless . . ."

Roger felt the unspoken alternative Lord Trenton obviously had in mind hanging in the air between them. This was an emergency. It behooved him to come to his father's rescue.

"I shall speak to Jane this very afternoon, Father," he said with more enthusiasm than he felt. "Once we are wed, you may rest easy again."

"Spoken like a true Hastings, lad," Lord Trenton remarked with an attempt at his usual joviality. "Your grandfather would have been proud of you."

Roger was not convinced by his father's false cheer, and as he strode down to the stables to take Jason for a gallop, he vowed to consult Doctor Graham, the family physician, on his father's obviously failing health.

Chapter Three

The Offer

Lady Jane sat back with a sigh and examined her half-finished sketch critically. It was not going well at all. Usually, she could lose herself in her work for hours on end, but this afternoon her attention kept wandering from the second purple orchid she had found that morning down near the stream to the scene she had stumbled upon several days ago.

She glanced at the small gilt clock on the mantel. It was nearly time for tea, and she needed to change out of her paint-stained smock. The less her esteemed papa was reminded of her literary pursuits, the less likely he would be to go off on a harangue about unladylike behaviour. As she had for the past two afternoons, Jane decided to take her embroidery down to the tea-table. Papa could not tell that her stitches were far from perfect, but this show of domesticity seemed to mollify him.

With luck, she thought, starting to put away her pencils and straighten her work table, Lord Penhallow might agree to allow her to visit Aunt Honoria for a few weeks. The London Season was well under way, of course, but Jane was not interested in the usual pursuits of young ladies. Her aunt would insist upon taking her to the most fashionable modiste, and parading her through the saloons of the *ton* hostesses, but Lady Jane looked forward to afternoons in the British Museum and the many libraries in the Metropolis. Aunt Honoria would not accompany her niece there, Jane was certain, not being given to reading anything more strenuous than the latest Minerva Press novels.

She glanced again at her sketch and shook her head. Her rendition looked more like a common spotted orchid than the early purple, which had fatter florets and a shorter stem. She would make a fresh start after tea and try to keep her mind on her work instead of—

Jane was interrupted by a knock on the door. Before she could respond, it opened and Roger Hastings stepped into the room.

For an instant, Lady Jane froze, her mind a jumble of conflicting emotions. Then she dropped her eyes to her cluttered table and reached blindly to gather discarded sketches and odd pencils together. She had not expected him to come so soon, and was still debating how she should receive the scoundrel. Why was he not out doing whatever it was he did with Lady Horton? Had he tired of her at last, or had his father reminded him that he was whistling a fortune down the wind? Neither explanation was flattering, and Jane ignored him.

"My dear Jane," he said with that disarming lilt in his voice that always caused Jane's heart to flutter, "your aunt told me I would find you here." He strolled over to her work table and glanced down at her sketch. "Still dabbling around with wildflowers, I see." He picked it up before Jane could protest and examined it, a half-smile on his face. "What is this supposed to be, a foxglove?"

"Foxgloves do not flower until June," Jane responded shortly.

"What is it, then?"

Jane glanced at him, deliberately ignoring the guileless smile on his handsome face. "Why this sudden interest in wildflowers? You have always despised my amusements, Roger, almost as much as I despise yours," she added daringly. She saw his smile fade and wondered if she had been too blunt.

"Exactly which amusements are you referring to, my dear?" His voice was soft, but his eyes were wary.

Jane raised an eyebrow. She knew she was treading a fine line, but she could not resist. "I am surprised you require me to point them out to you, my lord," she said stiffly. "The entire village is privy to your profligate ways."

Roger's face was pale now, his lips thin. He looked uncomfortable. "Am I to believe that you set any store by local gossip, Jane?"

"When I know it to be true, how can I not?" she answered blithely, her hands busy fitting her charcoals into their box. "Can you deny that you are extravagant beyond measure at a time when Lord Trenton's health is not the best?"

"What do you know about my father's health?"

"My father tells me he is feeling poorly, and when I saw him in church last Sunday, he appeared tired." In truth, Jane remembered, Lord Trenton had looked like an old man for the first time since she had known him.

"My father's gout is plaguing him," Roger responded lightly, "and he is depressed over his bad luck at cards."

"Ah, yes, I can well understand that," Jane said, her voice softening. "The word in the village is that your father dropped twenty thousand pounds the other evening. To Sir Robert Gardener, no less. I wonder that Lord Trenton had the temerity to play with that notorious card sharp. I have often wished to play a hand of faro with Sir Robert myself, just to see how good he really is."

Roger gave a snort of disgust. "I trust you will do nothing so foolish, Jane. I know you have the devil's own luck at cards, but the man is a menace. And how the word of my father's losses became common knowledge in the village is beyond me."

"The same way every other detail of our lives becomes known almost before we know it ourselves," Jane pointed out. "Everyone knows everything around here, Roger, as you must know. Absolutely *everything*," she added with feigned innocence. After a pause, during which Roger strode about the small room, his hands thrust into his pockets, Jane broached the subject that had tormented her for days. "I daresay the time has come for you to do your part to lighten your father's load, Roger."

He came to an abrupt halt and stared at her, a strange, almost hopeful expression on his face.

Fearing that he had misunderstood, Jane continued hastily, "Is it not time you went up to London to find yourself an heiress who might put things aright at Trenton Abbey? I would hate to see the grand old place—"

"I already have an . . . That is to say," he stumbled over his gauche remark, "I am glad you brought that up, Jane, for I wish to speak to you about that very matter."

Jane felt her heart race uncomfortably. Here it comes, she thought bitterly. The very offer she had wished to hear for so many years. But now her main concern was to fob it off.

"If you are asking my opinion, I suggest you seriously consider going up to London while the Season is in full swing, Roger," she said abruptly before he could say anything further. "Who knows how many beautiful heiresses are languishing there awaiting your arrival." She chuckled at the irony of her comment. "I may see you there, you know. Papa is on the brink of allowing me to spend a few weeks with Aunt Honoria. My mother's sister, remember? That eccentric old Tabby, Papa calls her. Most unfairly, I assure you—"

"Jane, do stop blathering on and listen to me for a moment." He had stepped closer, and she saw the deep cobalt of his eyes turning darker as it always did when he was angry or nervous.

"It is hardly polite of you to call my conversation *blather,* Roger." She looked up at him reproachfully. "Particularly when I am sharing the news of my London visit with you. I thought you would be happy for me."

"Over my dead body," he muttered under his breath.

Lady Jane quailed inwardly but held her ground. "I sincerely hope it will not come to that, Roger."

Her voice sounded calm, revealing none of the doubts that flitted through her mind. He was so very handsome, she thought wistfully, so much the man who filled her dreams with tenderness. So close and attainable. She longed to reach out and touch him, run her fingers down that rugged cheek, tangle them in his tawny, sun-bleached hair. The urge to step into his arms, to snuggle her face against his cravat was so strong, she felt giddy. Jane repressed a sigh.

Then the scene beside the stream flashed through her senses like a bolt of lightning. The memory of Lady Horton's bare back reminded Jane that this man was not everything she dreamed. He was a philanderer. A man in love with another woman. The question was: Did she want such a man for a husband? A few years ago she would not have hesitated, but now the prospect of spending her life as a complaisant wife galled her.

"Why must you go to London, Jane?" Roger demanded. "I realize you did not have your Season like other girls because you were caring for your mother, but you must see that there is no point now."

"No point?" Jane's voice was chilly. "I presume that is your evasive way of saying that I am too old for the Marriage Mart?"

Roger had the grace to blush. "I meant that there is no point in exposing yourself to ridicule—"

"Ridicule? I fail to see what is ridiculous about wishing to amuse myself at the opera, attend the *ton* parties, and see the sights. My Aunt Honoria knows everyone who matters in London. I shall not want for entertainment."

He gazed at her for a moment, and Jane could almost hear his mind turning over. Suddenly he smiled and reached out to grasp both her hands in his. "My dearest Jane, why did you not say so from the start? I shall take you to London myself to show you the sights. It will be our wedding trip," he added hastily, his eyes avoiding hers.

Jane's heart gave a frantic leap before settling into a wild thumping. She must nip this insidious maneuver in the bud. "Wedding trip?" She pulled her hands free and chuckled. "You must be jesting, Roger. Or have your wits gone begging?"

He looked chagrined, and Jane felt a pang of regret. "No jest, my dear," he said. "We have been betrothed since your birth, as you well know."

"I am sorry to disappoint you, Roger. Our fathers agreed on the match, 'tis true. In a drunken stupor, I am told. But you jilted me publicly when I was thirteen. Or has that conveniently slipped your memory?" she added with a hint of cynicism that surprised her. "You said—and I remember your words as though it were yesterday—that you would rather be nibbled to death by ducks than tied to a skinny beanstalk with a snub nose and freckles."

She watched as recollection seeped into Roger's memory and his face hardened. "I did not—"

"Do not deny it, you unfeeling oaf," she interrupted angrily. "I was known as *beanstalk* for months after that. I swore then that no drunken promise would force me to honour my father's agreement. And since you have said nothing since then to change my mind, I understood that you meant it. So do not try to bamboozle me with talk of wedding trips, Roger Hastings, because it will not fadge."

Realizing that she was close to tears, Jane turned away, only to feel his hand on her arm.

"You must have known I did not mean it. It was all in jest. Dash it all, Jane, we were children."

"Indeed?" she said icily. "Did you perchance hear me laughing? You were eighteen, Roger, and should have known better than to cheat a little girl out of her fantasies."

"It seems I was a thoughtless fool," he said after a pause, and the note of remorse in his voice caused Jane's resolve to waver.

Pulling herself together, she turned to stare at him. "Precisely. Now if you will excuse me, I must change for tea."

The second tea gong was still echoing in the halls as Jane made her way down the stairs towards the drawing room. She would have preferred to skip tea this afternoon, but she knew her father would be there. And so would Roger.

The thought made her pause on the first-floor landing, one hand on the dark oak banister. After their brief encounter earlier, Roger must be fully aware of her feelings on the matter of marriage, although like most gentlemen, he was probably convinced that he would prevail. Jane was still amazed that she had spoken as bluntly as she had to him. But then, she reasoned, if she could not be outspoken with Roger, who knew her better than her own father, whom could she talk to?

Roger stood up as she entered, but Jane merely nodded and sat on the brocade settee beside the teatable. Featherburton stepped forward to arrange the tray within easy reach, and Jane concentrated on pouring tea, ignoring the tension in the room.

"Roger and I were discussing the upcoming Hunt, my dear Jane," her aunt said brightly, evidently sensing that all was not well. "I told him that you would be attending this year on your new mare."

"I am still undecided, Aunt. Ginger is rather more skittish than I like, but she certainly is a splendid jumper."

"I told you she was, my dear, did I not?" her father broke in, entering in time to hear Jane's remark. "That mare comes from the best Irish stock, Jane, and, with a little patience on your part, should carry you over any fence in the county."

"That is more than we can say about some of the slugs that pass for hunters around here," Roger remarked, helping himself to a large slice of seed cake.

"I always marvel when old Cheswick's roan clears that first hedge."

Jane poured her father his tea, then took up her embroidery. "I wonder that you should notice," she remarked offhandedly. "You are always out in front of the pack, and Mr. Cheswick is usually trailing in the rear."

"I daresay you will be leading the pack yourself next week, my dear," Lord Penhallow said jovially, "once that Ginger gets a taste for the sport."

"I hope you are right, sir," Roger responded. "Between your Challenger and Jane's new mare, I look forward to some rare gallops. Dare I hope that you will give the mare her head, Jane? We could leave the field in the dust, I guarantee you."

"I have no intention of breaking my neck," Jane said dryly, "for you or anyone else." She bowed her head over her gaily coloured embroidery. "I understand Lady Horton is a neck-or-nothing rider—I am sure she would be delighted to accommodate you."

Jane listened to the frozen silence that followed this remark. She tied off the end of a red thread and measured out another at random. Only when she had her needle threaded with the light blue silk did she notice that her pattern of flowers included none with that colour. Well, it did now, she thought, purposefully jabbing her needle into a space beside a half-finished red rose. She would add a spray of forget-me-nots, a choice that appealed to her sense of irony.

Lady Octavia shifted uneasily, for once at a loss for words. Jane's father cleared his throat and passed his cup to be refilled, a sure sign of his inner turmoil, for he was not fond of tea. Jane glanced at Roger and blandly enquired if he would take another cup.

He passed his cup without a word. Jane marvelled at how easy it was to bring polite conversation to a standstill. All it took was the mention of that woman's name. She wondered what it might be like to be that notorious.

"Shall I ask Featherburton to bring up some of your favourite tarts, Papa?"

Lord Penhallow stood up abruptly, grim lines around his mouth. "Not now, Jane," he said brusquely. "Roger and I have things to discuss. Come, lad, I have a new case of brandy I want your opinion on." Without glancing at his daughter, he walked stiffly out of the room.

Roger murmured his excuses before following his host, but Jane ignored him, her attention riveted on the odd-shaped blue flower taking shape on her linen.

"Well, I must say your father seems to be in a rare pother, Jane," Aunt Octavia remarked as soon as the door closed behind the gentlemen. "Which is not to be wondered at, considering how you threw that woman's name in Roger's teeth without so much as a blush. I thought your poor papa would burst out of his waist-coat with pure mortification."

"Are we to pretend that we know nothing of Roger's dalliance with her, Aunt? I may be inexperienced in such things, but I am not a complete innocent. They were hardly exchanging polite conversation down by the stream that afternoon. You may take my word for it."

Jane threw down her embroidery and helped herself to a ginger biscuit. She did not for a moment believe that her father really wished for Roger's opinion on the brandy. No doubt they were even now discussing marriage settlements and other matters she would give her eye-teeth to have more control over. Things that concerned her future happiness, to which gentlemen seemed to give so little importance.

"Do not fret yourself into ribbons, my dear Jane," her aunt said gently. "Your father knows best, and you should accept his judgement and save yourself a lot of grief. Only consider what happened to me when I defied my father all those years ago. I sometimes wonder where I would be now had I accepted the husband he had selected for me."

Jane looked at her aunt in surprise. "You have al-

ways told me that Lord Jefferies was a toothless old
toad, who cared for nothing but his cattle and hunting dogs."

"He was kind and generous, too, dear, and as the
years passed, I learned to appreciate those qualities in
a gentleman. After all, it was not his fault he resembled an amphibian, which he undoubtedly did. His
penchant for wearing green did not help, but I might
have grown accustomed to such idiosyncrasies." She
sighed gustily and picked at the cake crumbs on her
plate. "I was young and foolish, which is hardly an
excuse."

"I am neither young nor foolish, Aunt. And Roger
has little to recommend him besides the charming
smile he bestows on any female who catches his eye.
I suggested that he repair to London and catch a rich
wife. I daresay that is the only way he may repair his
estate, which I understand from local rumours Lord
Trenton has run into the ground."

Lady Octavia stared at her. "Tell me you did nothing so vulgar, Jane. And why should Roger go to
Town for a bride? He has been betrothed to an heiress
for years."

"A very reluctant one, I assure you, Aunt," Jane
snapped crossly. "As you know, I am five-and-twenty,
which is definitely on the shelf. Do you not find it amazing that Roger has allowed me to waste away here if he
cared a fig for our so-called betrothal? The truth is that
he does not care, or at least did not do so until his
father frittered away the last of the Trenton fortune in
reckless gaming." She paused to catch her breath.

"But Roger is a dear boy, Jane—"

"Fiddlesticks!" Jane interrupted. "I had hoped for
your support in resisting this disastrous match, Aunt,
but I see that the rogue has bamboozled you, too. Can
you not see that all he cares for is my fortune? He
needs my dowry, Aunt, not me, but he cannot have
one without the other. It is as simple as that."

When her aunt did not respond, Jane blurted out
in a bitter voice, "Do you realize, Aunt, that I have

never enjoyed a single flirtation, or received a *billet doux* from a secret admirer? Or been kissed by some scandalous gentleman behind the potted plants at a masquerade ball?"—an exception came to mind, but she pressed on—"All I know of love is what I read in romantical novels, which always seem too bizarre to be anything like real life."

"My dear Jane," Lady Octavia murmured soothingly, sitting beside her niece and hugging her impulsively, "I should warn you that love has very little to do with real life. I thought you knew that. There are no tall, dark, mysterious strangers hiding behind the laburnum bushes, no dashing highwaymen who are titled gentlemen in disguise out for a lark. In short, there is no romance, or precious little of it, in real life."

Jane gazed at her aunt numbly. She had known this to be true, of course, but had deliberately ignored it. She had held firmly to the fantasy of finding the ideal man whose love would carry her through life on a cloud of tender passion. Roger had never shown the least inclination to fill this role—at least with her, but Jane had never ceased to dream. Until now.

Her aunt's words suggested that it mattered little whom she married, or whether she married at all. In any case the world would go on with or without her. A disheartening prospect. If she refused Roger, she might make a name for herself with her writing, become the national expert on wildflowers, not just in Devon, but in all of England. And why not Scotland, too?

If she accepted Roger, she would have to limit herself to wildflowers in Devon, but at least she would be a marchioness, as her father was forever telling her—not that she cared a fig for that—and she would be able to replace those tattered green curtains in the Great Hall at Trenton Abbey, an ambition she had harboured ever since setting eyes on them.

Either way, she told herself philosophically, reaching for another ginger biscuit, she had best put all romantical dreams out of her head. Then no man would disappoint her.

Chapter Four

Unwilling Bride

Roger followed Lord Penhallow downstairs to the library expecting to receive a severe lecture on the evils of neglecting one's duty. He was not disappointed. In short order his host worked up an impressive lather in describing the many disadvantages of allowing young ladies of breeding to reach the age of five-and-twenty without giving them a household to manage and a nursery full of little ones to raise.

"Females need a mission in life," Lord Penhallow pontificated sternly. "And if we men do not make them wives and mothers at the appropriate age, as the good Lord intended, they will follow some nonsensical whim or other that will lead them into useless occupations like collecting wildflowers, for instance. And before you know it, they have developed a mind of their own and begin to argue with you about things they have no business questioning at all."

"You may well be right, sir," Roger murmured, "but—"

"Of course, I am right, lad," his host interrupted. "Only look at my own daughter if you doubt it. Jane is pestering me to send her up to London to visit her aunt Honoria. Have you any idea what would happen if that tiresome old Biddy got her claws into Jane? She would parade her through all the saloons in London, with every fortune-hunter in Town at her heels. Before you know it, one of them would turn her foolish head, and then where would we be?" He paused to glare at Roger belligerently.

"Could you not forbid her to go, sir?"

Lord Penhallow grimaced. "I could, of course, but I made a foolish promise to her mother that Jane might have a Season in Town. It seems I may have to let her go, unless you can make her see reason. Jane can be stubborn, and I am reluctant to break my promise. Had you taken her to the altar seven years ago, as I have suggested to you several times, everything would have been plain sailing. I would have grandchildren by now, and you would have a pretty fortune to spend on Trenton Abbey. But no, you had to waste your time chasing every petticoat in the neighbourhood, where Jane was bound to find out about it."

"I was discreet about it, sir," Roger ventured to put in. This was not strictly true, of course, but he could hardly admit that his infatuation with Maud had made all else seem inconsequential.

His host snorted. "Not discreet enough, it appears. And to add insult to injury, you choose an *inamorata* from the local gentry, a woman Jane must needs encounter at any number of social gatherings. Lady Horton is not received here, naturally, and I doubt she is invited to dine at the Abbey, but old Horton—fool that he was to wed that lightskirt—has long-standing connexions with all the estates in the region. He simply cannot be snubbed because he has turned soft in his dotage."

Roger felt uneasy listening to Lord Penhallow discuss his lovely Maud as though she were some frivolous butterfly flitting from bed to bed indiscriminately. She was certainly not the lightskirt his host called her. Maud had sworn to that herself, her lovely eyes filling with tears. Never, since she wed Sir Giles, had she been unfaithful to her husband. Except with him, she had added coyly, a smile hovering on her perfect lips. Roger had believed her.

Had he perchance been *too* trusting? The notion was unsettling, and Roger quickly banished it. Maud had sworn. . . . His attention snapped back as he heard

Lord Penhallow mutter something about reading of banns and the wedding breakfast.

"I will do what I can, Roger, but I am depending on you to get my daughter to the altar with as little fuss as possible. Insist upon a June wedding in the Abbey chapel, my boy. That is bound to take Jane's mind off this nonsense of going to London."

"Yes, sir," Roger agreed cautiously. Even with the weight of Lord Penhallow's paternal authority behind him, he did not look forward to convincing Jane that she would be better off married to him than wasting her time sketching flowers. On second thoughts, that would not be the best approach to take with the lady after she had so recently called him an insensitive oaf. Perhaps he could persuade her that he had really cared for her all these years—which of course he had, but not in the way she probably expected—and was now ready to reform his ways. It was unfortunate that he had called her a skinny beanstalk, of course. That silly taunt seemed to have stuck in her mind like a burr and would be the very devil to dislodge.

"Well, what do you say, Roger?" his host was saying, evidently in the wake of another peroration on the advantages of getting himself riveted to Jane with all speed. Exactly what his lordship had said Roger could only guess, but he smiled anyway.

"You are absolutely right, sir," he stated with as much conviction as he could muster. "I agree entirely."

Lord Penhallow looked pleased. "Then I shall send Jane to you, my boy, and we can conclude this matter immediately." He drained his glass and turned to the door, looking well pleased with himself. "Use that famous charm of yours for a good cause, Roger. Make my little girl happy."

Roger stared at the closed door with rising alarm. Making females happy had always come easy to him. Now it loomed like an impenetrable briar patch.

Jane had just excused herself with the intention of resuming her sketch of the purple orchid, when the door opened and Featherburton entered with a curt summons from her father.

"I am called for in the library, Aunt," she explained, glancing ruefully at her aunt. "No doubt Papa wishes to pin my ears back for daring to sully my lips with the name of a harlot."

"Jane! Do not use such language, dear. Besides, it is not becoming in a lady to be unkind. I am sure that Lady Horton has some good qualities that you have overlooked."

Lady Jane stared quizzically at her aunt, wondering if this remark was as double-edged as it sounded. "She has gorgeous hair and a delightful singing voice, if that is what you mean, Aunt. Other than that, I can find little to commend in her. Perhaps you should apply to Roger, who doubtless could list a whole catalogue of the lady's virtues."

On that cynical note Jane swept out of the room before her aunt could reproach her for lack of Christian charity, which she was fond of doing.

Jane carried her annoyance with her down the stairs and into the library. As a result she was feeling anything but charitable towards the heir to Trenton Abbey and was prepared to tell her father that she would rather run off with one of the footmen than wed a man who had scandalized the neighbourhood for months with his immoral liaison.

Not that Jane would actually dare say anything so bizarre to her father, of course, but it was comforting to think that the mere hint of such a scandal would give Lord Penhallow an apoplexy. The trouble with that threat was that Jane doubted any of the footmen at Penhallow would run off with her, even if she begged them. Like most of the servants, the earl's footmen had either been born on the estate, or been in service for longer than Jane could remember. It was, nevertheless, a comforting thought, and she clung to it.

She glanced around the room, but it appeared to be

empty except for Roger, standing at the window with his back to her.

"Where is Father?" she demanded, a sudden prickly sensation invading her spine. "He said he wished to see me."

The moment Roger turned around, Jane realized that her father had led her into the trap. She stood very still, her heart beating rapidly. As Roger advanced towards her, she saw at once that he had lost some of his brash self-confidence. His paleness emphasized the cobalt blue of his eyes, which were fixed on her almost pleadingly. Pleadingly? Jane had never imagined Roger in the role of supplicant. To her knowledge he took what he wanted and worried about the consequences later. He had always seemed to her like an overgrown puppy let loose in a henhouse, not much caring which hen he caught, as long as he caught one of them. The chase, Jane suspected, was more important to Roger than the quarry.

Today he seemed different. For the first time Jane wondered what it might be like for a gentleman to be obliged to offer for a lady he did not love—except as a sister. With sudden insight she saw that she was indeed no more than a sister to Roger, and the thought cut through her like a knife. Jane felt her animosity melting away. Had she not herself loved him like a brother in the early days before she had discovered—with shattering intensity at fifteen—that it was not brotherly love she felt for Roger Hastings?

He came to a stop before her and smiled tentatively. "Your father asked me to talk to you in his place, Jane." He paused as if unsure how to begin. Jane held her breath, hoping he would not lie to her and profess undying love to advance his cause. She did not want to laugh in his face.

"Lord Penhallow has granted me permission to address you, Jane," he began formally. "He is desirous of fulfilling the agreement he made with my father of a match between us."

"Indeed?" Jane said icily, drawing herself up to her

full height. "So you took this step knowing full well
how set I am against it?" She paused, fascinated by
the darkening blue of his eyes. "Did I not share with
you only an hour or two ago my desire to spend a
Season in London with my aunt? You were good
enough to point out that I am firmly on the shelf—"

"I said no such thing," Roger protested, reaching
for her hands.

Jane hastily hid them behind her back. "You said I
would be ridiculous, which is worse. But it matters
little what you thought or what you said, Roger; it
should have entered your thick skull by now that I do
not wish to wed."

"I have your father's permission to make you an
offer, Jane." He looked so uncomfortable that Jane
wanted to take his head in her arms and assure him
that things would work themselves out eventually. It
took all her fortitude to suppress this piece of
foolishness.

"Then you had better do so this instant, my lord,
so that I may refuse your kind offer and go back to
my painting." This sounded harsh even to her own
ears, and Jane was not surprised when Roger reacted angrily.

"Your father is determined to have a June wedding,
Jane, so you had best set a date and cease this farradi-
ddle. Besides, it is nonsense to say you do not wish
to wed. All females wish for a husband and little
ones." He had the audacity to grin when he said this,
and Jane felt her cheeks grow hot at the intimacies
this picture conjured up.

"You sound exactly like my father," she fumed.
"But no female with any sense would wish to be in
my shoes, let me assure you."

"Now there you are wrong, my dear. I could name
any number of—" He broke off abruptly, as if realizing the impropriety of his remark.

Jane glowered at him. "I daresay half the eligible
females in London would agree with you, Roger. Why
then must you choose the only one who does not?"

Roger's eyes took on an anguished look that wrenched at Jane's heart. She reminded herself that this interview was as unpleasant for him as it was for her. After a long pause, she took pity on him.

"There is no need to answer that. We both know that you did not choose, and neither did I. We were not consulted, but are expected to live up to a maudlin promise made by two men in their cups. It simply is not fair." She felt her voice quaver and did not resist when Roger reached again for her hands and carried them to his lips.

How many times had she lived this moment in her dreams, and now that it had come, all Jane felt was a wrenching misery deep in her heart. His hands were warm, and Jane closed her eyes for an instant, letting herself imagine that this moment meant something special for both of them.

When she opened them again, she found him gazing at her speculatively. She dropped her eyes quickly, hoping he had not read her thoughts.

"No," he said softly, his breath warm against her fingers, "it is not fair. But your father wants you to be happy, Jane. He said so himself. *Make my little girl happy*. His very words. And on my honour, I shall do everything in my power to please you."

This promise sounded so stiff and awkward that Jane felt her throat tighten. Her father's words went straight to her heart; but he was so wrong to imagine that Roger could make her happy. How could he give her the love she needed when his heart belonged to another? A tear rolled unbidden down her cheek, and she stifled a sob.

"Please do not cry, love," Roger murmured, drawing her into his arms and cradling her against him. "I will be good to you, Jane, I swear it," he whispered into her ear, causing a tingling of desire to run through her. "You will not regret it for a moment. Here," he added, pulling out a fine lawn handkerchief, "take this and blow your nose, my sweet. Your father will have my hide if he thinks I made you cry."

Jane obeyed and dried her wet cheeks, relishing the subtle scent of him on the soft cloth. She held it to her face longer than necessary, before returning it to him without a word.

"Now, what do you say we get this over with so we can both be comfortable again?"

This brought Jane's head up, and she glared at him. "Get it over with?" she repeated. "I must say that is a curious way to address a lady you hope to wed, my lord."

Roger had the grace to look flustered. "I am not up to snuff when it comes to making marriage offers, Jane. I have never done so, you know. I am quite at a loss to know whether I should go down on my knees. You will have to be my guide, my dear."

Jane shook her head in reluctant amusement at the spectacle this conjured up. "I am no more *au courant* in such matters of etiquette than you," she replied, not knowing whether to laugh or cry. "And since I am less than eager to receive an offer, I suggest you start by listing the benefits I will derive from such a match."

"To begin with—"

Jane raised her hand in protest. "You need not list the title, for I care not a fig for that. What else have you to offer?"

Roger looked a little disconcerted. "You would have a home that dates back to the twelfth century and is listed in all the Guide Books."

"Yes, a barn of a place full of drafts and mouldy furniture. It will take me and an army of servants a year or more to make the place halfway habitable."

"You may have all the servants you wish, Jane," he replied, blithely ignoring the real point of her argument.

"And the gardens? I would want to see them full of flowers. All you have now are a few jaundiced roses."

"I shall give instructions to Crawford this very evening."

He was beginning to look rather pleased with himself, Jane noticed, but they had yet to agree upon the important things.

"What about my monograph on wildflowers? You have always disparaged my scholarly interests, Roger, do not deny it."

He grinned and Jane's heart jumped. "I can always learn to appreciate wildflowers, Jane. You can teach me, my dear," he added disarmingly, and Jane had visions of sunny afternoons in the woods together searching for rare specimens. The thought was wildly unrealistic, and she quickly suppressed it. "Besides," he continued, "I already recognize foxgloves and primroses, and those blue ones, what do you call them?"

"Bluebells?"

"Yes, and daffodils, of course." He grinned again, as though he had overcome a major obstacle. "Now shall I go down on my knees, love?"

Jane shook her head and walked over to the open window, wishing he would not call her his love. The afternoon had been exceptionally fine, and the warm air on her face felt soothing. She wondered how she could possibly tell Roger that she would never be happy unless he ceased his philandering. It was not something a lady of breeding would dare mention to a gentleman about to make her an offer of marriage. Ladies were not supposed to know about such masculine pursuits. But Roger was different. Jane had always talked to him as to a brother. She hoped she still could.

"No, Roger," she said hesitantly. "We have yet to discuss the most important things."

Roger said nothing, but he came to stand beside her, one hand resting on the stone casement. "Tell me what is bothering you, Jane," he said gently.

As if he did not know what bothered her, she thought, glancing up at him crossly. "The rumours, Roger," she said pointedly, feeling the colour flood her cheeks. "The rumours bother me, as you must know."

Jane looked away as she spoke, conscious of her heightened colour. When he did not answer, the silence seemed to stretch interminably.

Finally he sighed, and Jane knew that he would try to cover this ground as lightly as possible. "Rumours? I cannot believe that you would allow a few rumours to come between us, Jane."

He paused and Jane responded sharply. "Hardly rumours, Roger, as you of all people must know. As I said before, everybody knows everything around here, and I will not stand to be *pitied* by friends, neighbours, and even by my own servants." She hesitated, gathering courage to say what needed to be said. "If it is a complaisant wife you are looking for, Roger, then you had best go up to London for a bride. I have no stomach for such arrangements."

Jane had not once looked at him during this speech, which had sorely taxed her modesty. Now that it was all said, she felt weak and apprehensive. Part of her wished most intensely to call this man husband, to live with him and bear his children; another part warned her that if she wed Roger, she would be giving up her dreams of love. But had not Aunt Octavia assured her that love had little to do with reality anyway? Kindness and generosity appeared to count for more than love in her aunt's eyes.

The prospect of growing old like her aunt, regretting that she had not taken what Lord Jefferies had offered and made the best of it held no appeal at all for Jane. Roger may not offer love, but he was certainly kind and generous. Perhaps that would have to be enough.

"Neither do I," Roger said suddenly, shocking her out of these maudlin meditations. It was so unexpected that Jane could only stare at him, wondering if she had heard aright.

"Please do not say things you do not mean, Roger," she whispered.

He took her hand in his and held it companionably. "You can trust me, Jane. I had no notion how those rumours upset you, my dear. Once we are wed, I promise you will have no more cause for complaint."

"Are you *sure*?" she asked dubiously. "I know it is the fortune you need, Roger, and believe me, if I could, I would give it to you without . . . without . . ."

He smiled down at her, and her heart did a jig between her ribs. "I know you would, Jane. But I prefer to do this properly. And believe me, you will not regret it, love."

Jane returned his smile, suddenly sure that Aunt Octavia was right. If love was impossible, kindness and companionship would suffice. And at least Roger looked nothing like Aunt Octavia's toad. Jane was sure that toads never smiled so tenderly. Throwing caution to the winds, she decided to take a chance with him and trust him with her life.

"In that case, perhaps it is time for you to get down on your knees, my lord."

Chapter Five

The Hunt

Although rumours of the formal betrothal between Viscount Summers and Lady Jane Sinclair had seeped out to the village before Roger had even left Penhallow—thanks to the earl's under-scullery maid, who was sent home with a toothache—the actual announcement in *The Gazette* had yet to be sent off.

The morning after his offer to Jane had been tendered and accepted, Roger lay in bed wondering what sort of hobble he had got himself into. He had woken up with a megrim, which he attributed to the intense emotional upheaval he had experienced the day before.

To tell the truth, he had not expected Jane to capitulate so quickly. But she had, and Roger's hopes for a few more days of freedom were dashed. He could not make up his mind whether to be relieved that the whole ordeal was behind him, or aggrieved that he was about to be firmly leg-shackled. Either way he looked at it, his philandering days were over.

He sighed and clasped a hand to his aching head. Why he had made that insane promise, Roger could not fathom, but make it he had, and he intended— the Good Lord and his Guardian Angel willing—to keep it. He did not relish the inevitable moment when he would have to explain to Maud that their liaison, delightful though it certainly had been, was at an end. If he was right in suspecting that Lady Horton had set her sights upon him as a possible third husband, their interview was bound to be stormy.

Roger groaned and crawled out of bed. Had he not

accepted Lord Penhallow's invitation to dinner and drunk so much of the earl's excellent brandy, he might be in better shape to face the day. But it had been after midnight when Jason had deposited him at the front door of the Abbey. Luckily his father was not at home, and Roger had been glad to deliver himself into the capable hands of his valet, who had waited up for him.

An hour later he presented himself in the breakfast room with the intention of informing his father that the Trenton fortunes had taken a turn for the better. Collins informed him that Lord Trenton had not yet left his bedchamber. The butler had such a lugubrious expression on his gaunt face that Roger felt impelled to question him about his father's health.

"Not at all stout this morning, milord," Collins replied. "According to Foster, his lordship spent a restless night and did not fall asleep until after six o'clock this morning. I doubt we shall see him downstairs much before noon."

This was so unlike Lord Trenton that Roger sent for his father's valet. What he discovered from Foster alarmed him. His lordship had not been himself of late, the valet reported, but had refused Collins' offer to send for Dr. Graham.

"If he is not up to snuff by this afternoon, I shall ask Dr. Graham to look in on him," Roger said. "But let me know the minute he wakes up, Foster. I shall be with Peterson."

His father's estate agent occupied a small room at the back of the house and could generally be found there after ten o'clock. Roger sought him out as soon as he had finished breakfast, and Peterson rose to greet him from behind a desk piled high with ledgers and papers.

"Good morning, milord," the agent said cheerfully. "I am glad you are come, because I need a decision on the new roof for old Daly's cottage. The thatchers are all set to start tomorrow, but his lordship, your father, has been hesitant to spend any more money until the next quarter's rents come in. I warned his lordship that poor Daly will catch pneumonia if those leaks are not seen to before the next rains."

"Show me the figures, Peterson. We should be able to find enough for one small roof. I know my father intended Daly should have it." He drew up a chair and for the next hour pored over the ledgers, listening to the agent's explanations of why the rents would be low again this quarter.

Before he had become infatuated with Maud, Roger had accompanied his father on Lord Trenton's weekly consultations with the agent, and listened with half an ear to Peterson's explanations of which expenses were unavoidable and which might be postponed for another quarter. His father usually favoured postponing all expenditures until the last possible moment, and Roger had not cared enough to question the wisdom of this policy. This morning, however, he listened with more care than usual as the agent's voice droned on, and he was startled at the depressing state of the family fortunes.

At one point, he interrupted. "Are you telling me, Peterson, that most of the quarters' rents are spent before they have actually been received?"

"Yes, milord. 'Tis his lordship's way. I cannot say it is a prudent way to manage an estate the size of this one, which should be producing double or triple what comes in. And many's the time I have told him so, milord. But his lordship's idea of economy is to sell off some of the flocks, which reduces the production of wool, which in turn—"

"I think I understand what you are saying, Peterson. My father has not been well lately, as you know."

"Yes, milord. And disastrously unlucky at cards, too," the agent added disapprovingly. "Why, only yesterday his lordship demanded that I find him a surplus of twenty thousand pounds to pay off a gambling debt. 'Surplus?' I asked him. 'When has the estate had a surplus? Not for ten years or more,' I told him. Of course, he flew into a rage and told me he had to have it, even if it meant selling off the south meadow. You must know, milord, that the south meadow will not bring in a quarter of what his lordship needs. But I did not dare tell him so."

"You did right, Peterson." Roger hesitated for a moment before adding, "But things will be better from now on. You should know—if you have not heard it already—that I am shortly to wed Lady Jane Sinclair. On the strength of that, I think we may give Daly his new roof immediately. And I want you to make a listing of all the other repairs that are needed, and any other expenses you deem necessary."

By the time Roger had endured Peterson's lengthy congratulations, he was impatient to share the good news with his father. But when he tapped at Lord Trenton's chamber door, Foster reported that his master was still sleeping. So it was not until they gathered in the dining room for nuncheon that Roger was able to assure his father that Jane had accepted his offer.

"Of course she did," Lord Trenton remarked complacently. "There was never any doubt about it, son. I shall send off the announcement to *The Gazette* this very afternoon. And as for our friends and neighbours, I shall make a private announcement at the Hunt on Saturday. What do you say to that, lad? After all, Jane will be attending this year, or so Penhallow tells me."

Having no wish to hear his upcoming nuptials officially acknowledged in so bizarre a manner, Roger demurred. "Jane may not like it, Father, you know how shy she is. Besides, her father will naturally wish to make the announcement himself. She is his only daughter, after all."

"Fiddlesticks!" Lord Trenton exclaimed. "Penhallow may hold a soirée on Saturday evening if he chooses. In fact, I shall suggest that he do so. But that will not stop me from sharing your good fortune with our friends." His father seemed to have recovered his spirits, but he paused between mouthfuls of ham and pigeon pie to glance at his son across the table. "I trust you will be discreet about your little sorties among the ladies until the knot is tied, my boy," he said sternly. "And if the Horton wench gives you any trouble, I shall drop a word in Sir Giles's ear."

"There will be no need for that, Father," Roger replied quickly. "I fully intend to put an end to that connexion."

Lord Trenton raised one bushy eyebrow speculatively but said nothing. Roger gathered that his father did not put much stock in his son's good intentions.

Later, as Roger walked down to the stables, he wondered how he would get through the weeks before his marriage without the sweet dalliance with Maud, who had become so much a part of his life. Could he honestly keep his promise to Jane? Or was he deceiving himself—and Jane, too—in thinking he could put Maud aside so completely?

The day of the Trenton Hunt dawned cool and misty, but since weather was never a consideration in this popular annual event, which had been known to take place in pouring rain, Lord Penhallow did not for a moment suggest that Jane stay at home. He was in high spirits, and beguiled the ride over to the Abbey by retelling for her benefit some of the recent highlights of the Hunt.

Jane did not share her father's good humour and lent but half an ear to his stories, most of which she had heard before. Her mind was busy going over the list of tasks that still needed to be done before her Aunt Honoria and her elderly husband, Lord Bristol, arrived from London for the wedding. They were expected tomorrow afternoon, and Jane could only be thankful that her father's two married sisters from Yorkshire with their husbands and numerous offspring would not arrive for another week. She loved her cousins, but they inevitably shattered the tranquillity of Penhallow with their constant chatter.

"Ginger seems to be in fine fettle, m'dear," her father remarked as they cantered through the Abbey gates. "And you are looking lovely yourself, Jane."

"Thank you, Father," Jane said dutifully, although the compliment sounded very like an afterthought. "I trust Lord Trenton is feeling more the thing today," she added to change the subject. "Roger tells me his father has been off his food for days now, a sure sign that his lordship is out of sorts. He has also charged Roger with many of the estate duties, another indication that he is not himself."

"I have urged him do so many times, m'dear. It is never too early to let one's heir get a taste of the responsibility of running an estate that will eventually be his. Furthermore, I told Cedric that the boy needs something to keep his mind off . . . off frivolous pastimes."

Jane flinched. She knew what her father had been about to say. It was no secret that Roger had a roving eye.

"Roger has assured me that there will be no more of that, Papa."

Lord Penhallow glanced at her, and Jane read skepticism in his eyes. "I can guarantee that if the young rogue mistreats you, Jane, he will have me to deal with."

Jane laughed lightly, but said nothing. She had taken Roger's promise to put a stop to those rumours on good faith, but since she had accepted his offer, Jane had wondered, more than once, if perhaps she had been naive to believe a leopard would change his spots. Had she been too willing to believe Roger's promises? She had certainly been charmed by the notion of becoming Roger's wife, of fulfilling a dream that had been with her for years. But had he meant to keep them, or had he merely said what he knew she wanted to hear? And after all, she reminded herself cynically, what was a promise or two compared to the vast fortune she would bring him? Which he desperately needed.

"What the blazes is that woman doing here?" her father snorted sharply, jolting Jane out of her uneasy thoughts.

Jane quickly scanned the group of riders gathered in the old-fashioned courtyard between the Abbey and the long row of stables. There were about a dozen of them, but the one who drew her gaze flaunted a bright blue riding habit and rode a big black horse that was nervously pawing the ground as if to call attention to its rider.

"Lady Horton is an avid equestrienne, Father," she said mildly. "It would be odd indeed if she were absent from the Trenton Hunt." She did not add that she had not expected Roger's *ex-inamorata* to have the gall to appear at the Abbey in all her glory. Jane was not exactly sure of her facts, but she had assumed that a lady in Maud's delicate condition would not risk the arduous exertion demanded of any female daring to take part in this gentlemanly sport.

As they approached, Jane saw that Lady Horton had outdone herself. The long skirt of her velvet riding habit fell artfully along the voluptuous lines of her long legs, the military-cut jacket flared around her full hips, and a fashionable shako perched saucily on her luxurious red hair.

Not one to reprine on her own lack of sophistication, Jane felt a rare pang of jealousy at the sight of this magnificent creature. She herself had dressed with particular care that morning in a new green riding habit ordered specially for the occasion, and a matching felt beaver with green ribands and a curly feather. The reflection in her cheval mirror had gratified her, but the sight of Lady Horton's tall, buxom figure, and the sound of her melodious laughter as she joked with several gentlemen gathered around her caused Jane to wish she had stayed at home with her watercolours.

At least Roger was not one of Lady Horton's coterie of admirers, Jane noticed with relief. He was supervising the adjusting of Mr. Cheswick's saddle on the ancient roan their old neighbour had ridden for years. Lord Trenton was chatting with a group of his gambling cronies, but he came up to salute her most cordially.

"My dear Jane, delighted we could entice you away from your flowers this fine morning. Roger," he shouted over his shoulder, "look who is here, boy. Come and welcome our guest of honour."

Jane cringed as her host's jovial voice boomed across the courtyard, drawing everyone's eyes in her direction, but she kept her gaze fixed on Roger. She had dreaded this first public encounter with her newly betrothed husband, and today would be especially trying. Every member of the Hunt would know of Roger's connexion with Lady Horton, and it would take all the fortitude Jane could muster to endure the silent speculations.

Roger must have sensed her distress, for he squeezed her fingers as he carried them to his lips. "Welcome, my love," he murmured with a teasing smile that made her heart race. "You are looking quite charming today. I fear the gentlemen will be hard pressed to keep their eyes on the fox."

Jane returned his smile, but was saved from having to reply by the arrival of the liveried footmen carrying the traditional stirrup-cups of mulled wine. She endured with a fixed smile Lord Trenton's exhuberant confirmation of their betrothal, and the enthusiastic congratulations of all present. Soon after that, the Hunt Master appeared from the kennels, the famous Trenton hounds bounding around him, and Jane breathed a sigh of relief. As the party clattered out of the courtyard, she was able to smile more warmly at Roger, who rode close by her side.

"How is the mare holding up?" he asked, eying Ginger appreciatively. "She looks as though she could take the field with the best of them."

"I like her more each day I take her out," Jane confessed. "But I do not intend to demand too much of her on her first hunt. She is an eager little jumper and full of heart, so it will not be easy to hold her back."

"I cannot imagine why you would wish to hold a good horse back, my lady," a sugary voice remarked.

"Unless, of course, you fear the horse is too much for you."

Jane turned to find that Lady Horton had come up beside her. She smiled briefly, but made no reply to this veiled taunt.

Undaunted by this lack of response, Lady Horton laughed throatily, then lowered her voice. "I shall leave you to enjoy the attention while you may, my lady. Men are such fickle creatures, as I am sure you know, my dear. Who knows where their interests will lie tomorrow?" With another tinkle of cynical laughter, she moved forward to join a group of gentlemen who welcomed her boisterously.

Jane's fingers tightened on the reins and Ginger pranced nervously. She did not dare glance at Roger, who had been silent during this exchange. Had he overheard Lady Horton's snide remark? Jane feared he had been meant to hear it, and for the second time that morning wished she had remained at home.

The fox led the hunters a merry chase over the hills and downs and country roads surrounding Trenton Abbey, scattering sheep and geese and wide-eyed children in their wake. Jane made no attempt to lead the pack, preferring to hold her mare down to a brisk gallop and take each hedge and ditch with prudence rather than flair.

Roger remained at her side throughout the morning, rather than claiming his accustomed place at the head of the pack. Jane was by turns gratified that he seemed more interested in her company than in the sport, and resigned at the not-so-flattering alternative. He was unfailingly charming, but every time Jane found herself half believing that perhaps he actually did wish to wed her for herself and not her fortune, she would catch his eyes wandering to the figure in blue streaking along the crest of a distant hill.

Had she not been taught that to wish harm on others was base, Jane might well have wished that flamboyant female a serious tumble, perhaps even a fatal one, in the course of the morning. She gamely fought the temptation and took heart in every smile and teasing remark Roger threw her way. Perhaps with time he would forget about the beautiful Lady Horton, she told herself, knowing this to be wishful thinking. At most she could hope that he would keep his promise not to stir up rumours.

These troubling thoughts were interrupted several hours later by the distant shouts of the huntsmen and the excited braying of the dogs. Jane immediately pulled her mare to a halt.

"I do not wish to be in at the kill, Roger, if you do not mind. I have no stomach for the wanton slaughtering of that poor fox."

"Foxes are vermin that slaughter many a farmer's hens and geese," he responded. "But by all means let us return to the Abbey." He led the way through a small copse of ash and horse chestnut, dotted with clumps of elder and laburnum. Out of habit, Jane scanned the ground for wildflowers and was delighted to find a large clump of wild strawberries in bloom. She pointed them out to Roger.

"Remember all the strawberries we used to pick over near Hogdon Hill, Roger?" she exclaimed, memories flooding back. "We always intended to take a pail of them back to Cook to make tarts, but Tony Cheswick was such a pig, he could not stop eating them." She laughed. "You were no slouch yourself when it came to strawberries, I recall."

"At least I did not break out in hives like his sister Lizzie. Do you still hear from her, Jane? You used to be so close."

"We exchange letters quite often, although recently her little ones had the measles, which kept her busy." She paused, her thoughts on those happy childhood days. "Sometimes I wish she had not gone off to Yorkshire to live. I miss her."

"I wager you miss Stephen, too." Roger grinned, and Jane knew he was thinking of Sir Giles's only son, who used to join their rambles over the moors. "My father tells me he has become something of a legend over there in Wellington's army. Old Sir Giles is forever puffing him up.''

"Will Stephen come home now that the war with Napoleon is over, do you suppose?"

"I doubt it," Roger replied shortly, and Jane knew that, like her, he was remembering those rumours from long ago. Captain Stephen Horton had never approved of Maud and had advised his good friend David Danvers not to wed a female of dubious background. It had been whispered that the orphaned girl had set her sights on Stephen, but she had wed Danvers, who had been young and in love. Maud had been more than willing to follow the drum, and the couple had left for the Peninsula as soon as Danvers purchased a pair of colours.

Some malicious gossips had put it about that Maud Danvers urged her new husband to join the army so that she could follow Stephen when he rejoined his regiment. Jane had always considered this absurd. What self-respecting female would wed one gentleman and pursue another? Jane rejected the notion, at least until the grieving widow Danvers had returned to Torrington and three months later snared—there was no other word for it—the bedridden baronet.

Captain Stephen Horton had been noticeably absent from his father's second nuptials. Nobody blamed him.

The silence between Jane and Roger lasted until they had come out of the wood into the pale sunlight. The early mist had burned off during the morning, but the air up on Hogdon Hill was pleasantly cool. Roger paused on the grassy knoll overlooking the stone bulk of Trenton Abbey in the distance and glanced over his shoulder.

"Shall we go down through the meadow, Jane? Or would you prefer to take the high ground back to the Abbey?"

"Oh, let us go down, Roger," she cried excitedly. "I have not been here in ever so long. I wonder if our strawberries are still there."

He smiled a crooked smile that went straight to Jane's heart. "You may count on it, my dear. The birds have no doubt feasted on them for years."

"Well, this year the birds will have to feast elsewhere," she said gaily as she urged her mare down the grassy slope. "I intend to gather every single strawberry in sight and have them made into jam and preserves. Liz tells me that she misses our wild strawberries up in Yorkshire more than anything." She hesitated. "Liz will be coming down for the wedding," she added, suddenly shy at bringing up the subject. "I wish Tony and Stephen could be here, too. It would be quite like old times."

"I have invited both of them," Roger said. "Tony has promised to be here, but Stephen would never arrive in time, even if he could get leave."

They had reached a sheltered meadow with scattered oaks and clumps of hawthorn and gorse. On the far side Jane glimpsed the bright yellow of wild irises, and she felt her spirit rise at the sight.

"Look, Roger," she cried, pointing at the yellow flags clustered like sentinels in the marshy ground. "The pond! I wonder if the tadpoles are still there."

"Not the same ones, I can guarantee it," Roger said with a laugh. "But I'll race you over there and we can check."

It was only when they reached the secluded little pond surrounded by willows, and Roger had swung down and was reaching up to help her dismount that Jane realized how alone they were. Even the noisy shouts of the hunters did not penetrate this secret place, the scene of many childhood adventures. She trembled as his hands encircled her waist and she found herself standing close beside him, looking up into his blue eyes. She could not read his expression, but Jane hoped he was thinking of kissing her, something she had dreamed of for years.

When he grasped her hand companionably and pulled her along the bank of the pond to a half-submerged log, she sighed and told herself to be patient.

Was he still thinking of Maud and the kisses he must surely have exchanged with the voluptuous widow? Did he not *wish* to kiss her? Her mother had warned her that gentlemen would invariably take liberties with any young lady they could get alone. It did not appear that Roger had dalliance on his mind, however. He seemed to be more interested in tadpoles.

Standing on the log and gazing intently into the clear water, Roger reminded her forcibly of the happiness they had shared in the past. But this was not the past, Jane reminded herself. They were about to become man and wife and she had yet to be kissed by him.

"Are there any tadpoles?" Grasping his hand firmly, Jane leaned over his shoulder to stare into the murky depths of the pool. "Oh, there goes a minnow. And another. And two more. Oh, Roger, they do look hungry. I wish I had remembered to bring some bread crumbs for them."

After a while Roger jumped back to the bank, pulling her with him. "I suspect the tadpoles are in the spring, where they can avoid getting nibbled by enterprising minnows."

Hand-in-hand they strolled along the bank, overgrown with purple red-rattles on their tall stems, blankets of creeping grass-of-Parnassus, its white flowers not yet showing, and shade-loving clumps of angelica, as yet devoid of the flower stalks that would blossom like white balloons in late summer. A lone reed bunting favoured them with a burst of the harsh, disjointed jangle that passed for song from the canopy of willow branches overhead. The sight of the round basin of crystal water from which the spring bubbled up from underground to spill over into the pond below filled Jane with a nostalgia so sharp it was painful.

She crouched down among the maidenhair ferns covering the damp earth with their lacy fronds and gazed intently into the shallow pool. "There they are," she exclaimed happily, pointing at the score or more black tadpoles performing their energetic, squirming dance near the surface. "And look, Roger, there is a tiny froglet who has yet to discard his tail. He must be one of the first, would you not say?"

"I daresay you are right, Jane." His voice was warm and amused, and Jane was reminded again that down here in this special place of their childhood, they were very much alone.

Hastily she stood up, her hand still in his. "We should go back, Roger. They will be wondering where we are."

Roger laughed. "Oh, I think they know where we are, love." He tucked her hand in the crook of his arm, bringing her so close that she felt the movement of his hip against her as they walked. This was all highly improper, Jane thought, but the unexpected contact gave her so much dizzying pleasure that she would not protest for all the tea in China. This was Roger, after all. *Her* Roger, who would in a few short weeks be *her* husband.

Jane felt suddenly light-headed. She was walking on air. For a heady moment, all her doubts about the man at her side disappeared, and she let herself soak up the sensual pleasure of his touch. When they reached the horses, she was intensely aware of his hands on her shoulders, turning her gently to face him, his fingers tilting her face up to his. She lost herself in the blue depths of his eyes, her pulse fluttering wildly.

And when Roger bent his head to kiss her, Jane abandoned herself to him with a tiny sigh of rapture.

Chapter Six

The Rendezvous

Lady Jane heard the door click softly, and moments later the enticing aroma of hot chocolate filled the chamber. Jane buried her head beneath the covers, anticipating the instant her abigail would pull back the heavy curtains and let the bright sunlight stream into the room. Or the oppressive light from leaden skies, if the day was overcast and rainy.

"A good mornin' to ye, milady." Betty's voice rang out cheerfully, as it had every morning for as long as Jane could remember. "Cook is in a pucker about the new scullery maid this morning. Claims she is a saucy baggage more interested in flirting with the footmen than scrubbing pots. And Mrs. Daley is anxious to know if she might go into the village this morning. Her old mum came down with a colic last night. From eating spoiled fish, or so she claims. And—"

"Enough, Betty!" Jane sat up abruptly and flung off the covers. It was useless to try to catch an extra moment's sleep when Betty started on her morning rundown of the latest household problems. "I will not listen to any more complaints until I have had my chocolate." She slid out of bed and settled herself in her favourite armchair beside the window.

It was her custom, when the weather was fine, as it was this morning, to sit by the window while she drank her chocolate. From her window, which opened onto a small balcony, Jane could see the turrets of Trenton Abbey above the trees, and in the far distance, the green outline of Hogdon Hill topped by a darker shadow she knew to be horse chestnuts and an occasional ash. She could not see the meadow or the pond, but she knew they were there and wished she could escape into that magical world, which had become so much more enchanted now that Roger had kissed her there.

Jane had not been back since the day of the Hunt, but dreamed of it every night, reliving that kiss she had despaired of receiving. Her thoughts would often dwell on that precious moment while her hands were busy with other tasks. Her lips would tingle, and her heart race as if she were once again caught up in Roger's embrace there under the willows beside the still pool. For that brief moment in time, he had been all hers. She had sensed it and was exalted by the thought. He had been hers and no other's.

But the moment had passed, and Jane could not stop herself from wondering who else Roger might have kissed since then. She had not been alone with him after that wonderful moment there by the pond. They had met often enough, but always in the presence of the hordes of relatives who had descended upon both families for the wedding.

The weeks before the wedding had passed in a flurry of activity. Jane scarcely had a moment to herself from the instant she sprang out of bed in the morning to face a dozen different crises, like Mrs. Daley's colicky mum, until she retired at night, exhausted but secretly rejoicing that the most important day of her life was rapidly approaching. And now, two days before the great event, she had promised herself the indulgence of a short afternoon ride with Elizabeth, who had arrived two days ago, accompanied by neither her husband nor her three children.

"I regret that I can only stay such a short while, Jane," Elizabeth Wainscott remarked later that morning, as the two friends waited in the stable-yard for the groom to saddle their horses, "and I must confess that George was reluctant to allow me to travel so far with only the grooms and two outriders to escort me. He would have come himself, poor dear, but his mother is ailing, and let me tell you, Jane, you have no idea how lucky you are not to have a mother-in-law to find fault with everything you do."

Roger's mother had died of pneumonia three years ago, and Jane clearly remembered Lady Trenton's sweet and affectionate nature. She smiled as she allowed Tom to help her mount a skittish Ginger. "I fancy Lady Trenton would have made an ideal mother-in-law. She was like a second mother to me when we used to spend much of our time at the Abbey with you and Tony. Do you remember the time I broke my ankle?"

"You are naive if you think the marchioness would not have made subtle suggestions on how to manage her household once she became the dowager, Jane," Elizabeth objected gently. "Besides, no mother likes to admit her son's wife is perfect."

"That has been your experience, no doubt, Lizzie, but since it never happened to me, I shall have to take your word that some females naturally turn into shrews when a younger woman takes their place in the house," Jane admitted as they rode across the Park towards Trenton land. "But I do think we should enjoy ourselves this afternoon, and forget about our troubles."

"Speaking of trouble, my dear Jane," Elizabeth said after a pause, "how is your nemesis, Lady Horton, adjusting to your marriage to Roger? You have told me so much about her, I feel as though I would recognize her anywhere."

Jane smiled. "You could not help but do so, Liz. But I believe that woman has realized that she is no longer important in Roger's life. He assured me himself that there will be no more ugly rumours on the subject." She spoke with confidence, but the memory of Roger's eyes following the dashing, blue-clad figure of Lady Horton nagged at the back of her mind.

"I trust you are right, Jane. But as you say, no more talk of trouble. If only we had brought Tony and

Roger with us, this visit to the pond would be just like old times."

Jane heartily agreed and was only too happy to spend the rest of the ride to Hogdon Hill dredging up escapades from their childhood. As they rode through the little copse towards the grassy summit of Hogdon Hill, Jane enjoyed the more recent memory of her visit to the secret pond with Roger. Her heart swelled with happiness as she relived the kiss he had given her, so special to her that she had not yet confided in her best friend.

"I have missed all this so much, Jane," Elizabeth was saying. "And there is the strawberry patch we used to raid every summer. Tony will want to stay on here at home until they ripen. You know how much he loves strawberries."

Jane, who was dawdling in the rear, halted beside the strawberry patch. "I do believe they have spread since your brother made himself sick that time, remember, Lizzie? We had best—"

Her remark was cut short by an exclamation of annoyance from Elizabeth, who had reached the top of the hill. "Oh, botheration, there is someone down by our pond," she said, glancing back at Jane, her brows drawn together. "I had so looked forward to seeing the tadpoles again. Do you know them Jane? Perhaps they are trespassing and we can scare them off."

Jane urged her mare forward and stopped beside her friend. Her gaze was drawn to the figures standing beneath the weeping willows. They stood close together, and it was not hard to imagine that they were enjoying an intimate moment together. Not hard at all in this case, because Jane could not pretend she did not recognize them.

Her heart seemed to freeze in her breast.

"Is that not . . . ?" Elizabeth began, then stopped abruptly, glancing at Jane with eyes full of shock and a hint of pity.

Even as they sat there on the brow of Hogdon Hill overlooking the idyllic scene, Jane saw the woman in blue mount her black horse and gallop away towards the woods on the farther side of the pond. She did not seem to care that she had been observed. In what looked to Jane like an act of sheer bravado, the woman pulled the black to a prancing halt and raised a blue-gloved hand in a mocking salute to the man standing by the pond. Then she whirled and disappeared into the trees.

"What bare-faced effrontery," Elizabeth gasped after the woman had gone. "I gather that must be the infamous Lady Horton."

Jane could not respond. Her mouth was dry and her throat full of unshed tears. She felt as though her face had turned to marble, unable to move a muscle. Then the man beside the pond turned towards the hill and Jane knew that worse was yet to come.

How could she possibly face Roger after this?

The movement on the hill drew Roger's attention from the angry woman who had, moments before, thrown her arms about his neck and kissed him with sensuous abandon. He had instantly felt the old pull of desire Maud had always aroused in him, but he forced himself to push her arms away.

"I am to be wed in two days, Maud," he rebuked her. "This cannot be. I thought I had made it clear to you that—"

"Aye, clear enough for the likes of you, my lord," Lady Horton had snapped back sarcastically. "I never would have taken you for just another randy bastard, all smiles and charm when it suits you to roll a poor girl in the hay for your pleasure, but quick to cast her aside as soon as some rich hoity-toity bag of bones agrees to let you into her bed."

"That is not the way it happened, Maud," Roger protested, suddenly ashamed that she had come so close to the truth. He had been supremely careless in his liaison with her, as he had with all his amorous adventures, drugged by her overt sensuality, with never a thought for anything but his own pleasure. He

had enjoyed Maud more than any of his other con-
quests, and it had bothered him not a whit that she
had a husband. She had been the ideal mistress; he
had always thought so, and if he could keep their affair that way, he would have done so without hesitation, wife or no wife.

But there was that promise he had made to Jane.
Why he had done anything so foolhardy was beyond
him; but he had promised, and he knew as truly as if
she had confessed it herself, that Jane had accepted
his offer of marriage because of that promise. She had
trusted him. Roger had given his word, and a Hastings
never went back on his word. Never.

But what was a man to do when a voluptuous hussy
flung herself at him and molded every luscious curve
against him invitingly? He was not cut out for celibacy,
and it had been nearly two months since he had broken with Maud. Two whole months without a woman.
Roger could not remember suffering such deprivation
since that fortuitous afternoon he had come upon one
of the milkmaids asleep in a haystack, her skirts rum-
pled around her thighs. What he learned that afternoon at fourteen had made him a firm believer in the
delights of the flesh, and he had not stinted himself
ever since. Until now.

He had wavered, he admitted, when Maud offered
herself so brazenly, blue jacket already unbuttoned
and lips eager and demanding against his. It had taken
every ounce of fortitude he had not known he pos-
sessed to deny her. And now she turned bitter and
argumentative.

"That is exactly the way it was, do not deny it, you
rogue. You are no better than the worst of them, taking advantage of a married woman for your vile pleasures, with nary a thought to the consequences."

This was so blatantly untrue that Roger opened his
mouth to protest, but Maud continued without a
pause.

"Yes, it is the babe I am talking about, and well you

know it, Roger. What am I to do with your bastard I carry in my belly?"

Taken aback by the virulence of this accusation, Roger responded in kind. "You have no proof at all that the child is mine," he said harshly. "And I suggest that you do not put that falsehood about in the village, my girl, for you will only make yourself out to be the slut you are. You have a husband who may well be the father. Indeed, more than likely Giles did father the child if you will only admit it."

"Bah!" she broke in angrily. "What do you know about it? Anyone with half the sense he was born with would see that the old man is beyond fathering anything. Heaven knows, I tried my best, but it was worse than a wet dishrag flapping around on my belly. Never could get him to hold the course. The child is yours, I swear."

"Sir Giles will doubtless acknowledge it as his and be pleased as punch to do so," Roger said dryly, more than a little shocked at the coarseness of his former beloved's speech.

It was then that Roger recognized the two riders on the hill.

When Maud saw them, too, she laughed with reckless abandon, looking at him with those startling violet eyes of hers filled with mockery and something else. Could it be that she was glad they had been caught together? Was it her way of getting back at him for ending their affair?

Roger had a sudden premonition of catastrophe. Had her promise of returning the letters he had been rash enough to pen over the months they indulged in their sexual fantasy been merely a pretext to lure him here? She had mentioned something about a small compensation—a parting gift. Something to prove there were no hard feelings between them.

He had believed her. After all, the fifty pounds he had been prepared to give was little enough to express the pleasure she had given him. But now he wondered if his devious Maud had not perhaps some other plan

in mind. Had she intended to seduce him again? She
might well have done so, he thought ruefully, had not
he remembered his promise to Jane. And even then,
his flesh might have been too weak to resist had there
been time for Maud to work her intoxicating magic.

But he had been saved from this ignominious defeat
by the chance appearance of the last person he would
have wished to discover him in yet another compromising assignation with Lady Horton. The irony of this
situation was not lost on him.

"You must leave at once, Maud," he said in a low
voice, as if Jane were within earshot. "Give me the
letters, and I will send you fifty pounds next week."

Lady Horton's laughter turned decidedly cynical.
"Fifty pounds, love? You expect to get off so lightly,
do you? I think not, my lord. I shall keep your sweet
notes to remind me what pathetic creatures men are."
She turned, her swirling skirts brushing his boots, and
setting one foot in the stirrup scrambled into the saddle before he could help her. "I would advise you to
mend fences with your virgin heiress, my dear. That
is, if you intend to wed her in two days," she called
over her shoulder. "I fear you will have to grovel."
She seemed to find this amusing, for she laughed
immoderately.

She urged the big black horse round the bank of
the pond, kicking him into a canter on the other side.
At the edge of the wood that separated Trenton land
from the Horton estate, she paused, raising a gloved
hand in an impudent gesture of farewell or triumph—
it was difficult to tell. Roger could still hear her laughter after she disappeared into the trees.

He mounted his own horse and rode out from under
the willows into the sunlight. No amount of sunshine
could warm him now, he thought, urging Jason into a
canter up the gentle slope of Hogdon Hill. Before he
was halfway across the meadow, he saw Jane disap-
pear from the summit. Elizabeth paused for an instant
to gaze down on him and then she was gone, too.

Roger kicked Jason into a gallop but his heart was

heavy as he crested the hill and saw nothing but emptiness. Jane was gone, and knowing her as he did, Roger feared she was racing that mare of hers with total disregard for life and limb.

He would never catch her before she reached the safety of Penhallow. And even if he did, he knew his promised bride was in no mood to listen to him. Roger had serious doubts that she would ever listen to him again.

Lady Jane jumped at the light tap on her bedchamber door. She had been closeted there since returning from her ride with Elizabeth, sitting in her favourite chair, staring out of the window at the distant turrets of Trenton Abbey. Beyond, in the mellow light of late afternoon, Hogdon Hill rose up, a silent reminder of the betrayal she had suffered there. Try as she might, Jane could not rid her mind of that wrenching scene of the couple beside the pond. Had anyone reported Roger's perfidy to her, she never would have believed it. Had he not promised? And she—blind, lovelorn fool that she was—had believed him. But witnessing the scene under the willows herself had burned the memory of it into her mind irrevocably. There was no excusing this treachery.

The tap came again, but Jane did not respond. She did not want anyone to interrupt her misery and persuade her that there must be a reasonable explanation for Roger's secret assignation with Lady Horton in the very place that was so special to her. The place where he had kissed Jane.

The door opened a crack and Elizabeth stuck her head in.

"Please go away, Lizzie. I am not in the mood for company."

Ignoring this surly remark, her friend stepped into the room bearing a tea-tray, which she set down beside Jane's chair. "Since you missed your tea, my dear, I have brought you a fresh pot and a piece of seedcake. The tarts were all demolished by your little

nephews and nieces. I cannot imagine why your Aunt
Honoria permits her grandchildren to invade the tea-
table when they should be upstairs in the nursery.
Poor Lady Octavia had something to say about that,
I can tell you."

Jane remained silent. She knew her Aunt Honoria
liked to provoke her father's unmarried sister at every
opportunity. The two ladies had been archenemies
ever since her mother arrived at Penhallow as a bride.
They clashed over the most insignificant issues. Only
yesterday morning, Jane had been forced to intervene
when the two ladies could not agree where a vase of
lilies should be placed. In her present state, she did
not find her aunts' petty rivalries amusing.

"I do not wish to hear it, Lizzie. Neither do I wish
any tea, thank you."

She might as well have held her peace, for Elizabeth
settled herself on a straight-backed chair and poured
two cups.

"I thought I would have another cup with you, Jane.
Those children quite ruined my first cup downstairs
by racing round and round the pianoforte and yelling
as if the devil himself were after them. Lady Octavia
was beside herself, I can tell you. You would have felt
sorry for the poor dear."

Jane turned to stare out of the window, but the
sight of Hogdon Hill did not improve her spirits. She
wrenched her eyes away and watched numbly as Elizabeth cut a slice of cake and passed it to her on one
of her mother's favourite Sèvres plates.

"I truly cannot eat anything, Lizzie. I simply
cannot . . ." Jane felt a wave of despair threaten to
engulf her, and she choked back a sob.

She felt her friend reach over and clasp her hands.
"I know you are upset, my dearest Jane, but so is
Roger. He has told—"

"Oh, is he indeed, the wretch?" Jane burst out angrily. "I can well imagine he is upset that I caught
him dallying with that Horton woman again. And after

he had promised me . . . Oh, Lizzie, he *promised* me that he would not . . . I cannot bear it."

"Tell me all about it, love," Elizabeth said gently, squeezing Jane's rigid hands. "You have yet to tell me how it happened with you and Roger. You wrote that he had finally made you an offer, and that you accepted, but what really happened? I want to know all the details."

"There is nothing to tell," Jane answered shortly. "Roger Hastings is a liar and a deceiver. He made me a promise never to see that woman again." She laughed humourlessly. "And then with my own eyes I see him . . ." She swallowed the lump in her throat. "Oh, how dare he take her *there*? To our special place. I will not stand for it, Lizzie, I swear I will not." Now that she had started talking, she could not seem to stop. "Oh, Lizzie, whatever am I to do?"

"First of all you will drink your tea, Jane," Elizabeth said bracingly, handing her the steaming cup. "You are in dire need of a restorative, and a good strong cup of China brew is what my grandmama always gave me when I was feeling blue-devilled." She smiled when Jane took a tentative sip from the delicate cup. "And then you must promise to let me tell you Roger's side of the—"

"No!" Jane cried out in alarm. "I have no desire to hear anything that wretch has to say. I saw what I saw. *You* saw him, too, Lizzie. What more is there to tell?"

"If you will not fly into the boughs, dear, I shall tell you what Roger told me. *Please* listen." She raised both hands before Jane could utter the angry retort that came to her lips. "You are right, I did see him with that woman, and I was as disgusted as you, believe me. And when he approached me after tea and asked about you, I was hard pressed not to give him a piece of my mind. But he looked so very dejected that I could not help but take pity on him."

"I am not the least surprised," Jane snapped. "He is a consummate charmer and could make you believe

that up is down if he had a mind to it. I daresay he
had an entirely plausible explanation for meeting that
woman alone at that particular place. Is nothing sacred
to him?" Her voice broke. How naive she had been
to believe that first kiss from the man she loved had
meant anything to him.

"As it happens, he did have an explanation that
sounded very reasonable to me, and remember, Jane,
I was not disposed to believe anything he said. But in
the end I did, and I promised I would speak to you
about it." She paused. "Roger begged me to give you
this," she added, pulling a folded paper from her
pocket and handing it to Jane. "Will you read it,
dear?"

Jane stared at her friend as though Elizabeth had
suggested something obscene. "No, I will not. He is
wasting his time sending *billets doux* to *me*. He would
get better results addressing them to his *chère amie*,"
she said waspishly, ignoring the note that Elizabeth
placed on the table beside her. Part of her heart
wanted to snatch it up and peruse it for something,
anything that might allow her to understand, to believe
in him again, even to forgive. But the part that had
been so badly hurt wanted to hate him for that blatant betrayal.

"Then please listen to what he told me, Jane. You
should at least know what really happened at the pond
this afternoon."

"What he *says* happened," she said bitterly. "Not
necessarily the same thing, remember."

Elizabeth obviously took this for the reluctant con-
sent it was, for she started talking, and Jane sat silently, sipping her tea and trying to hate the man
whose excuse sounded increasingly convincing the
more she heard.

"Love letters?" she murmured when Elizabeth was
done. "Are you telling me the rogue wrote love letters
to that female?" The notion of Roger, *her* Roger,
being in love with Lady Horton had never occurred
to her. She had imagined these illicit liaisons gentle-

men so often indulged in to be entirely carnal in nature. But what if she was wrong? "Do you think he loves her, Elizabeth?" she demanded.

Elizabeth shook her head. "Not in the way we ladies mean when we speak of love, dear. George hinted at it when he made me his offer. Everyone knew he kept a mistress in London, but he swore he loved me. Mama explained it all to me afterwards, and I know for a fact that he broke with her before he married me. Animal passion is what Mama called it, and some gentlemen have an excess of it. But it is not love, or very rarely. More like an infatuation with some buxom wench who attracts their eye." She paused for a moment before adding, "Nothing like what Roger feels for you, Jane, you can take my word on it."

"Roger does not feel *anything* for me," Jane responded prosaically. "He needs my fortune. More so if he must pay off the dozens of discarded lightskirts who threaten to blackmail him."

Elizabeth raised a hand impatiently. "Matches are arranged every day among families of the *ton*, Jane. You know that. If all the silly chits I know were allowed to choose for themselves, what a disaster their lives would be. Many of them would elope to Gretna Green with their dancing masters. You are lucky that Roger cares enough about you to break off his liaison, which he assures me he has done."

"He does not love me," Jane repeated stubbornly.

"Give him time, dear. I think you will find marriage to Roger very much to your liking." Elizabeth smiled shyly. "Especially the marriage bed. I do not doubt for a moment that Roger is adept at pleasing a female. And believe me, if he is anything like my George, you will have no cause for regrets, Jane."

Lady Jane had lowered her eyes during this frank speech, conscious of her hotly flushed cheeks. This aspect of her relationship with Roger had occupied her thoughts increasingly as the date approached. She had no mother to guide her on the intimate side of marriage, but Aunt Honoria had taken it upon herself to override Lady Octavia's scruples and lay out everything that would be expected of a bride, sometimes in frightening detail. Elizabeth's quiet assurance that Roger would give her pleasure made Jane suddenly eager to pass into womanhood as soon as possible. To do so, of course, she would have to go to the altar with Roger, and to do that, she would have to forgive him, or at least try to do so.

"Well?" Elizabeth gently prodded. "What shall I tell Roger? That you want nothing more to do with him, or that you will be his wife?"

"Tell him that I will talk to him after dinner," Jane heard herself say, all her reservations melting away. "And thank you, Lizzie. You are the best of friends."

Only after Elizabeth had gone, and Jane sat gazing at the turrets of Trenton Abbey, did she realize that she had effectively burned her bridges. She would marry Roger, not because her father had so decreed, nor because Roger needed her fortune to restore his estates, but because she wanted to be his wife more than anything she could name and had for as long as she could remember.

She smiled as the outline of Hogdon Hill disappeared into the dusk. It would be her choice after all.

Chapter Seven

The Wedding

Jane stepped gingerly down from the carriage, holding her father's hand tightly. Her two contentious aunts, who had arrived at the chapel earlier to attend to last-minute details, fussed around her, carefully lifting the small train of her wedding gown and settling it in creamy folds of satin around her feet.

"The gown is too long," Lady Octavia remarked for perhaps the tenth time since Jane had put it on that morning. "I told you it would be, Honoria. The poor gel will trip all over herself walking up the aisle."

Lady Bristol's face mottled in anger. "It is *not* too long," she declared forcefully. "Madame Clothilde assured me it was all the crack in Town, and she should know. After all she *is* the premier modiste in London. I insisted upon the very best for my poor Claire's little girl."

Lady Octavia was evidently not convinced, for she frowned at her niece. "I cannot understand why it is so plain. One might mistakenly think that the bride's father had pockets to let, which of course is absurd. If you were short of the ready, Honoria, I wish you had applied to me. I would have been more than happy to—"

Lady Bristol instantly bristled. "That was not the case at all, Octavia, as you must know. Your brother insisted upon having the bills sent to his London agent, but I refused. I wanted the gown to be my gift to my dear sister's daughter."

"Well, I still say the train is altogether too short.

A few more yards of satin could not have been so very expensive."

"And the gown is not plain, my dear Octavia," Lady Bristol continued condescendingly. "The word is *elegant,* as anyone with the least sense of fashion would recognize. Madame Clothilde was quite adamant about it. Flounces, frills, bows, and ribbons are for tradesmen's daughters, she told me. And long, elaborate trains might do very well for St. George's in Hanover Square, but for a simple country wedding in a family chapel, yards and yards of train would only be an encumbrance. It was not a matter of expense at all."

"Indeed?" Lady Octavia murmured. "I am *so* glad to hear it."

Suddenly tired of this senseless bickering, Lady Jane glanced imploringly at her father.

Lord Penhallow took immediate action. "That is quite enough of your silly quibbling, ladies. I will not tolerate any criticism of Jane's gown. It is quite lovely, and you are even lovelier, my child." He smiled, and Jane felt a lump in her throat.

She glanced around at the crowds of relatives and guests, now thinning rapidly as everyone moved into the chapel, children yelling and pushing to get in first. For a terrifying moment, Jane felt an irrational urge to jump back into the carriage and run home again, back to her workroom, where the sketch of the purple orchid lay unfinished on her desk. Back to the bedchamber decorated in blue and gold where she had slept most of her adult life.

"Oh, Papa," she whispered, so faintly that the earl had to bend his head to hear, "I am so scared."

"Nonsense, child, everything will be all right," he said gruffly, patting her cold hands. "It is only natural for young girls to be nervous on their wedding day. But Roger will be a good husband to you, Jane, never fear. Everything is as it should be. I only wish your mother were here to see her little girl make such a splendid match."

He smiled fondly at her, and Jane did not have the heart to tell him that her mother would certainly have insisted that the earl keep his promise to give his daughter a Season in London. Jane had mentioned it several times herself, but Lord Penhallow had argued that there would be time enough for a visit to the Metropolis once she was a married lady.

On more than one occasion, Jane had been on the verge of telling him that she did not wish to be a married lady. And certainly not to Roger Hastings. At least until she could be sure—quite, *quite* sure—that he had put his philandering ways behind him. All she had was his promise, renewed as recently as two evenings ago, that his affair with Lady Horton was definitely over.

After a few false starts, a wave of organ music suddenly poured out of the chapel and washed over her. Mrs. Ogden, the organist from St. Matthew's in the village, was in fine fettle. At the sound, her father moved nervously. " 'Tis time to go in, Jane. Roger is waiting for you."

In a daze, Jane clutched the bouquet of pink rosebuds and forget-me-nots their head gardener had so carefully prepared for her himself. He had presented it to her just before she stepped into the carriage this morning, surrounded by the entire garden and stable staff. Her eyes had filled at their simple yet sincere gesture, and it was then that the irreversibility of her marriage had impressed itself upon her most forcibly. She was leaving her father's house, the home of her childhood, and although she would naturally visit her father often, her home from that day forth would be Trenton Abbey. With Roger.

There was no turning back now. Roger was waiting for her in there beside the ancient stone altar—where, legend had it, one of his ancestors had wed a lady won from a rival knight at sword point—probably impatient at the delay.

Two evenings ago she had intended to tell him she could not wed a man whom she did not trust. This had seemed the wisest course. But he had been so contrite, so tender, so sincere that she could not bring herself to cast his betrayal in his teeth. Jane had finally believed his tale of the incriminating *billets doux,* and the threat of blackmail. And when he had given her the emerald ring, an heirloom from the Trenton coffers, she had felt her resentment waver and dissipate. Then he renewed his promise, and she had allowed herself to dream again.

That change of heart had brought her to the steps of the chapel this morning, and as Jane moved out of the sunlight into the small vestibule, she was conscious of the coolness closing in upon her.

Behind her, Jane heard the muted voices of her aunts, still arguing, but she no longer cared. Beyond the archway, she could see the blur of faces on either side of the aisle, relatives and friends towards the front, retainers and tenants from both estates at the back. The music took on a solemn measure and Lord Penhallow moved forward.

Jane felt as though she drifted rather than walked down the aisle. She was in a daze. Though conscious of the murmurs from the congregation, she did not see any of them clearly.

And then she was there. Her father stood by her side, but Jane's eyes were drawn to Roger, resplendent in pale blue and silver. After that first glance, Jane dropped her eyes to his waistcoat, glittering with silver embroidery. He was magnificent, she thought. His tawny blond curls were neatly arranged for once, instead of flying wildly around his head like a halo. There was no doubt in her mind that he was the handsomest man she had ever seen, even more so than Stephen Horton, whose dark good looks had beguiled her as a young girl, and who had stolen a kiss in the shrubbery during one of Lady Penhallow's annual masquerade balls. She felt a fleeting stab of pity for Maud Horton, who had been abandoned by both these men.

Jane heard the Reverend Johnson's voice through

a fog of memories that flooded her mind and made her feel giddy and detached from what was going on around her. She heard Roger's deep voice pronouncing his vows, and somehow she must have given her own correctly, for before she knew it, Jane heard the collective sigh of the congregation behind her as Roger leaned forward and kissed her chastely.

And then all was chaos. Jane was swept out of the chapel on her new husband's arm, and everyone crowded around her to offer congratulations. Tony Cheswick, with his teasing grin, Elizabeth, smiling and crying at once. Lord Trenton with a bear hug, welcoming her into the family, her aunts, both in tears, Roger's sisters and their husbands, and numerous cousins calling out to her as Roger eased her through the crowd and into his father's open landau with the Trenton coat of arms emblazoned on its varnished doors.

All too soon the doors were closed and the stately coach, drawn by Lord Trenton's four best horses, pulled away from the chapel, set on its hill overlooking the placid expanse of lake that separated it from the Abbey.

Local rumour had it that the third Earl's second countess had tossed her young stepson into the deep waters to ensure that her own son would inherit the title. As a child, Jane remembered rowing out to the centre of the lake—where the tragedy was said to have occurred—with Roger and Tony, who were convinced the boy was still down there somewhere. Roger claimed that the child's grave, next to his mother's in the Trenton cemetery, was empty because the body was never recovered. Some villagers swore to have seen a small figure rising up out of the waters on moonlit nights, crying for his mother. Jane had tried hard not to believe such superstitions, but as the coach passed along the lake shore, she shuddered.

"You are not cold, are you, Jane?" Roger leaned over to clasp her hands in his. "Your hands are freezing, my dear. Here, let me put a rug over your knees."

"I was thinking of that poor wee mite who drowned

here," Jane murmured. "How different things might have been had he become the fourth earl instead of his brother, your ancestor."

Roger shrugged. "Indeed they would, my dear. You would not be sitting in this carriage with me, I daresay. Some other Hastings would be enjoying that honour; perhaps some dreadfully boring fellow who would prose on and on about how fortunate you are to be his chosen bride. Naturally, he would not be half as handsome nor charming as me, so you can count yourself lucky that the dull fellow's ancestor was cut off in his youth four hundred years ago."

Jane shuddered again, and wrapped the rug more tightly about her. "How callous you are, Roger, to speak so ill of that poor boy, murdered by your direct ancestor."

"The records say it was an accident, Jane."

"Nobody around here believes that Banbury tale, Roger. You do not believe it yourself; I remember you saying so."

There was a sudden silence in the carriage, and Jane regretted bringing it up. It was not until they reached the outskirts of the village that Roger spoke again.

"This is hardly a topic of conversation appropriate for a wedding day, Jane, my love," he said smoothly. "We are about to enter the village—Father insisted we keep that tedious tradition alive—so I suggest we try to look as though we are as happy as newlyweds are supposed to be."

His words left Jane stunned. She gazed for an endless moment into his dark blue eyes, hoping to find the teasing gleam that would assure her Roger was funning. There was none. She turned away and waved mechanically at a group of villagers gathered beside the road. She forced herself to smile. "Yes," she murmured, determined not to cry on this of all days, "we must both learn to pretend, must we not?"

Roger observed the streams of relatives and neighbours milling around the long trestle tables set up under the gaily-coloured marquees on the freshly manicured lawn. From his position beside Lord Penhallow, he could appreciate the clash between the chaotic throngs converging on the loaded tables, and the orderly contingent of footmen marching with military precision from the kitchen bearing the silver platters of delicacies most of the guests had never tasted before.

In the shade of the centennial oaks that dotted the Park, a harried-looking string quartet did its best to rise above the sounds of squealing children, chattering guests, and the occasional shrill bark of Aunt Octavia's ancient pug, Sunshine. Roger felt a keen empathy for the little dog, trailing around after his mistress, a monstrous pink satin bow around his neck. He hoped his own misery was not writ large upon his face as it was on poor Sunshine's. His lips set in a permanent smile, and his patience running dangerously thin, Roger glanced at his new father-in-law, wondering how the earl could sound so jovial after more than four hours of fielding inane comments from his guests.

He looked around for his wife—he was still having difficulty with the idea that Jane really was his wife—and saw that she had changed into a pale green muslin with sprigs of yellow rose-buds around the neck and hem. She looked cool and collected as she strolled with her aunts among the guests, stopping to speak to little groups that gathered around her. Roger found her utterly charming in her simplicity, and he looked forward to the moment he could tell her so.

She had said little to him since they completed the traditional ride in the open carriage through the village, and Roger had the uneasy feeling that Jane was unhappy under the serene exterior she presented to her father's guests. He had tried to catch her eye several times, but she seemed in no hurry to leave, for she ignored his silent plea. Roger had ordered the landau a full half hour ago, and it was standing under an oak, the horses lazily whisking their tails in the shade.

Everything was over but the shouting, as his father

liked to say. It was high time Roger pried his bride
away from all these relatives and carried her home to
Trenton Abbey. He thought he understood Lady
Jane's reluctance to make this final break with her
father's house, but that breach had already been made
this morning at the altar of the chapel. She belonged
with him now, as Lord Penhallow would be the first
to agree.

He turned to his host. "I think it is time for us to
leave, my lord."

"If you can get Jane away from her friends, boy."
The earl chortled good-humouredly. "Very popular
with the locals is my gel. Always had a soft heart for
the children, too. No wonder they all love her."

Roger had to admit that Jane had attracted a crowd
of young people around her. Some of the younger
ones—her nieces like brightly-coloured butterflies in
their new silks and muslins, and his own nephews in
velvet suits and frilly lace collars—clung to her skirts
with their tiny fingers, loath to let her go. All appeared
to be talking at once, vying for her attention, but
Jane's smiling face showed no sign of the impatience
that was eating him up.

In a flash of insight, Roger imagined his wife surrounded with their own children on the lawns of Trenton Abbey. A happy picture that made him smile,
until it was clouded by the shadow of that other
child—purportedly his—that Maud carried. And by
the ghost of another child, that young boy of long
ago whose spirit had not found rest in the Trenton
family graveyard.

At that moment, Jane raised her eyes, and their
gazes locked. Was it his imagination, or had some of
the joy gone from her face? Roger wondered if she
could possibly have read his thoughts. But that was
impossible. He waved at her, and she reluctantly—or
so it seemed to him—started moving in his direction.

The public rituals demanded by Church and family
were behind them, Roger mused, watching his bride
make her way across the grass. But the time had come

to perform the private rituals in the privacy of their bedchamber. He felt an unaccustomed nervousness. In his time, Roger had bedded dozens of females, but nothing in his experience came close to this act he was expected to perform on the girl who was his bride. For some reason he had never thought of Jane in that way before. Marriage to her had always been a constant in his life, but until recently, he had given the actual mechanics of it little thought.

Her eyes were downcast as she stood before him, and Roger wondered if she was as nervous as he. He took her hand and smiled. "It is time to go, my dear," he murmured, pulling her hand into the crook of his arm. Before he could lift her into the carriage, he had to endure yet another tearful scene from both her aunts and from Elizabeth, who promised to visit them before returning to her family in Yorkshire.

Jane was silent during the drive back to the Abbey, and Roger was relieved when they stopped before the massive carved door to find Collins waiting to usher them in. The housekeeper had lined up the female servants to receive their new mistress, and Jane greeted them with a smile as they bobbed their curtseys. Mrs. Collins herself wore her usual sour expression, which had always reminded Roger of a particularly bad-tempered bulldog his father had owned years ago.

"Show her ladyship up to her apartments, Mrs. Collins," he said as soon as the welcoming ritual had concluded. "And Collins, there is a basket of food in the carriage. Have it taken down to the kitchens, will you?" His eyes followed Jane as she mounted the stairs in the housekeeper's wake, and then he turned into the library and allowed the butler to serve him a glass of brandy.

What was Jane thinking? he wondered. Was she as nervous about their new relationship as he was? Roger longed to dash up the stairs to assure her that she had nothing to fear from him. He wanted to put his arms about her slender form and bury his face in her hair, to breathe in the elusive perfume of spring flowers that she always wore, to touch her cool lips with his as he had done at the chapel. Most of all he wanted to make her smile again, to banish that hint of unhappiness that clouded her amber eyes.

The unexpected rush of tenderness that engulfed him took Roger by surprise. He could not recall feeling quite so affected by a woman before. His reactions were usually far more carnal, as they had been with Maud—no, he must not think of Maud. That was all in the past, especially since she had shown herself so mercenary and grasping over those dratted letters. He had not heard from her since that unfortunate meeting beside the pond, but he did not doubt for a moment that she would not let the matter drop.

But there he was thinking of that delectable hussy again when he had the sweetest girl in the world waiting for him upstairs. He wondered how soon it might be appropriate for him to join her. Summer twilight was only beginning to fall in the Park outside the library window, and the warm stillness of the air was filled with sounds of birds roosting in the oaks. Was it too early to retire? Perhaps he would find Jane already asleep after the excitement of her wedding day. Roger smiled at the thought of waking his wife with warm kisses on those cool lips. Waking her body to passion, teaching her to enjoy his touch, to welcome it, showing her the secrets of desire.

Roger glanced at the gilt clock on the mantel. His impatience was suddenly a palpable thing. He took a turn about the room, then stopped abruptly, grinning to himself. His father had stayed on at Penhallow and planned to make a night of it at the card-table. Lord Trenton had deliberately arranged things to leave the newlyweds alone. There was no one to raise an eyebrow if the groom chose to go up betimes to his bride. He was behaving like the veriest moonling, Roger told himself disgustedly, and reached for the bellpull.

Before he could order Collins to send up a dinner-tray to the viscountess's sitting room for them, the butler cleared his throat. "Beg pardon, milord, there is a lady to see you."

Roger turned away from the window and stared at the butler, who looked uncomfortable, his mouth puckered in disapproval. "A lady? At this hour? Tell her that her ladyship has retired already."

"I did so, milord. She says it is you she wishes to see."

Roger felt a cold hand clutch at his insides. "Me? Is something amiss at Penhallow perchance, Collins?"

"Oh, no, nothing like that. It is Lady Horton, milord. Shall I send her away?"

"Please do," Roger replied coldly. "And, Collins, I believe I gave orders that this woman was not to be admitted to the Abbey."

"Yes, milord. I shall see to it." Then he extended his silver salver. "The lady left this for the viscountess, milord. Shall I take it upstairs?"

Roger knew what it was instantly. He picked it up. "No. And no other letters that woman leaves are to be taken to the viscountess. Is that clear?"

"Yes, milord," the butler replied stiffly.

After the door closed behind Collins, Roger looked down at the letter in his hand. It was as he thought. His own handwriting stared back at him, and he wondered which of the damning missives he had foolishly written at the height of his infatuation with Maud it was.

He had to admit that her timing was exquisite. What better moment for a discarded mistress to make her presence felt than when he was about to join his wife in her sitting room on their wedding night? And to deliver the letter herself. The audacity of it was monstrous, but so like her. At least he now knew that she intended him as much harm as could be wrung from his indiscretion.

Roger held the letter to a candle flame until it flared up. Once it was burning strongly, he tossed it into the empty grate and watched it curl, turn black, and fall apart in grey ashes. So much for his thoughtless appetites. As a married man, he had other responsibilities and duties, and one particular duty was waiting for him upstairs.

He climbed the stairs to his wife's chamber with deliberate nonchalance. There was no need to confirm what the servants probably had already guessed: Roger Hastings was as eager as any new husband to taste the pleasures of the marriage bed.

Chapter Eight

The Viscountess

The twilight deepened perceptibly as Jane stood on the balcony outside her apartments in her night rail. She held her breath as the full moon finally rose from behind the dark shape of the chapel and hung above the lake, a huge yellow eye in the black sky.

She sighed and pulled the silk shawl closer about her shoulders. The summer evening was not cold, but there was an eerie feel to the scene before her that caused her to shiver. The moon gazed down at its reflection in the still waters now coated with a glittering silver veil that hid the dark and dangerous depths beneath. Would that little boy—rumoured to lie at the bottom of the lake—be staring up at the moon with sightless eyes? How many times had those dead eyes watched this same moon wax and wane over the centuries? Did his ghost really rise from the lake at midnight, as the villagers claimed, to visit the lonely graveyard where his mother lay?

Jane shuddered. She should be in bed, waiting like a good wife for her new husband, who might even now be mounting the stairs. Yet she could not drag her eyes away from the moonlit lake or dispel thoughts of that fatal night when a mother became a monster.

Absorbed by these morbid thoughts, Jane flinched when a warm arm circled her waist, and she felt herself pulled against a lean masculine form.

"What are you doing out here alone, my love?" Roger murmured close to her ear. "We cannot have you catching cold, you know." He nuzzled her play-fully, and Jane felt a frisson of pure joy.

"I was watching the moon rise over the lake and . . . and thinking," she replied, glancing up to admire the sheen of his tousled hair in the moonlight.

"Thinking about me, I trust," he said teasingly, but his voice was deeper than she had ever heard it. "I was thinking about *you*, my sweet," he whispered against her hair, and the words stirred her blood and made it pulse wildly in her veins.

He turned her round to face him, pressing her fully against his body with both hands. Jane realized imme-diately that he must be naked under his blue dressing robe, for she felt the outline of his hardness against her belly. She gave a little gasp that was cut short when his mouth covered hers. His lips were no longer cool as during their first kiss by the pond, or at the altar when he claimed her as his wife. They were hot and wet, and Jane felt a wave of dizziness invade her senses as his tongue traced her mouth, gently coaxing it open until she relaxed against him with a sigh. With-out conscious thought, she found her arms on his shoulders, then round his neck, clinging to him as the erotic sensations rippled through her body.

For what seemed an eternity, Jane felt his lips ex-ploring her mouth, then moving over her eyes and forehead, gradually down her cheeks to her neck. He paused briefly, and Jane felt the warmth of his tongue nestled in the hollow of her throat. Her thoughts were no longer on the moon, the mysterious lake, or the boy who had perished there so long ago. Her entire being was focused on Roger and what he was doing to her with his mouth and hands. Any apprehension she may have had slowly melted away under this tender assault until Jane felt that her whole body was on fire.

When Roger gently pushed open the bodice of her night rail and ran his mouth over her exposed breasts, Jane could not stifle a low moan of pleasure. At last, she thought dreamily, at last she would learn the mys-teries of her own body, and the desires that drove

In the light of the candles burning on the dresser, Roger's tawny hair shone like burnished bronze as he trailed kisses over Jane's exposed breasts. He was quite the most beautiful man she had ever seen. Even more breathtaking undressed than she had dreamed; and he was about to make love to her, the same little Jane Sinclair he had once called *beanstalk*. He may not love her in the romantical sense of the Minerva Press novels, but he definitely desired her. Jane could see it in his eyes, and it made her whole body tingle.

His hands were warm and tender as they roamed her body, and Jane closed her eyes, giving herself up completely to the sensuous pleasure of his touch. She gasped as his fingers brushed over her most secret parts, but she made no protest, moving instinctively against his hand and uttering a little moan of delight when his fingers found a particularly sensitive spot. He teased it gently and seemed to know exactly how to give her the most pleasure.

When he eased over her, nudging her knees apart, Jane felt as though her bones had turned to jelly. She felt the hard heat of him pressing against her. A tremor of delight ran all the way down to her toes.

Roger drew back slightly. "You do know what will happen here, Jane?" he murmured against her mouth. "One of your aunts must have told you about the marriage bed, surely. If not—"

"Oh, yes," she interrupted quickly, anxious to feel him against her again. Anxious to feel him enter her—as Aunt Honoria had described in graphic detail—anxious for the pain that would proclaim her a wife. Roger's wife. The marriage vows might speak of worship, but the solemnity of the word seemed so inappropriate for what Roger was doing to her now.

He pushed inside and Jane felt the precise moment when he breached her maidenhead. The brief pain was insignificant beside the burst of joy she experienced in this act of possession. Roger was finally all hers. He moved further into her and Jane gasped and arched her back to accommodate the full, incredible length of him. Then he began to move, slowly, rhythmically, his breath coming in hot bursts against her ear.

Jane felt her own muscles moving her body in a matching rhythm, as if by some preordained design. This seemed to please him, for Roger groaned and brought his mouth up to kiss her, his tongue hot and demanding. She felt a mounting tension as her body gradually surrendered to the sensuous haze that seemed to have wrapped the two of them in a warm cocoon, cut off from the rest of the world. Jane wished this ecstasy would go on forever, and deliberately blocked every other thought from her mind.

At one point, Roger's hands had slipped under her, and now he raised her up as his movements began to quicken. Jane sensed his growing urgency and pressed herself upwards to meet his thrusts. He groaned and plunged deeply, then shuddered and held still. Jane felt him gradually relax upon her until she had to shift to breathe. Immediately his weight lifted and Jane looked up to find him regarding her tenderly, a crooked smile on his face.

"Well, Jane, we are truly man and wife now, are we not?" He dipped his head and kissed her gently. "I did not hurt you too badly, did I, sweetheart?"

Jane shook her head. Her heart was too full for words, and even if she could have spoken, what does a new bride say to the man who had just been so very, very intimate with her?

She felt herself blush at the memory of it. Would she ever get accustomed to the rush of pleasure she had felt at that first contact with Roger?

"After you get more practice, love—and I can guarantee that you will"—he added with a chuckle—"you will experience more pleasure and less discomfort." He settled down beside her, one arm holding her against him, and in a short while, Jane heard his breathing grow shallow and knew that her new husband had fallen asleep. Just as Aunt Honoria had warned her he would.

Sleep eluded her, however, and Jane lay awake for some time, pondering Roger's words. Perhaps she should ask him, she mused, snuggling against her husband's warmth. Then again, perhaps she should wait and see. Roger had said that pleasure came with practice. She could find no fault with that. And if he planned to come to her bed every night, might not he eventually learn to love her as well as desire her? Jane was not sure how these things worked, but the notion of gaining Roger's love cheered her.

Jane smiled to herself and closed her eyes, suddenly drowsy.

In the weeks that followed, life assumed a definite pattern for Roger. His marriage to Jane was turning out to be far more pleasant than he had anticipated, and he actually looked forward to their evenings together in the drawing room after dinner. Unless they had guests at dinner, Jane would order the tea-tray early and after playing an air or two on the pianoforte, or making a pretence at her embroidery, she would excuse herself and retire to her room. Roger took this as an invitation, and often skipped his glass of port with his father to follow her upstairs.

She was a beautiful little thing, small boned and delicate, and any fear he might have had of bedding a beanstalk quickly fled after that first night together. She had none of the reluctance he had expected in a virgin bride, and had quickly responded to his lead. He actually enjoyed teaching her the finer points of coupling, and spent a not inconsiderable amount of every day as he went about the estate thinking up new ways of giving his wife pleasure. Furthermore, Roger derived a great deal of pleasure himself from her uninhibited response to anything new he might suggest.

The only thing that marred Roger's enjoyment of his new life with Jane was the deterioration of his father's health. Since the wedding breakfast in the Penhallow gardens, which he had attended to celebrate the culmination of a promise made years ago,

Lord Trenton rarely left the house. Roger would often find him sitting in the morning room with Jane when he came in from his rounds with Peterson. The marquess doted on his daughter-in-law, whom he had known all her life. As her godfather, he had always had a proprietary interest in her, but since she had moved into the Abbey, that bond between them had grown stronger.

"Your father is lonely," Jane had said one evening as they sat in her private sitting room prior to going to bed. "And his failing health has made him melancholic. He talks often of your mother, Roger, and regrets that she is not here to help me settle into the Abbey."

Roger took a sip of the brandy he had brought upstairs with him. "I regret that, too, Jane, as I am sure you do about your own mother. Dr. Graham tells me there is little he can do, particularly since Father refuses to give up his port and takes no exercise or fresh air. There is a lethargy about him that I do not like. It is almost as though he has given up."

"At least your father has no other worries, at least none that we know of." Jane paused and looked at him sharply. "Lord Trenton is not in debt again, is he, Roger?"

The idea had already occurred to Roger, but his father had told him not to worry, he would not again make the mistake of sitting down at the card-table with captain sharks like Sir Robert Gardener. "He says he is cured of high stakes after Sir Robert fleeced him. It is not debts that has Father in the doldrums, my dear," he added with a grin, "but grandchildren." He watched her blush and lower her eyes. "No doubt when his grandchildren cluster at his knee, Father will find a renewed interest in life." He paused, waiting for Jane to look up. When she did, as he knew she would, he stood and offered his hand, grinning suggestively. "I suggest we do not disappoint him, my love."

Later, after Jane was sleeping peacefully, curled up beside him, Roger's thoughts drifted back to his father. Lord Trenton had given up any pretence of managing his estate. That responsibility had fallen entirely upon Roger's shoulders. He was gratified to discover that he had a natural aptitude for being a landowner. Peterson now consulted him on everything, and Roger took a deep-seated pleasure in his growing competence in estate affairs and in dealing with his tenants. He had known most of them when he was a boy, but now they no longer called him Young Master Roger, and teased him about his latest escapade, but came to him with their problems, which they evidently trusted him to resolve.

Responsibility had changed him. Roger felt it in the way his mind turned, not to the excitement of London and his friends there, or to missing the hunting season at Melton Mowbray, or the races at Newcastle, but to the Abbey and all that needed to be done to restore it. The task had seemed insurmountable at first—the estate had been too long without an aggressive master—but he was beginning to see that, with the capital his marriage had brought to the Trenton coffers, the Abbey might one day rival Penhallow. Roger intended to try, to prove himself to his father.

And then, of course, there was Jane. He glanced down at her affectionately. Her lips looked soft and warm, and the shape of her body next to his made him restless. He wondered if tonight his seed had taken root in her. He was increasingly anxious for a son, but he refused to tease her, confident that sooner or later it would happen.

This train of thought inevitably brought him back to Maud. He had seen her only sporadically during the summer months, and had managed to avoid being alone with her. But he could not fail to notice that she was increasing rapidly and could not be far from her time. Sometime before Christmas, he would become a father. He did not know which he regretted most, the fact that he had carelessly impregnated another man's wife, or that his firstborn would come into the world under another man's name.

What if the child was a boy? Of course, he hoped Jane would soon give him a son, but the thought of having to watch his first son grow up as Sir Giles's heir would be galling to the extreme. He would never be able to acknowledge the child, for to do so would be to brand him a bastard. It was an unthinkable stigma that Roger had not given any thought to during his years of sowing wild oats among the local lasses. Maud's claim that she carried his child had forced him to consider the consequences of his hedonistic way of life. It was useless to tell himself that most young men of his station were equally heedless in their pursuit of pleasure. While it was true that a number of them provided for their by-blows, it was also true that too many young women were left to fend for themselves. At least Maud would bear his child in the protection of marriage, and Roger supposed he should be thankful to old Sir Giles for that blessing.

He looked down at his wife and a lump formed in his throat. As he gently stroked a strand of hair away from her face, Roger saw that Jane's eyes were open and that she was smiling at him. His response was immediate. She did not protest when he rolled her over on her back, and he suddenly wished he had wed Jane years ago, especially before he became entangled with Maud Horton.

"I have the premonition that we are making a child tonight, my love," he whispered softly, his lips feathering across her small, shapely breasts.

"You are anxious for a son, are you not, Roger?"

"Any man would be anxious for an heir, Jane. But I would welcome a girl if she looks like you."

She smiled and he knew he had pleased her. "I would prefer her to have your hair. And if she is lucky enough to have your eyes, too, Roger, we will have no trouble at all in firing her off when the time comes."

"Let us hope that whoever is in charge of these things is listening carefully tonight," he murmured, lifting her night rail and moving over her. "All we can do is keep trying and hope for the best."

Later, when Jane had gone back to sleep, Roger lay awake wondering what his wife would say if she knew that he was so close to being a father with another woman. It was not a subject he could ever discuss with her, of course, but he wished he could. Jane was so sensible and compassionate, he knew she would understand his anxiety over the complicated mess he had made of things. But Maud Horton was a forbidden topic between them, and Roger had vowed never to give his wife cause for distress ever again.

It was a promise he firmly intended to keep.

Chapter Nine

The Letters

Jane soon discovered that the role of mistress of Trenton Abbey was not to be made easy for her. Accustomed to the efficient staff at Penhallow, under the sage guidance of Mrs. Daley, her father's longtime housekeeper, she was startled at Mrs. Collins's habit of arguing with every command she gave. She got little support from Roger, who confessed to being terrified of the woman.

"She is a veritable dragon, my dear," he explained apologetically one morning at the breakfast table, when Jane brought up the matter. "I should have warned you about her. Father and I avoid dealing with her whenever possible. We had hoped that you would know how to handle her, Jane. We gave up long ago."

"I suspect you have allowed her the running of the household for too long without supervision," Jane remarked. "Naturally she resents any challenge to her authority. But that has to change; and if she becomes too troublesome, I shall have to let her go. If you have no objection, of course, Roger."

"As long as you do not dismiss my father's valet, or my own Greyson, who is the best valet outside London, you may do anything you choose, Jane. I know the house is sadly in need of refurbishing, and Father has agreed that you may do as you see fit. He is only too happy to have you here to keep him company in the mornings. He is very fond of you, as am I." He said this with a smile that made Jane's heart flip.

She blushed and rang the bell to order more toast.

She knew that Lord Trenton had a soft spot for her; she had been a favourite with him ever since she could remember. But she wondered how long, if ever, it would take Roger's fondness to grow into love. She wanted so much more than fondness from him. She wanted his heart as well as his body.

Armed with Roger's approval, Jane adopted a more stringent manner with the housekeeper. It was, after all, her money that paid the wages of all the staff, so she had every right to demand their obedience and respect. But Mrs. Collins continued to defy her, and things came to a head the morning Jane had gone into the formal dining room to plan the changes she wanted to make.

"We can begin by removing that dreadful epergne from the dining table, Mrs. Collins," she said pleasantly. "I am sure our guests dislike having snarling dogs and dead fowl staring at them throughout their meal as much as I do. John," she continued, addressing one of the footmen, "will you and Timothy lift it over to the sideboard, where it will be less objectionable?"

"Milady," the housekeeper protested in that acid tone of voice she always used to address Jane, "the epergne has always been on the table. Lady Trenton had it set there herself."

"Really?" Jane kept her voice pleasant. "I am glad to know that, but I cannot see the relevance. Please remove it." When the footmen hesitated, she added softly, "Now, if you please."

"Lord Trenton will only have it replaced, milady," Mrs. Collins said shortly, "and we will have done all that work for nothing. His lordship will not be pleased, I can tell you. I never thought to see the day when her ladyship's house would be turned topsy-turvy," she added under her breath but loud enough for Lady Jane to hear.

"Since her ladyship is no longer with us," Jane said briskly, keeping her temper in check, "I believe you should concern yourself with doing things as I see fit, since I am now mistress here." She paused, signaling the footmen to move the epergne a little to the left. "And if you cannot be happy with that, Mrs. Collins, I am sure there are other positions available in the neighbourhood."

A shocked silence followed this veiled threat, but Jane could see from the housekeeper's pinched expression that the battle had not been won. The most she could hope for was that the news would reach belowstairs and that she would encounter less opposition from the staff.

For several days after she laid down the law with Mrs. Collins, Jane felt that perhaps the staff was beginning to accept her. Until one morning she walked into the music room and discovered Mavis, one of the most rebellious of the downstairs maids, in a shockingly immodest position with one of the footmen. They pulled apart when they noticed her presence, but Jane did not miss the defiant smirk on the girl's pretty face as she straightened her skirts.

Jane frowned at the guilty pair for a moment, then pointed to the door. "You will both present yourselves immediately to Mr. Peterson and tell him that you have been turned off. He will settle any wages owed you." This was the first time Jane had ever had to dismiss a servant, and she was loath to do so, but she knew that if she tolerated lax behaviour, she might as well hand over the reins of the household to Mrs. Collins and go back to Penhallow.

The girl Mavis had the audacity to whine that she was Mrs. Collins's niece and had a bedridden mother and six siblings to support in the village. Jane did not believe a word of this, but was intrigued to know that the housekeeper had relatives on the staff besides her husband, the butler.

She turned to the footman. "And I suppose you are Mrs. Collins's nephew, Joseph, is that right?" she enquired sarcastically.

"Aye, milady," the young footman stammered, very

red in the face and evidently more aware than Mavis of the enormity of their transgression.

Over the next weeks, Jane found it necessary to dismiss several more of Mrs. Collins's relatives, who had basked too long in their favoured position and become lazy and impertinent. She also acquired the habit of running her finger along the furniture and banisters—something she had never done at Penhallow—to keep the maids on their toes. The hiring of a dozen young girls from the village to replace those dismissed restored the household to a more comfortable footing, and Jane turned her attention to the gardens.

There she encountered the same reluctance among the gardeners to follow her instructions to add rosebeds and borders of perennials to the Park. By the end of the summer, after several dismissals, and a good deal of arguing with the head gardener, Jane felt she was beginning to make some headway in setting the Abbey to rights.

In the Trenton stables, however, Jane encountered a different kind of obstacle. Her mornings were taken up with household duties, but when the weather was fine, she tried to spend a part of each afternoon either riding or driving her little tilbury around the countryside paying calls on friends. Roger had wanted to order an elegant phaeton from London, but Jane had balked at the unnecessary expense.

"I am accustomed to my tilbury, Roger," she insisted when the subject came up, "and I have no burning need to impress the neighbours. After all, I am not the Duchess of Devonshire," she added with a smile. "And I can trust Primrose not to take exception to the sheep and geese we encounter on these country roads, which is more than I can say of that high-bred pair you drive in your curricle."

Roger had insisted upon teaching Jane to drive his curricle, and although she was quite happy with her tilbury, she was delighted to humour him. When he gave her the reins and guided her on the intricacies of handling a pair of Welsh-bred high-steppers, Jane glowed at the warmth of his hands covering hers.

"You must keep your eyes on your horses, Jane," he often scolded her. "Until you establish a rapport with them, you must not even glance at the scenery or you will soon find yourself in the ditch, my dear."

Jane obediently fixed her gaze on the horses, although she would much rather look into her husband's deep blue eyes, and watch his lips curve seductively into a smile. They found so much to laugh at during these times together that Jane was reminded of the bond that had joined them during their childhood. They were no longer children, of course, as Jane was reminded every night when Roger walked into her bedchamber and climbed into her bed. He appeared content to spend so much of his time with her that Jane could not help wondering if perhaps he had truly banished Lady Horton from his mind. Perhaps, just perhaps, her husband was beginning to love her and had not realized it yet.

This fantasy was shattered the very next afternoon.

The morning had been misty and damp, but soon after nuncheon, the sun came out, and Jane was smitten with the urge for a canter up to Hogdon Hill to look for late strawberries. This was only an excuse, of course, for Jane was sure there would be no berries left after the heavy picking they had endured that summer. Whatever late ones may have ripened since then would have been eaten by the pheasants and grouse that were fattening for the November shooting season. Nevertheless, she had an invigorating gallop and returned to the stables intending to walk up to the house.

She missed young Tom's cheerful face and wondered, not for the first time, whether she could persuade her previous groom to come and work at Trenton Abbey. There was something about the groom assigned to her that made her uneasy. A great, hulking fellow, with an unruly shag of hair and buck teeth, Jimmy Barnes was all too often rude and unmannerly.

That afternoon Barnes was lounging against the pump in the stable-yard picking his teeth when Jane returned from her ride. He pushed himself to an upright position, as though the whole thing was too fatiguing for words, and ambled over to take Ginger's reins. At the very last possible moment, he touched his forelock, but the gesture of respect was marred by a suggestive grin that sat oddly on his pockmarked face.

Jane usually tried to ignore the boy's impertinence, but that afternoon he was particularly loquacious. The stable-yard was empty, and Jane listened impatiently as Barnes recited a meandering tale, the gist of which Jane was hard put to follow. All the while his eyes surveyed her so insistently that Jane became uncomfortable. Tired of this insolence, she dismissed him with a wave and turned towards the house.

"Wait, milady," he muttered, thrusting a grubby hand into the pocket of his jacket and pulling out a piece of paper. "Almost fergot to give ye this, I did." Thrusting the missive at her, he stepped so close that Jane caught a whiff of sour ale.

She stepped back hastily. "Who sent it, Barnes?" she enquired, looking at the crumpled paper dubiously.

"One of the lads from 'orton 'all brought it over this mornin', milady," came the surly response.

"You should have sent him up to the house to deliver it," she said, twitching the paper from his fingers and turning away.

"The lad said I should give it to ye in person, milady." The smirk that accompanied this remark sent a chill through Jane's heart. She stuffed the note into her pocket and almost ran up to the house.

When she reached her chamber, and submitted to Betty's fussing at her for riding around without a groom, Jane was tempted to throw the mysterious letter into the grate and forget it. Curiosity was too strong, however, and as soon as Betty had gone off to brush her mistress's habit, Jane broke the seal and spread out the crumpled sheet of cheap paper.

Maud Horton had signed with a bold, aggressive flourish.

Jane stood for a long moment staring at the signature before reading the contents. Lady Horton congratulated her upon her new husband, but immediately warned her to make the most of the initial months of marriage. Leopards never *ever* changed their spots, she wrote, and Lady Summers would do well to abandon all hope of keeping a gentleman like Roger Hastings, whose roving eye was common knowledge, under her thumb for long. Her fortune had bought her a husband, the letter went on to say, but money could never buy love, as perhaps Lady Jane had already discovered. There was a distinct sneer to this piece of advice that chilled Jane to the bone.

Her first instinct was to rip the offending missive to shreds. Her second was to run to Roger and demand assurances that this was nothing more than a mean and envious trick from an abandoned lover.

In the end, Jane did neither. She had worked too hard to establish harmony in her marriage to allow a bitter woman to ruin everything. The fact that Maud Horton had voiced some of her own fears did not make it any easier to fold the letter and hide it away at the bottom of her jewel-box.

Running to Roger with the letter would probably achieve exactly what that woman hoped for: to plant seeds of mistrust and sow discord at Trenton Abbey. Lady Jane Summers was not about to let that happen.

One afternoon towards the end of August, Roger was riding home from the monthly fair at a nearby village where he had gone to look at some sheep. He was in high good humour.

"Well, Peterson, I acquitted myself reasonably well for a novice sheep buyer, would you not agree?" he remarked, feeling rather pleased with himself.

"And that you did, milord," the agent replied.

"Farmer Brown is a cantankerous old bird who has been known to refuse a sale if he don't like the cut of a man's jib. You got a fair price out of him, I would say." After a pause, he added with a dry chuckle, "The ale helped, of course."

Roger laughed. He was feeling a little lightheaded himself. The local ale they had sampled at the King's Arms had been rich and strong, and Farmer Brown had shown amazing stamina in putting it away. If negotiations—traditionally carried on over a tankard of local brew—had lasted much longer, Roger might have needed assistance in climbing back on his horse.

This feeling of well-being lasted all the way back to Trenton Abbey, where Peterson left him. Roger continued on to the stables, thinking how amused Jane would be when he recounted his first successful foray into sheep trading. He felt a sudden urge to see her smile and hear her soft voice praising him.

His exuberance diminished abruptly when he saw Barnes waiting for him in the stable-yard. The burly groom had become increasingly surly of late, and Roger had begun to regret giving in to Maud's pleas to find a position at the Abbey for her cousin. The lad had fallen on hard times, or so she claimed. Roger thought it more likely that Barnes had been dismissed for laziness. He seemed to do little but lounge about the stable-yard, broom in hand, a vacant stare in his eyes.

He ambled over and took Jason's bridle. "Afternoon, milord," he mumbled, looking at Roger with a vacuous smile. " 'ave a nice ride, did ye, sir?"

Roger did not bother to answer this impertinence and would have turned away had not a sly expression on Barnes's face detained him.

"Well, what is it, Barnes?" he said impatiently.

The groom grinned, showing two large gaps in his teeth. "Got a letter fer ye, milord," he said in a horse whisper, glancing over his shoulder. He made much ado about searching through his pockets. "Aha, 'ere it is, milord. A secret message from someones as knows ye well." His expression became a leer as he held out the crumpled paper, and Roger felt a stab of apprehension.

"Messages should be left up at the house," Roger said curtly. He took the folded note between thumb and forefinger. The writing on it was Maud's untidy scrawl. He grimaced and shoved it in his pocket.

He did not open it until Collins had closed the door of the library behind him. The number of crossed out words and smudges gave clear evidence of Maud's distress. Sir Giles had confronted her about the child, she wrote. He had been enraged at a trifling bill from the modiste and lectured her for hours on her failure to live up to her duties as a wife. She had reminded him that she was about to present him with a son, but Sir Giles had fallen into a livid rage. He had not been hoodwinked by her attempts to coax him into her bed. In spite of her diligence, he claimed their union had never been consummated. Hence the child was not his. He threatened to deny paternity. Her life was in danger, she wrote. Would Roger meet her in the abandoned gatehouse that very evening?

Roger's first instinct was to consign the letter to the grate. Had he not promised Jane that this clandestine activity was over with? As he stood there gazing at the childish scribble, he caught a whiff of Maud's perfume, and the tantalizing scent reminded him so vividly of their many amorous encounters that he felt his blood stir again. By Jove, she had been a tasty armful, he thought ruefully. He would not mind reliving some of their more lusty couplings.

If it were not for Jane and the promise he had made.

He would be foolish indeed to meet with Maud. The mere scent of her perfume had a dizzying effect on him; what her presence would do, even in her present state, could not bear thinking of. He read the letter again. There was no hint of threat in it, and this surprised him. Perhaps this was not the trick he had first imagined. Perhaps Sir Giles was truly about to disavow his paternity of Maud's babe. The old man would come off as a cuckold, of course, but what else did he expect when he wed a young, lusty woman with Maud's looks? The outcome might have been no different had Sir Giles been twenty years younger, Roger thought cynically. Knowing Maud as he did, this was a distinct possibility.

Would Sir Giles dare to name Roger as the other man? For himself he cared little what the gossips said; they could prove nothing. And Maud had always seemed as careless as he of public censure. Of course, that was before the baby. And before his marriage. He owed Jane the loyalty he had promised her; but what did he owe his baby?

Roger was well aware that many gentlemen of his class would wash their hands of both mother and child, but he had been too close to this miracle to take a cavalier attitude. He had placed his hand on Maud's gently distended belly and imagined he felt the life burgeoning there. The experience had thrilled and humbled him. He was prepared to do whatever possible for the babe, but what good would it do an innocent child to brand it a bastard by acknowledging it?

Suddenly Roger wished he could take his dilemma to Jane. His wife had a practical and generous nature, he knew from experience. But even the most understanding wife might not welcome the burden of her husband's by-blow. And what could they do, anyway? It was not as though he had any legal rights to the child. In the eyes of the law, it was Sir Giles's heir, and the gossips might chatter all they wished.

A gentle knock brought Roger out of his brown study, and as Lady Jane entered the library, he thrust Maud's letter into his pocket.

"My dear Roger," she said cheerfully, "Collins told me you were home, and I am all agog to hear of your adventures with the sheep. Did you purchase any? Is Farmer Brown as fearful as people say? When can I see them?" She paused to catch her breath and regarded him steadily. Roger wondered if his thoughts were written all over his face.

"You look tired, Roger," she said softly. "Do come and have your tea. Your father and I have been waiting for you upstairs. I have finally bullied Cook into making a decent batch of strawberry tartlets like those we used to eat at Penhallow. Remember?"

Roger smiled. He remembered many other things about his wife at that moment, and the knowledge that he cared for Jane more than he had intended to only added to his dilemma.

Arm in arm they strolled upstairs together to the small drawing room where tea was generally served. Roger's thoughts were bleak. Should he keep his assignation with Maud in the gatehouse tonight? He saw no other alternative unless he ignored her summons entirely. He could hardly call upon her at Horton Hall.

His instinct told him that trouble lay ahead whether he met her or not. But how he could do so without hurting Jane, Roger was at a loss to decide.

Chapter Ten

The Ghost

Jane stood before the cheval-glass in her bedchamber and regarded her reflection with approval. Marriage definitely agreed with her. She could not remember ever looking or feeling as well as she did now. Her hair, gathered in curls on top of her head, glowed a rich chestnut in the candlelight. Her face and form had gently rounded out, and although still slender, she had a subtle elegance about her that was noticeably different from her earlier girlish grace. At least it was to Jane's eyes. It must be happiness. And probably other things, too. She blushed, even though she was alone, at how much she enjoyed those *other things* that came with marriage.

In a few days she would celebrate her third month as Lady Jane Hastings, Viscountess Summers of Trenton Abbey. A grand title, to be sure, but Jane was less impressed with it than she was at being Roger's wife. Finally. She wondered if Roger noticed the improvement in her looks. Or if he ever wished she were taller, more buxom, or more this and less that. Did he ever compare her with Maud? Jane tried not to, but it was inevitable when everyone in the village knew what Lady Horton had been to him. His whore, some ungenerous souls called her. Jane could not being herself to be so critical. Too well she knew her husband's charm and seductive powers. Had she not become addicted to them herself in an alarmingly short time?

She smiled at Betty as the abigail opened her jewel-box and examined the contents critically. "The emeralds, milady? They match that gown to perfection."

"Too formal for a family dinner party with my father, I think," Jane said. "This gown is really too formal, too, but Father has not seen it yet. The pearls he gave me last Christmas will please him. And the ear-bobs to match."

"And the gold silk shawl in case it turns cold later?"

"Yes, and with the new gold reticule, I shall be fit to meet the Queen, if Her Majesty knew of my existence, that is," she added laughingly.

"Oh, Her Majesty will meet you soon enough, milady, when his lordship takes you up to London next Season."

"His lordship shows no sign of wishing to go anywhere," Jane replied without rancour. "Much less to the Metropolis. He is too taken with the idea of filling every available Trenton meadow with sheep. It is his latest obsession. I must take up my sketching again, Betty. I have sorely neglected it over the past months."

And so she had, Jane mused as Roger entered her chamber to escort her downstairs. She was too enthralled with this new husband of hers. She glanced up at him as they trod down the stairs, her hand on his arm, only to find him gazing at her quizzically.

"Are we attending the Duchess of Devonshire's grand ball tonight, my love?" he teased. "Had I known, I would have donned my finery." He smiled crookedly, and Jane's heart gave its familiar leap.

"You are a sad tease, my lord," she replied, trying not to laugh with joy. "This is merely a new gown Madame Clothilde made for me. It arrived from London last week and I was anxious for your opinion, Roger."

"It looks very fine to me, my dear, but we must ask my father. You know he is the acknowledged expert in this house."

Much later, as they gathered round the dining table at Penhallow, Jane garnered fulsome compliments from both Lord Trenton and her father, but it was her Aunt Octavia's comment that bothered her.

"You look blooming, my gel," her aunt said as the ladies retired to the drawing room after dinner. "Can it be that you are not telling us something, child?" she added coyly.

Jane shook her head. She had tried not to let her failure to conceive disturb her, but it was so obvious that everyone else was breathlessly awaiting an announcement from her to that effect that it was hard to remain cheerful.

"Never mind, dear," Aunt Octavia murmured, patting her hand comfortingly. "It will happen in good time, no doubt. We must be patient. Come and play something for me, Jane. I have missed it."

When the gentlemen joined them, the talk turned naturally to sheep. Jane regarded them affectionately, the three most important men in her life. Lady Octavia sat plying her embroidery until Featherburton brought in the tea-tray. Jane sat near her aunt, listening with half an ear to her chatter about village affairs. She kept the other open to the gentlemen's talk, especially to Roger's amusing recounting of his encounter with some sheep farmer at the fair.

"The rumour is that there is trouble at Horton Hall," her aunt said suddenly, claiming Jane's full attention.

"What kind of trouble, Aunt?"

"Something about the babe Lady Horton is expecting. Or so Molly, the cook's helper, told my abigail only yesterday. Molly has a sister employed at the Hall, as you know. Apparently Sir Giles took exception to something his lady did and went into one of his rages. Dr. Graham has warned him that his heart will not withstand these explosions. He told me so himself. But does that foolish old man listen—"

"What about the child?" Jane interrupted, suddenly recalling the ugly letter she had received from Lady Horton hinting that it was her fortune, not her beauty that had captured the roving heart of Roger Hastings.

Lady Octavia leaned over and lowered her voice dramatically. "You will never guess, my dear Jane.

Indeed, I could hardly credit it myself. Molly swears that there is talk at the Hall that Sir Giles is *not*"— her voice dropped even lower—"the father of the babe. All nonsense, I am sure, but there you have it."

Jane's breath caught in her throat, and she stared at her aunt in consternation. Surely even the flamboyant Maud Horton would not deal her husband such a crippling blow to his honour. Instinctively, she glanced over at Roger, noting that he seemed distracted tonight. Did he perhaps know more than he had told her about this fresh scandal? Then the thought that had been lurking on the fringes of her mind would not be silenced any longer. Was Roger in some way linked to this scandal, too? Was he perhaps not only the lady's ex-lover, but also the . . . ? No! Her mind screeched to a halt. What was she thinking?

Abruptly she set down her empty cup and stood up. "I think it is time we left, Aunt. Roger looks tired, and I have had a pretty strenuous day myself supervising the hanging of the new curtains in the formal drawing room. The yellow brocade you helped me select is exactly the right shade. That room no longer resembles a drafty medieval hall, and with the windows open—I swear they have not been opened since the Crusades—the room is actually quite pleasant."

"I am glad you chose to leave early, Jane," Roger remarked during the short drive to Trenton Abbey. "Peterson wants me to ride all the way down to Okehampton tomorrow. I am loath to go, love, since we will have to remain overnight, but Peterson assures me that there is to be an important auction at one of the Hampton estates. Devon is full of Hamptons, you know. I am related to them through a distant cousin, but I was up at Oxford with Willy Hampton and know him to be one of the most successful sheep breeders in the south of England. This is a rare opportunity to obtain some of his premium stock."

"Then you must certainly go, Roger," Jane said, although she dreaded spending even one night without him.

Later that night, after Roger had returned to his room—to get a good night's rest for his journey, he assured her—Jane lay awake trying to make sense of the rumours she had heard from her Aunt Octavia. It did not seem reasonable that a man like Sir Giles would shame both himself and his wife by denying that he had fathered her child.

It was true that the baronet had long been in bad health and frequently spent extended periods in his sick-bed, but Lady Horton had herself confided to Jane soon after her marriage that her main goal was to present her husband with a son to insure her future at Horton Hall. Not that Sir Giles needed an heir, since he had Stephen.

How would Stephen react when he heard of this latest scandal in his family? He must surely know by now of the rumoured affair between his father's young wife and his own childhood friend. Elizabeth had confided that her brother corresponded regularly with Captain Horton, still stationed with Wellington in Paris. Jane was confident that Tony had relayed all the local gossip, including the notorious escapades of Lady Horton.

And now this. Jane felt a deep compassion for the unborn babe. What a tangle it would encounter when it finally entered the world. First a mother with a tarnished reputation, then a father who disowned it, and finally a true father—if indeed Roger was that man—who could not come forward without setting the entire neighbourhood on its ears. Poor little mite, she thought, before slipping into an uneasy sleep.

She woke up with a start. The room was filled with moonlight, a full moon, Jane remembered. She shuddered, not from cold but from the terrifying dreams that had plagued her. Half expecting her night rail to be soaking, she threw the covers back. It was quite dry, but she was shaking as she recalled the waters of the cold lake closing about her. She had been boating on the lake with—of all unlikely people—Lady Horton. Like all dreams, this one had no rhyme or reason, but Jane remembered vividly that Lady Horton had a babe in her arms. The horror of it was that the child, wrapped in a plaid rug of yellow and purple, the Hastings' colours, had Roger's eyes. It smiled up at her as babies do, all plump cheeks and cherub lips, and Jane had felt a moment of sickening premonition before Lady Horton tossed it into the lake.

Jane had stood transfixed watching the yellow and purple rug slowly become waterlogged and sink into the clear depths. She remembered uttering a wail of despair and jumping into the lake, clothed only in her night rail. She remembered thinking that she was drowning, too, but then her arms and legs came alive and she dived down after the pale sinking form.

And then came the thrill of joy when she grasped the soggy bundle and pushed herself upwards to break the surface close to the boat. At least she had saved this child from the dreadful fate of that other boy.

What happened next was the worst nightmare Jane could ever recall. She heard Lady Horton scream, her mouth wide, and the sound echoing across the water in waves of terror. Then she had laughed, a hysterical reaction that still chilled Jane's bones, and pointed at the bundle in Jane's arms.

Jane had looked down at the babe. Only the bundle in her arms was no longer the cherub baby of a few minutes before. She must have fainted, for the next thing she recalled was Stephen pulling her out of the cold water. Lady Horton had gone, as had the apparition she had retrieved from the lake.

Stephen had held her cradled in his arms, like the child she had brought out of the lake. He was crooning something Jane could not understand. Her mind was focused on Roger. Where was he? Why was he not here when she needed him?

She stood up and stumbled out onto the balcony. The moonlight glittered on the water and Jane shuddered, her dream still vivid in her mind. She stared at the vast expanse of silvery water, the night fog already rolling in from the cemetery beside the dark chapel.

And then she saw it. She closed her eyes quickly, willing it to go away. But when she dared to open them again, the pale form was still there, poised on the surface of the lake, the fog swirling around it.

Suddenly it seemed to move towards her, drifting lazily across the water. Was this the *thing* she had held in her arms in her nightmare? A wave of panic shook her and she ran into her chamber, slamming the door to the balcony. Then she was standing by Roger's door. Without waiting to knock, Jane wrenched it open and rushed in to stand at the foot of Roger's bed.

"Roger!" She tried to scream, but little sound came out. "Roger, please help me." Still only a whisper escaped her. Then she saw how pointless it was to call on her husband to save her. His bed was empty. She drew closer and saw it had not been slept in.

Frantically Jane looked around the room. There was no one there. By the light of the moon, she saw what appeared to be scraps of paper in the empty grate. It must have been a letter, she thought, crouching down to examine it. Someone—Roger perhaps?—had attempted to burn it, but several scraps remained intact.

Carefully Jane picked them out of the ashes and collected them in the palm of her hand. She carried them back to her room and placed them on her escritoire. Lighting a branch of candles, she sat down and pushed them around, turning them over until all displayed signs of writing. Lady Horton's handwriting. Jane recognized it instantly. Unfortunately she could decipher only a few words. Some were whole words, others fragments. These she carefully lined up: *Sir Giles enraged; modiste bills; a son; deny pater . . . ; gatehouse; Roger*. And the bold letter *M* of what must have been the signature at the bottom of the letter.

Jane sat for a long time staring at the evidence of Roger's perfidy. The obvious conclusion stared her in the face. Her husband had been in touch with Lady Horton after promising her he would not. A worthless promise it had been to be sure. What was even more

difficult for Jane to accept was the proof that Roger
had gone to rendezvous with Lady Horton. The empty
bed, the burned letter, his excuse that he needed to
rest. Even now they might be at the old gatehouse
together. Jane had no doubt that the "gatehouse" in
the letter referred to the abandoned cottage on the
Horton estate where they had often played as children. How convenient. And how treacherous of him.
So Maud had been right after all.

She stood up, her feet chilled. Carefully folding the
incriminating pieces into a sheet of paper, she slipped
it into her writing case. What was she to do? Knowing
that she would hardly fall asleep again—and not really
wanting to if it brought more nightmares—Jane put
on her slippers and snatched up a woollen shawl. She
opened the door to the balcony and stepped out into
the cool night air, too numb with grief to feel fear.
The lake looked so placid in the moonlight that Jane
felt foolish for having believed the gruesome scene in
her dream.

Jane forced herself to examine the lake carefully.
Covered by a diaphanous blanket of fog that swirled
and shifted eerily, the lake seemed empty. That mysterious pale figure—if it had existed at all outside her
dreams—was gone. She pulled the shawl more closely
around her. The scene was not for the faint of heart,
and it took all Jane's rational powers to look upon it
without recalling the horror stories of her childhood.
The dark bulk of the chapel at the far end of the
lake was clearly visible, its tall stained-glass windows
reflecting the moonlight like so many ghostly eyes.

Nervously, Jane shifted her gaze to the graveyard
beside the chapel. She had played there often as a
child and knew each headstone as well or better than
she knew those at Penhallow. Both tragedy and romance were recorded at Trenton, and Jane remembered the fanciful stories she had woven around the
brief epigraphs carved into the mossy stones. The
place held happy memories for her; sweet violets and
wild pansies carpeted the grass in the spring and sum-

mer, and someone long ago had planted crocuses and
snowdrops, which she had often gathered to place on
certain tombs whose occupants had caught her fancy.

Tomorrow, she told herself, she would place flowers—wild poppies now in late summer—on that empty
grave beside the long-dead countess whose son's body
was said to be lying at the bottom of the lake. Local
superstition, of course, she reminded herself quickly.
But the story had always intrigued her, so much so
that it often coloured her dreams, although never
quite so vividly as last night. She shuddered at the
memory.

Jane had no idea how long she stood there before
a movement in the graveyard froze her. A shadow
moved among the graves. A horseman. Frantically she
racked her brains, but she recalled no story from long
ago to account for the ghost of a solitary horseman.
Abruptly she saw that this apparition was no ghost.
The horseman had come down the hill to the lake and
now approached the Abbey along the path beside the
water. As he drew closer, Jane recognized Roger, and
breathed a sigh of relief.

This was short-lived when she remembered the fragments of Lady Horton's letter in her escritoire. What
does one say to a roving husband caught inflagrante?
Would he only lie to her again? As she pondered the
alternatives, the horseman glanced up at the battlements. Had she been discovered? Well, she thought
defiantly, watching the dark outline of horse and rider
as it rounded the corner towards the stables, so had
he.

Throwing off her shawl, Jane crawled back into bed.
She was too distraught to confront Roger tonight. Her
first inclination was to accuse him of betraying her and
heap insults on his head. But just as it had with Lady
Horton's letter, her good sense prevailed, and Jane
decided to set aside her anger until she had recovered
her equanimity. Perhaps Roger had seen her on the
balcony as she suspected, and would come to her with
a plausible explanation of his nocturnal rambles. And

perhaps he would grow wings and a halo, too, she
thought cynically. He would need them if he were to
convince her that he had not been at the gatehouse
with Lady Horton that evening.

Jane curled herself into a ball and pulled the covers
over her head. If she were lucky, Roger would be
gone tomorrow morning before she awoke. In the
meantime, she squeezed her eyes shut to prevent the
tell-tale tears from escaping.

Roger pulled Jason down to a walk as he crested
the rise and entered the family graveyard. The tombs
of his ancestors lay scattered around him in untidy
rows. The most ancient hugged the dark wall of the
chapel where, three months ago, he had been wed.
The most recent, his mother's, was visible farther
down the slope, next to the spot reserved for his father. His own was nearby—a sobering thought. Before
him the lake spread out in the moonlight, still and
shining. Beyond that the grim battlements of Trenton
Abbey rose high into the night sky, its pennant motionless in the still air.

His visit to the gatehouse had been pointless. And
dangerous, to boot. He had waited for an hour in the
damp, dilapidated ruins before a scared-looking lad
appeared to report that her ladyship was on her way.
When she did arrive, Maud was accompanied by an
old dragon of an abigail who supported her mistress
solicitously and glowered at him when he sent her
away.

Roger had questioned the elaborate attempt at se-
crecy when it was clear that the entire staff at Horton
Hall must know the exact time and place of their
meeting. Maud had dissolved into tears, which was
very unlike her, and had clung to him tenaciously,
weeping all over his cravat.

She looked pale and drawn, complaining that her
condition had seriously debilitated her.

"Had I known I would feel this ill, I would never
have kept the brat," she snapped pettishly, mopping

her face with his handkerchief and sinking down on an old bench that had withstood the ravishes of damp and neglect.

Startled at the implications of this casual remark, Roger was not sympathetic. "Then you should not be out in the middle of the night, Maud. This rendezvous here was a bad idea."

"I had to see you, Roger," she moaned, ignoring his caution. "Giles is making life miserable for me, and you have abandoned me. How am I supposed to go on, can you tell me?"

"I am a married man now, Maud. You knew that would happen sooner or later. It is not as though this complication came as a surprise to you. I thought you wanted a child to secure your position at Horton Hall."

"A lot of good it has done me when my own husband refuses to acknowledge it as his." She pouted prettily, but for some reason Roger was no longer charmed. His mind was too full of Jane and what she would say if she ever found out about his latest transgression.

"It is up to you to change his mind, Maud. Use your charm on the old man. Now, tell me why you sent for me. You cannot stay out here in the damp. It was foolishness to suggest it. What was so urgent that you could not put it in a letter?"

As he watched, two large tears welled up in her beautiful eyes and trembled in the moonlight shining through the broken window. Roger watched in fascination. This was a truly stellar performance, and in spite of himself, he felt the old magic tugging at his heart again.

"You are so unfeeling, Roger," she murmured softly, reaching for his hand and pressing it to her bosom. "I thought you were happy the child was yours."

"I am, Maud, but let us not forget that legally Horton is the father. There is no way I can claim it, as you well know. Now tell me why you wished to see me, for I must be going."

Her fingers tightened on his hand, and her expression hardened. "Afraid that mousy little wife of yours will discover you are not as true to her as she imagines?" Her smile was a grimace. "I want a promise from you, Roger," she said after a pause. "And I think you owe me that much. After all, you did get me *enceinte.*"

"Anything within reason, Maud, you know that."

She gazed at him steadily, then sighed. "I am not well, Roger. Some mornings I can barely leave my bed. I am afraid. Promise me that if Giles casts me out, as he threatens to do, you will take care of me. And if something should happen . . ." She stopped, and Roger saw a flash of real fear in her violet eyes. "If anything happens to me, Roger, promise me you will take care of the babe. I fear Giles might do it harm."

Her fingers again clutched at his hand, and Roger felt her nails dig into his skin. Her request startled him. He had never imagined that his moral responsibility for Maud's child would ever become a physical reality. He had been quite prepared to provide for the child, but what else could he possibly do, especially if Sir Giles changed his mind and accepted it?

He had promised, of course, and Maud had wept again, making him repeat the promise over and over. When she finally let him go, Roger put spurs to his horse and raced across Horton Park, which marched with Trenton land, and did not pull up until he reached the chapel.

He had been unwise to meet with Maud, but he was home again now, and found himself wondering if Jane would be still asleep. Doubtless she was, but he toyed with the notion of rousing her with kisses along the sweet curve of her neck. Lost in these pleasant thoughts, Roger was startled to see the figure in white on the balcony overlooking the lake. He passed beneath one of the chestnut trees bordering the path, but when he emerged again into the moonlight, the figure was gone. He had the uncomfortable feeling of having seen a ghost.

Roger rode round to the stables, and as he handed Jason over to a sleepy groom, he wondered how he was going to explain his midnight ride to Jane. If he knew anything about women, his wife would assume the worst, that he had been to meet Maud. Which of course he could not deny. But would Jane understand his need to keep this particular assignation? Would she believe that it had nothing to do with any feeling he might still have for his former mistress, and everything to do with the child she carried? Could he reasonably ask a wife to believe such things?

The glimpe of Jane—if indeed it had been her—on the balcony had brought home to him with sudden clarity how much she meant to him. Roger wanted to tell her the truth, but would she believe it?

Chapter Eleven

Wild Pansies

Contrary to her expectations, Jane slept soundly and awoke to find the day well advanced. Her first thought was for Roger, but when she rang for her chocolate, Betty informed her that his lordship had ridden off at dawn with Peterson and would be gone for two days.

"He left you these, milady," the abigail said with sly smile, indicating the small posy of wild pansies in a glass vase on her dressing table. "Found them on your pillow, I did. Early this morning. You were fast asleep so I put the wee things in water."

Jane stared at the delicate yellow and violet pansies in astonishment. It seemed so unlike Roger to pick wildflowers, especially in the middle of the night. Perhaps he had a guilty conscience for breaking his promise to her. Nevertheless, the gesture touched her deeply, and she smiled at this evidence that he had come into her room last night after all. He must have seen her on the balcony and come to explain his absence from his room when he said he needed to rest before his journey.

Betty picked up her mistress's shawl, which had fallen on the floor, and glanced at Jane. "Wild pansies signify love and loyalty, milady," she murmured and blushed profusely.

"That sounds wonderful, but we should not put too much stock in old wives' tales, Betty," Jane remarked as she swung her legs out of bed. Love and loyalty indeed. In her experience, Roger paid scant attention to either, and after last night's escapade—at which she had caught him red-handed—he had better not pretend to be innocent.

But the sweetness of her husband's gesture lingered on, causing Jane to remember all the happy hours she had spent in his company since their wedding day. And all those delicious nights. Perhaps there had been a good reason for Roger's absence last night. Perhaps she did not know all the facts. And just perhaps she had been too quick to attach more significance to that charred letter than it actually had.

This benign frame of mind took Jane up to the small room she had chosen for her paints and easels. The large windows let in plenty of light and she spent several peaceful hours transferring Roger's pansies onto a small canvas she planned to hang in her bedroom. In accordance with superstition, she intended to call the painting "Love and Loyalty," and hoped that Roger would appreciate the gentle irony.

A timid scratching at the door around mid-morning broke her concentration, and when the door opened to admit one of the downstairs maids, who had no business on the third floor, Jane sensed that her peace was over. She put down her brush and racked her brain for the girl's name.

"Sally, is it?"

"Aye, milady," the girl whispered, bobbing an awkward curtsey.

Jane waited expectantly, but the girl appeared tongue-tied. "Well, what is it, Sally?"

Eyes lowered, the girl curtseyed again. "I was told to bring you this, milady," she murmured in a voice that trembled audibly. She fished in her apron pocket and pulled out a piece of paper.

"A letter?" Jane held out her hand, but for some reason she felt a great reluctance to touch the paper.

"Aye, milady. I was to bring it to you private-like." The girl glanced nervously over her shoulder. "He said Mr. Collins were not to catch me, or he . . . or he . . ."

"Who is this *he*?" Jane wanted to know. "And what did he threaten to do to you, Sally?"

"Barnes, milady," the girl—who could not be more than fourteen, Jane suspected—muttered so low that Jane barely caught the name. "And he will smack me, milady, he swore he would, if I got caught."

Jane felt her anger rise at this bully who threatened young girls. "Barnes does not give the orders around here, Sally. And if he hurts you in any way, you are to come straight to me. Is that understood?"

The girl bobbed her head. "Aye, milady," she whispered.

Jane took the letter and Sally vanished from the room like a shadow. She held the piece of paper in her lap for several minutes before looking at the bold script scrawled across it. The handwriting was Lady Horton's, and it was addressed to Jane. She sighed. What new impertinence had the woman thought up? she wondered, reluctant to open the missive.

When she finally did so, Jane wished she had left it unopened. With deliberate spite, the writer thanked her ladyship profusely for permitting her husband to tryst with his *inamorata* last night. In exchange, the writer continued with sugary sarcasm, her ladyship might enjoy perusing the enclosed *billet-doux*. After all, second-hand love was surely better than no love at all, the writer added. The malice of this remark drove the colour from Jane's cheeks.

The enclosed *billet-doux* was from Roger, and after scanning the first line or two, Jane hastily refolded it and thrust it into her pocket, her face flaming. She had never imagined that a gentleman could or would express himself so grossly to a female with any pretensions of gentility. Lady Horton must be quite utterly lost to all sense of modesty. At the first opportunity, Jane took both notes downstairs and hid them in her jewel-box with the first one.

The letters left an unpleasant taste in her mouth that lasted the rest of the day. Roger would be back tomorrow, but what use would it be to complain about the letter? This must be one of the letters he had expected Lady Horton to return that afternoon they met beside the pond. She had not done so, he confided, first to Elizabeth and later to her. Well, Jane thought grimly, she had returned one of them now, if not quite as Roger had hoped she would.

After a restless night, Jane rose the following morning determined to confront Roger upon his return with Lady Horton's unseemly behaviour. If there was to be peace and harmony at Trenton Abbey, she would tell him, such scandalous annoyances must cease. He had made her a promise, and she expected him to honour it. If not . . . Here Jane's resolution faltered. What would she do if her husband took up with his former mistress again, as Lady Horton appeared to suggest he already had? She brushed this uncomfortable thought aside.

She must be practical and patient, Jane thought as she made her way up to her studio after breakfast, two virtues in which Maud was pitifully deficient. Of course, what man would value practicality and patience when Lady Horton could boast stunning beauty, vivacity, and sensuous allure, all things she lacked, Jane reminded herself with painful honesty. But she did have the huge advantage of being Roger's wife. This thought gave her less comfort than it should. Jane wanted to be so much more than a wife to Roger. She longed to be his one and only beloved, the centre of his existence.

Now she was being highly impractical, she thought with a deprecating smile, seating herself at her easel. The wild pansies in their vase seemed to be laughing at her. On the canvas she had captured some of their free spirit and insouciance, and wished she could borrow their delicate beauty and air of careless gaiety. Since this was never going to happen, she told herself resolutely, she had best learn to live with herself and make the most of what she had. Make the most of Roger. She smiled softly to herself as she worked, thinking of the end of the day when Roger would be home, and they would go upstairs together, and . . .

When Roger had not returned by tea-time, Jane

began to worry. Had he suffered an accident? Been taken sick? Encountered highwaymen? Was he even now lying dead in a ditch somewhere?

"Do not fret, milady," Collins surprised her by saying as he poured her tea for her in the solitary drawing room. "More than likely his lordship has been detained at Okehampton longer than he planned."

"How long does it take to purchase a few sheep, Collins?" Jane replied, her tone anxious.

"Well, you never know, milady," the butler responded soothingly. "Perhaps Mr. Hampton attended the auction himself. He often does, Peterson tells me, being a gentleman as likes to keep an eye on his affairs."

After the butler had left, Jane realized he had been trying to warn her that his master might well have run into his Oxford crony and extended his stay in Okehampton. Even now he might be at the Hampton estate, drinking and swapping stories of their college days. He would hardly refuse a dinner invitation, and that would necessitate spending another night away from home. Away from her, Jane thought crossly, silently wishing this unknown Mr. Hampton in Jericho for keeping Roger so long.

Feeling abandoned and lonely—since Lord Trenton was also away that afternoon—Jane finished her second cup of tea and, ignoring the stale-looking seedcake, made her way downstairs. She could avoid needlework this evening, there being no visitors to impress with her ladylike skills. Instead, she would indulge herself with one of the books Aunt Honoria had sent down from London last week. As yet she had not even opened the parcel, and her spirits rose at the prospect of finding one of Mr. Scott's latest novels.

As she reached the front hall, Collins was opening the door to a frantic knocking, and she paused, fearful that it might be a message from Roger. The groom who stood on the threshold looked flustered at the sight of her as he handed a letter to the butler. Recognizing the groom as one of Sir Giles's servants, Jane's suspicions were instantly aroused, and she came forward.

"What is it, Collins?"

The groom ducked his head and vanished, and the butler turned to regard her stiffly. "Only a letter for his lordship, milady," he said in his driest tones.

Jane was not deterred, and held out her hand. "I will take it, Collins, thank you."

The butler hesitated, holding the letter tightly against his chest. "There is no need to inconvenience yourself, milady. I shall take it up to his lordship's room myself."

Jane remained with her hand outstretched. "I believe I said I will take it, Collins." She stared at him steadily until he relinquished the letter with extreme reluctance.

"As you wish, milady."

Jane tucked the letter into her pocket and entered the library. The parcel of books from London she had hoped to enjoy still stood on the desk where she had left it a week ago. Jane ignored it. The letter was burning a hole in her pocket, and she knew she was going to open it in spite of everything her conscience was screaming at her.

The letter was indeed addressed to her husband, and as she had guessed, in Lady Horton's flashy scrawl.

Firmly brushing her scruples aside, Jane ripped it open, expecting to read a love letter full of immodest and scandalous propositions. She was surprised and affected by the desperation evident in the short note. Lady Horton begged Roger to go to her at once. She was dying, she wrote, and feared that without her to protect it, her child would die, too. Sir Giles would carry out his threat to destroy it. Roger was the only one who could save the babe, she wrote, evidently in tears, for the paper was blotched and damp.

Jane reread the letter, trying to dismiss it as the ramblings of a hysterical woman. She could not do so, however. There was too much panic and despair in

the note, which sounded more convincing the more
she read it. Would Roger have felt the same way had
he received it? And if so, what would he have done?
Jane felt foolish asking such a question when she knew
very well what he would have done. He would have
gone to Horton Hall and the devil take the consequences. If Lady Horton could be believed, not only
her own but the baby's life was at stake. A babe who
was in all likelihood his own.

Yes, she thought stoically, Roger would have answered his former lover's frantic call for help. And
since he was not here, and might not return before
tomorrow, Jane could not escape the obvious conclusion that she owed it to him to go in his place. The
thought appalled her, but the more she considered it,
the more convinced she became that this was not the time
for squeamishness or false modesty. It was not the
time to consider what the gossips might say. Would
inevitably say.

Before her courage failed her, Jane walked out into
the hall and ordered the carriage. Then she ran upstairs to change her gown and fetch her shawl. The
air would certainly turn cool later on.

During the drive to Horton Hall, Jane deliberately
suppressed all thought of Roger's involvement with
the unfortunate woman. She concentrated on the babe
and tried to devise an explanation for her presence at
the Hall in case she encountered Sir Giles.

As it turned out, Jane need not have worried about
Sir Giles. His lordship had retired early, the butler
informed her, after she was admitted to the Hall.

"Her ladyship is confined to her bed, and the doctor
is presently attending her," he added when Jane explained her business was with Lady Horton.

Jane was not phased for a moment. "She is expecting me," she lied blithely.

Dr. Graham was leaving the lady's chamber when
Jane arrived, and he looked relieved when he saw her.

"Things do not look good for her ladyship," he replied in answer to Jane's query. "She will not take the

potions I give her, and accuses me of being in league with her husband to kill her child. Pure delirious nonsense, of course. Actually, Sir Giles has ordered me not to call again, and refuses to pay my bill if I do."

Jane's hackles rose at this show of insensitivity. "You may send your bills to me, Dr. Graham," she said at once. "And please continue to do all you can for the poor lady. I will not stand to see her treated so callously at such a time."

The physician gave her a strange look, but promised to do his best, and Jane entered Lady Horton's chamber, despite the assurances of the flustered abigail that her ladyship did not wish to receive anyone.

"She will see me," Jane announced, surprised at her sudden assertiveness. She marched over to the bed. The sight that met her eyes deprived her momentarily of speech. The gaunt woman who lay there as though she had already given up the ghost bore little resemblance to the vivacious Lady Maud Horton Jane was accustomed to. This woman appeared listless, her beautiful face pallid and lifeless.

"She will not take her medicines, milady," the old abigail whispered. "And how she is to get well if she does not heed the doctor, I am sure I cannot tell."

As Jane observed her, the invalid's eyes fluttered open, showing a flicker of alarm. "Come to gloat have you?" she muttered.

Jane was unprepared for the spiritless voice.

"No, of course not," she said bracingly. "I have come to see that you take your medicines. Dr. Graham tells me you are being naughty."

Lady Horton waved her away with one limp hand. She pouted, but Jane realized it was no longer the flirtatious gesture of a lovely woman, but the grimace of a fractious child who could not have her way.

"Where is Roger?" the invalid muttered suddenly, her voice weak and petulant. "Why is he not here? Have you locked him away so that he cannot come to me when I call, as I know he would not hesitate to do?"

"Oh dear," the abigail murmured, glancing apologetically at Jane. "She is delirious, milady, and does not mean anything she says, I am sure."

Jane ignored her. Lady Horton had said nothing that she did not know already. Roger would certainly have come to her, regardless of any promises he had made to his wife. This truth no longer bothered her. The woman in the bed was obviously very ill indeed, and no woman should have to go through any illness, and especially not the trials of childbirth, without emotional support from her family. Poor Maud had no mother, and her husband had practically cast her off. And her lover had married another woman. It was hard to imagine a worse fate, and Jane felt an unexpected rush of sympathy for the woman she had envied for so long, and despised, too, if she were honest about it.

"Which is the medicine Dr. Graham instructed her to take?" she demanded, anxious to keep her mind occupied with something useful.

The abigail indicated several flasks on the bedside table, and Jane read each of the instructions carefully. She rinsed out a cloth in the bowl of rose-water and wiped the invalid's face. Then she forced the reluctant woman to swallow several spoons of tonic and a little laudanum. With the help of the abigail, she stripped off the covers and changed the soiled night rail, after giving the patient a thorough wash.

As she gently passed the cool cloth over Lady Horton's distended belly, Jane was thrilled to feel a slight movement. In spite of its mother's frail health, the babe appeared strong and lively. She wished there was more she could do to insure its safety.

Jane sat with Maud for over an hour, listening to the woman's uneven breathing. When she finally rose to leave, she gave specific instructions to the abigail.

"If your mistress does not obey the doctor's orders, send for me immediately. We must watch her carefully, or she will cause the babe's death with her own foolishness."

On the drive home, Jane prayed that she would be able to prevent this disaster to the innocent child.

The night was far advanced when Lord Summers and his agent rode into the stable-yard at Trenton Abbey. Roger was glad of the bright moonlight that had persuaded him to risk riding home at such a late hour. The stables were dark when they arrived, and finding no groom on duty, Roger unsaddled his own horse, and was rubbing it down when a bleary-eyed Barnes stumbled down the stairs from his room in the loft.

"Beg pardon, milord," the groom muttered his excuses in a surly voice. " 'Er ladyship told me not to wait up for 'er, and we dinna expect ye home tonight, milord."

Roger paused in his work and stared at the groom. "Her ladyship is out visiting? At this hour?" He should have waited to ask Collins for this information, but the groom's words took him by surprise.

"Aye, milord," Barnes replied, with a smile that Roger did not like the look of. " 'Er ladyship ordered the carriage and rushed off in a bang straight after tea, she did." He leered at Roger quite as though they shared a dirty secret.

"Where did she go?" Roger snapped, too alarmed at his wife's absence to pay attention to protocol.

" 'Orton 'all," the groom answered, with a smirk that Roger ignored.

"Saddle Ajax for me," he ordered, forgetting how tired and hungry he was. The groom obeyed and, refusing Peterson's offer to accompany him, Roger galloped off in the direction of Horton Hall.

The horse was fresh and it took Roger less than ten minutes at the rate he was going to reach Sir Giles's estate. As he approached the gate, he saw a carriage turn out of the driveway onto the main road. Instantly recognizing it as one of his own, Roger waved the coachman to a halt and flung himself from his horse. Jerking the door open, he peered into the dim interior.

His wife was sitting there by herself, clutching a dark shawl round her shoulders and staring at him with wide, frightened eyes.

"I apologize for alarming you, my dear," he said hastily. "I have only now returned from Okehampton and they told me you were here."

She said nothing, and Roger wondered what had happened in his absence to bring Jane over to Hampton Hall, the home of a woman she could have no love for. "What brings you here at this time of night?" He sounded harsh to his own ears, and she flinched.

"Lady Horton was taken ill." Her voice was expressionless, and even in the dimness of the coach, she looked fatigued. Roger wanted to take her in his arms and kiss all her cares away, but her coolness deterred him.

There was another pause, during which he became increasingly uneasy. "Was it the babe?" He was not sure he wanted to hear the answer to this, but he spoke what was uppermost in his mind.

Jane shook her head. "No. At least not yet. Dr. Graham assures me it will certainly come early, but whether or not it will live he could not say."

"And the mother?" This was the first time he had spoken so openly to his wife about Maud, but the time for roundaboutation was long gone.

"Lady Horton is resting," Jane replied woodenly. "Dr. Graham will keep me informed, as will her abigail."

Roger was startled. Before he could demand an explanation of his wife's sudden involvement with his former mistress, Jane raised a gloved hand. "I am tired and have missed my dinner. Shall we continue this conversation at home, my lord?"

The formality of that speech was an obvious dismissal, he thought as he rode along behind the carriage. What had Maud told his wife that had brought on this cool reserve? Roger felt an unfamiliar ache settle in his heart. He had thought it would be so easy to close that illicit and highly irresponsible chapter of his life and start afresh with Jane. It was not as though Maud had been ignorant of his long-standing betrothal to Penhallow's daughter. Everyone within a hundred miles knew of it. He had felt safe to enjoy this passionate liaison with Sir Giles's wife before his father's pressing debts had forced him to take a step he had postponed for years.

Now he not only had a wife of his own—one he was well pleased with—but by some ironic twist of Fate had fathered a child with his mistress. Roger thought of the female in the coach ahead of him, and a tenderness such as he had never experienced before overwhelmed him. He had known Jane all her life, but since their arranged marriage three months ago, he had discovered that he had not known her at all. He had looked at her and seen Jane the childhood companion, the *beanstalk,* as he had called her. But the woman in the carriage was a stranger to him.

With a flash of insight, Roger discovered that he did not want Jane to remain a stranger. He had visited her bed practically every night for the past three months, and had confidently assumed that there was nothing about his wife he did not know. What an arrogant fool he had been. He began to understand why he had been so reluctant to rendezvous with Maud at the gatehouse, and why he had dismounted to gather the wild pansies in the graveyard upon his way home. He had been thinking of Jane.

He was thinking of Jane now as he rode alone in the moonlight, feeling as though she had abruptly cut herself off from him. The thought of an abyss opening between them intensified the ache in his heart. He would not let it happen. She was too important to him.

Roger did not dare put a name to what he felt for his wife. It was too elusive, too precious. She had taken over his heart, and he had never noticed. Till now.

Chapter Twelve

Estrangement

The next few days came and went in a blur for Jane. It was as though the normal pattern of her life as mistress of the Abbey had been suspended. The formal drawing room she had been in the process of refurbishing looked like an abandoned furniture warehouse, bolts of cloth on the floor, pictures stacked in corners, carpet samples awaiting her decisions, and gutted chairs against the wall, their stuffing hanging out indecorously.

Her painting suffered, too. No longer could she slip away to her studio to lose herself in her flowers. Roger's wild pansies shrivelled in their glass vase, and were thrown out by the maids. The warm glow Jane had experienced at his tender gesture faded, too, and slipped away from her, leaving her feeling cold and unloved.

Emotionally she felt drained. It did not help that Roger seemed to have distanced himself from her. Ever since that moonlit night she had seen him riding back from the forbidden rendezvous with Maud, their relationship had faltered. Those wild pansies had touched her romantic heart, and Jane had been fully prepared to believe her husband innocent of betrayal. She had even vowed to forgive and forget those vicious letters his former love had sent to harass her. But he had offered no explanation for that stolen night at the gatehouse. How could she forgive if Roger would not confess?

"I cannot," she murmured, her heart breaking at the rift that had come between them.

"Beg pardon, milady?"

Jane started from her reverie to find Betty gazing at her anxiously. The abigail stood behind her, brushing out her hair for bed. Jane shook her head and smiled faintly. "Oh, nothing. I am afraid Lady Horton cannot live much longer. Dr. Graham is amazed she has lasted this long."

"Never fret yerself over that woman, milady," Betty said with unaccustomed fierceness. "Nothing but trouble she is—beggin' yer pardon and all—ever since she arrived in these parts. First to young Stephen, Captain 'orton as 'e is now. Fair drove 'im off to war she did, the scheming 'ussy. Then up and married that poor old man as should have known better than to take a wife 'alf 'is age."

With every accusation, Betty applied a vigorous sweep of the brush, until Jane felt she was in danger of losing all her hair.

"Lot of good it did 'im," Betty muttered, carefully brushing out an obstinate tangle. "And then the shameless piece went out of her way to dazzle 'is lordship with her wanton ways. Begging yer pardon again, milady, for speaking my mind, but 'tis common knowledge."

"I know, I know, Betty," Jane felt obliged to say. "But the viscount was not a married man at the time, you must remember." She had no idea why she felt impelled to defend Roger to a servant.

"Aye, but *she* was, and still is, the immoral vixen. But sins have a way of coming 'ome to roost, milady," the abigail said sententiously. "And good riddance, I say."

"You are forgetting the innocent babe, Betty," Jane said, shocked at this virulence. "No child should have to suffer for its mother's mistakes."

"Mistakes? Bah!" Betty scoffed. "That is not what the Good Book says, milady."

The abigail's words filled her mind long after she had climbed into bed and pulled up the covers. It should not surprise her that the servants knew all about Lady Horton's checkered past. There was nothing new in Betty's tirade except the part about Stephen. Jane had no recollection of saucy red-haired Maud Barnes, later widow Danvers, having caused the Horton heir to join Wellington's army. Jane knew that she had urged her new husband, Peter Danvers, to buy his colours immediately after Stephen left. What was the connexion?

Tired of speculating about the past, Jane burrowed her head into the pillow and thought about the present. Her own miserable present. A deep and wrenching sadness overtook her every time she found herself alone in her bedchamber. And she had found herself alone there for over a week now. Ever since that appalling night she had gone to Lady Horton's sickbed and encountered Roger on the way home. He had looked at her strangely but shown little interest in her. Instead he had asked about the babe, and then about Maud. How pleased Maud would be if she knew. But Jane had no intention of telling her.

As for Roger, a layer of ice had formed around her heart that night, and her husband made no attempt to thaw it. He stayed away. They had not had the conversation she had requested that night in the coach. After a hasty meal of cold cuts, during which he had barely answered her questions about the sheep he had bought, he had excused himself and gone to Peterson's study. There were papers that must be attended to, he had muttered. And she had let him go without a word.

What was the use? she had thought. Perhaps later, when he came to her room. But he had not come, neither that night nor the nights that followed, and Jane had sought to shore up her defences against the sudden indifference of the man she had come to love.

The following morning, as she had every morning that week, Jane called for the carriage and, accompanied this time by her abigail, drove over to Horton Hall and climbed the oak stairs to the second storey where Lady Horton lay in her tester bed, her flame-

coloured hair a tangle on the pillow. Whenever Jane
entered the chamber, the invalid invariably called for
Roger, and this morning was no different.

"Roger?" The voice seemed weaker today, and
Jane quickly shed her cloak and gloves and approached the bed.

"My husband is busy this morning and could not
come," she replied softly, as she always did. Pity
welled up in her as she saw Maud's eyes fixed on
the door.

"What do I care about your husband?" Lady Horton muttered fretfully. "I want *Roger*. Where is
Roger? Why does he not come?"

"She is feverish again, milady," the Horton abigail
whispered. "And has not taken her potions this
morning."

"I thought I told you to insist upon it," Jane replied,
annoyed at the abigail's apparent incompetence. "Get
another maid to help hold your mistress still if you
must. But she must take the tonic."

"No other maid in the house will help, milady," the
abigail whined.

Jane turned from mixing the restorative powders to
stare at the maid. "Why ever not?"

"Master has threatened to dismiss them if they do,
milady."

"Nonsense, girl!" Jane snapped, frustrated by this
foolishness. "Sir Giles is also confined to his bed, is
he not?"

"Most of the time, milady. But sometimes he gets
his valet to wheel him around in his chair."

"How can he expect Lady Horton to get well if he
does not allow her proper care? Help me give her this
potion, will you?"

"Oh, he does not expect it," the maid whispered as
she held her mistress down while Jane administered
the medicine. "Nor does he wish it, if you were to ask
me, milady. A regular tartar he is and no mistake."

Further comment was cut short by the arrival of Dr.
Graham, who looked relieved to see Lady Summers.

To Jane's enquiry about the invalid, he shook his grey head.

"I see no reason to delude you, Lady Summers. Her ladyship is weaker now than yesterday. She seems to have no will to live, and will not accept any food except under protest. I do believe she would have been gone a week ago had you not come to insist upon medicating her. A blessing that is, I can tell you, my lady. Every day she lives increases the chances of the child surviving. But she cannot last much longer." He shook his head again and went away.

By mid-afternoon Jane was exhausted. Not having eaten anything since breakfast but a bowl of chicken broth and an apple pilfered from the kitchen by Lady Horton's abigail, she was also hungry. She eagerly looked forward to the arrival of Mrs. Johnson, the vicar's wife, who came in the afternoons to sit with the patient and relieve Jane from her thankless vigil. The older woman never failed to praise Jane on her Christian charity and forbearance.

"I cannot tell you how much my husband admires your fortitude, Lady Summers," the old lady said as she entered the chamber just as Jane was despairing of getting home for tea. "And generosity, of course," she added, glancing at the bed where Lady Horton slept fitfully. "Only someone of your generous spirit would have put your personal feelings about this woman aside, my dear. We all respect you immensely. Frankly, I do not know how you stand her rambling on about his lordship in that shameless way she has. No breeding, that is her problem, my lady. Mr. Johnson said only this morning over his breakfast that you will surely be rewarded in heaven for your charity."

As the carriage covered the short distance between Horton Hall and the Abbey, Jane pondered Mrs. Johnson's words. Would she have to wait until she got to heaven to receive her reward? Was she worthy of a reward at all? She knew her motives for her daily pilgrimages to tend Lady Horton were ambiguous. She could not like the woman, but she certainly pitied her.

And she was beginning to understand all too well the pain and desperation of losing the man she loved. What good would a heavenly reward be to her, if what she yearned for, what she needed, was a little happiness now? A little love and tenderness. Roger's love. And if love was not in the cards, Jane told herself prosaically, she would make do with his tenderness. Anything would be possible if only he would come to her at night as he had those first delirious months of their marriage.

For now, however, she would be happy enough if Roger joined her at the tea-table.

"The devil take it, Roger, what are you doing to the gel?" his father demanded at the breakfast table a week later, as soon as Jane had excused herself and left the room. "She looks downright mopey, and a sparrow has more appetite than your wife."

Roger glanced up from his plate of York ham and coddled eggs. He had little appetite himself and had been pondering the same question. As yet, a satisfactory answer eluded him. "Jane is spending far too much time at Horton Hall," he offered. "Lady Horton is doing poorly and Jane seems to think it is her duty to share the burden of tending her."

Lord Trenton snorted. "There is no reason for her to spend every single day over there. What is Mrs. Johnson doing? I thought the duty of the vicar's wife was to tend the sick and ailing." He glared across the table at his son. "And how it comes about that your wife is putting herself out for that woman, I cannot for the life of me understand."

"I do not understand it myself, Father."

His father regarded him sharply. "You have not done anything foolish, have you, son? Jane told me you promised there would be no more rumours," the old man continued in a sharper tone. "And I warn you, she is not one to take it mildly if she hears you have taken up with that hussy again." When Roger made no response, Lord Trenton insisted. "Tell me you have not offended her with your dalliance, Roger."

"No, Father. I may have offended her, but not with any dalliance. I can swear to that."

Roger spoke nothing less than the truth. For over a week he had not had a meaningful conversation with his wife, much less with any other woman. He saw her only fleetingly at the breakfast table, where they spoke nothing but trivialities. He avoided the tea-table because he could not bear it that she conversed with her aunt and his father but ignored him. And after dinner, she always seemed to have an excuse for retiring after drinking a single cup of tea.

"If that is true, can you tell me why your wife has the hangdog look of a woman who fancies herself betrayed, unloved, or neglected?"

Roger had no explanation that he could share with his father, so he said nothing. He could hardly confess that he had indeed betrayed Jane with his secret assignation at the gatehouse, and that he had neglected her by avoiding her bed. He simply did not have the courage to confess his guilty feelings about Maud. Had he not been so cavalier about seducing another man's wife and bedding her at every opportunity, Maud might not be carrying his child. If he had done his duty when he ought, Jane would be carrying it; he might have been a father long ago, and none of this embroglio would have happened. And poor Maud might not be at death's door even as he sat eating his breakfast. The thought took away his remaining appetite.

"Jane is a good girl," his father said after a long pause. "Much too good for you, if you want my opinion. And if you are such a muttonhead as to lose her affection, I can guarantee you will regret it for the rest of your life, son. The rest of your life."

Lord Trenton pushed his plate aside and rose to leave. When the door closed behind him, Roger was left to mull over his father's advice. It was all true, of course. Jane *was* too good for him. Luckily she did not seem to know it, and had put on a good face when she was forced to wed him. Roger did not delude himself that she had been overcome with delight at the prospect. She had, he remembered wryly, flatly rejected him the first time he asked. Marriage to him could not have been the romantic event young girls were said to dream about. He had not even attempted to woo her with the trinkets and flowers and flattery she must have expected from a lover.

Now he came to think of it, he had never given her anything except his name, which, according to general rumour, was severely tarnished. The pansies he had impulsively gathered from the graveyard on his way home that night and laid on her pillow had been as much to assuage his own guilt as to please Jane. She must have realized this, for she had never mentioned the flowers.

It was a sobering thought for Roger, who had long seen himself as a dashing conqueror of female hearts—and bodies—to admit that his own wife might well view him as an unavoidable encumbrance.

The thought stayed with him as he stood at the window moments later and watched his wife whisked away in the carriage on her errand of mercy. Roger longed to unburden himself to Jane, to tell her why he had felt obliged to go to the gatehouse that night; to assure her that Maud's tears and exhortations had moved him to nothing but pity. And to make her believe that the whole while he was with Maud, his thoughts were with her. How could he make her believe this when it sounded like a Banbury tale even to him, who knew it to be true?

Roger sighed and turned away. He needed the intimacy of her bedchamber to broach these private matters, and he had denied himself that pleasure for days. Something warned him that Jane would expect a full explanation if he ventured into her room. She might not demand one, but the question would be in her soft amber eyes, and it would throw up a barrier between them that physical passion alone would never bridge. And Roger was beginning to realize that he wanted more than a physical unity with his wife. Jane had offered an unexpected emotional harmony that he had never enjoyed with other women. He panicked every time he thought of losing it.

He grimaced at the notion of spending many more nights like last night, alone and restless in his cold bed. He could always insist, as was his right, and in moments of intense desire he had thought about walking through that door and climbing into her bed. As if nothing had happened. She was his wife, after all. But perhaps for that very reason, and because she was Jane, not some saucy tavern wench who would welcome him as well as the next man, Roger could not bring himself to the point.

Thus he found himself on the horns of a dilemma: he yearned to confide in Jane, to return to her good graces, but his courage failed when he considered how contemptible he must appear in her eyes for breaking his promise. He could not bear it if she refused to believe him.

The worst trial would come when he admitted to Jane that Maud's child was his. He had made up his mind to do so as soon as the babe was born. He wanted no secrets between them, but feared that such an admission would destroy her affection forever. But then perhaps Maud had already taken care of that. It would not surprise him, for that was precisely the kind of vindictiveness Maud seemed to relish.

These and other morbid thoughts harried Roger as he went about the estate with Peterson, listening to tenants and making decisions on the autumn plantings. He took his midday meal with Peterson at a tavern in the village, and did not return to the Abbey for tea, although he knew that his continued absences strained his relationship with Jane beyond endurance.

"Reverend Johnson tells us that poor Lady Horton is not expected to last the week, Roger," Lady Octavia—who had invited herself to dine with them again—remarked as soon as the party gathered in the small drawing room after dinner. "Such a pity, would you not agree, my lord? Who would have guessed last summer that she would never see Christmas again? So full of vigour as she was, poor thing."

Lord Trenton snorted. "A mite too vigorous if you ask me, Octavia." He said no more, although the glance he shot at Jane told Roger that there was a lot more on his father's mind.

"My dear wife reports that her ladyship is failing rapidly," the vicar said in his deep, ponderous voice. "I have upon several occasions offered to attend her to discuss the salvation of her soul, but her ladyship is disinclined to dwell on heavenly matters. We can only hope and pray that the poor lady has made her peace with her Maker."

The vicar—who dined at the Abbey as often as he could—pursed his thin lips and threw a speaking glance at Jane. Roger wondered if the man had honestly tried to comfort Maud, or whether he had unleashed one of his endless morality sermons on her captive head. Like many of the gentry in the area, the vicar did not approve of Lady Horton, but unlike them, he was obliged by his profession to camouflage his dislike with pious blatherings.

"More tea, Mr. Johnson?"

Jane had said hardly a word all evening, and Roger tried in vain to catch her eye. As soon as she had refilled the vicar's cup, he rose and approached the tea-tray, cup in hand. Ignoring the surprise on his father's face, Roger handed Jane his cup.

"I believe I will have another cup, too, my dear." He almost never had a second cup, preferring a glass of brandy with his father, but Jane did not so much as look up at him. Dutifully she filled his cup, and he was forced to sit and drink tepid tea while Lord Trenton motioned to Collins to serve him another brandy.

As soon as Collins removed the tea-tray, Jane rose, as Roger knew she would.

"I wonder if you would care to help me decide on

a colour for the morning room curtains before you leave, Aunt," she said, her soft voice stirring memories of happier times.

She had escaped him again, Roger thought much later, as he sought his room. Another solitary night. Another night without his Jane in his arms. Unwilling to endure another lecture on acceptable husbandly behaviour, he had declined his father's invitation to a game of billiards after the vicar left. Instead he instructed Collins to bring him a decanter of brandy and settled down with a book, determined to drink himself to sleep if necessary.

He must have dozed off, for he woke with a start to find himself slumped before the dying fire still in his clothes. The door opened and his valet, Greyson, stuck his head in.

"Beg pardon, milord. This just arrived from the Hall." Advancing into the room, he held out a note on his salver.

Roger sat up, abruptly wide awake. The handwriting was not Maud's. Possibly Graham's, he thought, unfolding the paper and scanning it hastily. The physician's message was terse and to the point. Lady Horton had given birth prematurely to a baby girl, he wrote in heavy script. Unhappily, the new mother had not lived to enjoy her daughter, having succumbed almost immediately to complications. In one of her lucid moments, Lady Horton had asked that his lordship be notified and reminded of his promise. His lordship's presence was urgently requested since none of the servants at the Hall would come near the babe.

"Order Jason saddled and brought round at once," he commanded. "And fetch my hat and cloak." He glanced at his valet, who, like any good servant, showed not a flicker of curiosity at the news that took his master out in the middle of a rainy night. "Have her ladyship's maid inform my wife that I have been called to Horton Hall. Tell her I shall come to her as soon as I return." Roger did not wish for any further misunderstandings to arise between them.

He stood for a moment, hesitant as to whether he should go into Jane's room and tell her himself. Deciding against it, Roger strode to the door that his valet held open. "And, Greyson," he added over his shoulder as he started down the stairs, "do not wait up for me. I may be very late."

He hoped not, Roger thought, jumping astride Jason and clapping heels to the horse's glossy flanks. It would all depend on what he found when he arrived at Horton Hall.

A daughter. He had a baby daughter. Holding Jason down to a steady canter through the damp, blustery night, Roger knew that the time had come, ready or not, to face up to his responsibilities. To keep the promise he had made to a dying woman.

Maud was gone now, and he would mourn her. But Jane was still with him, as was his innocent daughter. Roger prayed for the strength to bind these two remaining females in his life into the happy, loving family they both deserved.

Chapter Thirteen

The Baby

Awake and filled with a vague uneasiness, Jane lay in her bed long after Betty had helped her change into her night rail and brushed out her hair. A single candle burned on the dresser, and Jane wondered if she should get out of bed to douse it. Would she sleep any better in the dark? Or would she simply lie there listening to the old house settle around her with familiar night noises?

Hours ago she had heard Roger retire to his room, but he had not come near her. Jane had kept her eyes glued to the connecting door, as she did every night, hoping that this would be the night her husband would come through it. But he had not done so. Every night he failed to come to her increased the panic in her heart. Were they to be forever estranged? Was Maud, even on her deathbed, to come between them every night?

The thought of Lady Horton sobered her and calmed her latent hysteria. The days Jane had spent at the dying woman's bedside had softened her hostility towards her rival. Active dislike had dissolved into pity as the days passed, and Jane began to understand something of the despondency the once beautiful woman suffered. With neither husband nor lover to support her, Maud had slipped into deep despair and seemed to relinquish her will to live a little more each day. Her daily demands for Roger's presence became less strident, and a note of hopelessness crept in that touched Jane's heart.

Lady Horton had not appeared to derive any comfort at all from the babe she carried. She rarely spoke of her condition and then only in terms of the inconvenience the child caused her, blaming it for Roger's absence. This lack of natural motherly instinct was incomprehensible to Jane; it appalled her. Had she been in Maud's shoes, she would have fought tooth and nail, both for herself and her child. Particularly had she been—as she now had no doubt that Maud was—carrying Roger's child.

Her thoughts were interrupted by a door opening down the hall. Someone had entered Roger's room. She was tempted to throw on her robe and go into their sitting room to hear better, but the cold deterred her. A few minutes later she distinctly heard heavy steps descending the stairs. Was Roger going out? Where would he go at this time of night except to Horton Hall? If Lady Horton had taken a turn for the worse, why had they not sent for her?

Her questions were answered ten minutes later when Betty, dressed in her nightclothes, entered the room. The abigail appeared wide awake, and Jane could see she was bursting with news.

"What is it, Betty?" she demanded with trepidation.

"Oh, milady, a groom from the Hall came with a message for 'is lordship from Dr. Graham. It seems 'er ladyship 'ad a baby girl."

Jane sat up and threw back the covers. "Help me get into my clothes, Betty," she commanded. "I must go to her at once."

"'Is lordship says 'e will come to you as soon as 'e returns, milady. It's raining something awful, it is. Besides, 'er ladyship is beyond 'elp, milady. Greyson says she went to 'er rest an 'our ago."

Jane sat immobile, her breath caught in her throat. She let it out slowly. Although she had known Maud's death was imminent, the news was a blow. "And the babe?"

"Must be alive, but 'eaven knows how the poor wee mite will go on without a mother."

Getting over her initial shock, Jane stood up and

reached for her robe. "Have the fire built up in the
sitting room, Betty. I shall wait there. His lordship will
be cold when he returns, so ask Collins to send up
the brandy."

After this initial bustle of activity, quiet again settled over the Abbey. Jane sat before the blazing fire,
absentmindedly nibbling at the seedcake Collins had
brought up with the brandy. One eye on the brass
clock on the mantel, she spent the time speculating
about the motherless baby girl Lady Horton had left
behind.

What would happen to the poor child? she wondered. Would Sir Giles relent and claim it as his
daughter? Or would he continue to deny the child the
protection of his name and roof? If this happened, as
Jane feared it would, having witnessed the baronet's
stubborn vindictiveness against his wife, what would
Roger do?

Drowsy with the warmth of the fire, Jane was lost
in these uneasy speculations when the sound of voices
in her husband's chamber startled her. She rose as the
door opened, and then he was there, poised on the
threshold, his handsome face lined with worry.

"My dear Jane," he said, striding across the room
to stand before her. "I apologize for taking so long.
Horton Hall is in an uproar. Never have I seen so
many foolish servants all in one establishment. None
of them seemed to know what to do, and they refused
to take my orders. They all appear to be scared to
death of old Giles."

"I know," Jane murmured. "He threatened to turn
them off without a reference. Dr. Graham thinks he
is senile."

"No doubt about it," Roger agreed. "He raised the
devil of a rumpus when he saw me. Swore like a ban-
shee and told me to get out of his house. I thought
he would go off with an apoplexy. Quite deranged,
poor fellow."

There was a sudden silence, and Jane noted that
Roger looked uncomfortable. He had not stopped to

change his clothes. His breeches were damp, and his black Hessians glinted with raindrops. Damp curls plastered his forehead, and he looked chilled.

He still had not broached the real reason for his presence in her sitting room. Jane guessed he found it awkward to speak of his mistress to his wife. She had no such compunction; she needed to know.

"The servants are saying that Lady Horton . . ." She paused, noting that his cobalt eyes had clouded.

"Yes," he cut in, voice thick with emotion, "she is dead." He turned to the fire and placed one booted foot on the fender, an arm resting on the mantel. He looked drained and vulnerable. Jane's heart went out to him. She ached to put her arms around him, to hold him, to comfort him. But she knew too well—remembering her mother—that some losses were beyond comfort.

"Did you arrive in time to . . . ?"

"No, she was already gone when Graham sent his message."

Jane waited for more details. When none were forthcoming, she asked. "And the child?"

"A girl. Alive but not strong, Graham says. She will need extra care. Lord knows she will not get it there."

"Is Sir Giles so very set against her, then?"

"Oh, yes." He sounded bitter, and Jane wondered what had passed between him and Maud's husband. Nothing pleasant, if her rare encounters with the irate baronet were any indication.

"Where is the poor little thing, then? You cannot have left her at Horton Hall."

He came to her and caught both hands in his, pressing them against his damp waistcoat. "Forgive me, Jane. None of this can be pleasant for you. I brought her back with me." He hesitated, then continued in a rush. "I could think of no other place to take her." He gazed down at her anxiously. Jane felt her heart slowly warming again.

"I trust you did not bring the child home on your

horse." She smiled faintly at the picture that rose in her mind.

"Oh, no, I sent for the carriage. That is what took me so long. Maud's abigail, Mrs. Watson, accompanied her. I have promised her a position here. It seems Sir Giles has turned her off. I hope you do not mind, my love," he murmured softly, pressing her fingers gently.

Jane would have agreed to anything Roger asked if he spoke to her in that tone of voice. "Of course not. Why should I mind?" She saw a smile flicker on his lips, and knew he was thinking of any number of reasons why she should mind very much. None of these seemed to matter any longer. All she cared about was Roger smiling at her again, holding her hands, and mesmerizing her with those cobalt eyes of his. Jane felt a glow of happiness invade her whole body, bringing a happy flush to her cheeks, and a smile to her lips. Now if only he would kiss her . . .

"You are too good to me, Jane," he said with a crooked smile. "Father is always telling me so, and now I believe him. I did not know what else to do with the poor little mite. She is so tiny and quiet it breaks your heart." He regarded her steadily and a frown marred his forehead. "If you dislike it, my love, I promise to take the child to Mrs. Johnson in the—"

"Oh, no, you will not, sir," Jane interrupted sharply. "You must know that the Johnsons will consign her to the poorhouse, and heaven knows what will become of her. She must stay here, Roger, I insist upon it. After all . . ." She hesitated and felt the colour rush into her cheeks. "After all, she is . . . she is yours, is she not?"

Jane gazed up steadily at him as she spoke and saw the flicker of hesitation in his eyes. *Please do not lie to me,* she prayed, willing him to trust her with the truth.

He nodded slowly. "I wish I could spare you, Jane, but the child is mine." His voice was firm, and Jane relaxed. "I promised you no more scandals, my dear," he continued softly, "and I tried, believe me, I tried.

But if the babe stays here, it is bound to kick up the devil of a dust. I can still take her to the vicar if you feel you cannot bear it. Or I can arrange to have her raised by one of the tenants.'' His gaze wavered as if he expected rejection.

"Nonsense," Jane exclaimed. "She is your daughter, Roger." She paused. "You are quite sure of this?"

"Oh, yes." He managed a wry smile. "When you see her, you will know beyond a doubt. She has the Hastings' nose, and my hair. Of course, she is so small, it is hard to be sure, but—"

"Well, that settles it," Jane interrupted, guessing that Roger saw what he wanted to see in his child. But that would not bother her, just as long as this daughter she was determined to welcome as her own did not have red hair. That constant reminder of Maud she would have found difficult to live with.

"We will have to find her a wet-nurse, of course, and have the nursery refurbished immediately. I think I shall call on my old nurse to come and help me, since I know next to nothing about babies." She grinned up at him. "But I will soon learn. I will have to." Jane stopped abruptly. Now was not the time to tell him that he might well be a father again in a few short months. For the first time, her courses were two days late, but it probably meant nothing. Jane hurried on. "Mrs. Watson will stay with the child, of course. But first I want to see her, Roger. Where is she?"

Roger laughed and suddenly his arms were about her, and Jane felt his damp cravat against her cheek. She snuggled into the warmth of his embrace, her blood singing. He had come back to her. He needed her. And though this was not quite the same as loving her, Jane was content.

Suddenly she thought of something and raised her head. "We will have to find a name for her, Roger. And she can be christened in the Abbey chapel. What do you think?"

"I think we should discuss all this in the morning, love," he murmured, kissing the tip of her nose. "For now, I suggest we go to bed, Jane. We have some catching up to do, would you not agree?"

Jane could not have wished for a better ending to a momentous evening.

Roger attempted to dissuade his lady from attending Maud's funeral two days later, but Jane was adamant.

"When has a little rain prevented us from doing what is right?" she asked defiantly.

They stood together at the breakfast parlour window watching the misty drizzle turn the shrubbery into bedraggled clumps of greenery along the side of the house. The weather had been uncertain for over a week, but since the night of Maud's death the rains had begun in earnest and were expected to last for several days. The funeral, scheduled for eleven o'clock, was bound to be a wet one, and Roger was not looking forward to it.

He glanced down at the woman beside him and his heart contracted. They had bridged that dreadful gap that had come between them the night of his rendezvous with Maud at the gatehouse, and life at the Abbey had settled back into a comfortable routine. Roger had done his best to explain why he felt he had to meet Maud that night, and Jane appeared to understand. He also spoke of his feelings of guilt over the child and over Maud's death. Jane said she understood that, too, and Roger hoped this was true. He had discovered during the past weeks that he needed his wife's understanding and support more than he realized. There was something infinitely reassuring about Jane's smile, and the knowledge that she trusted him again. Roger vowed to be more worthy of her trust in the future.

She turned to him and smiled that sweet smile of hers that made Roger's insides turn upside down. "Why so gloomy, Roger? You cannot seriously consider not attending the funeral, surely?"

He returned her smile. "All I said, my dear, was

that this drizzle will turn into a downpour at any moment, and is valid enough reason for staying at home where it is warm and dry. I do not want you to catch a cold standing ankle-deep in mud at the parish cemetery. I fear it is not as well kept up as it might be."

"Then you must speak to the vicar about it, Roger. I will do so myself if you prefer. Reverend Johnson needs reminding more often that his living depends on your father's goodwill."

"What is all this about my goodwill, my dear?" Lord Trenton came over to the window and hugged his daughter-in-law affectionately.

"Good morning, Father," Jane greeted the marquess with a warm smile. "Roger was complaining that the parish cemetery is badly in need of repair, and I suggested that the vicar needs to be reminded of his duties."

"You are probably right, my dear. And Collins informs me that we can expect heavy rain this morning. I wish you would reconsider, Jane. There is no need for you to stand about in the wet. Roger and I will be there. That should be enough to satisfy formalities."

Roger glanced at his father in surprise. Only last night at dinner, the marquess had promised Jane he would not expose himself to the weather. He saw his wife bristle, and knew that his father was in for a scold.

"This is far more than a formality, my lord. Lady Horton is—was the babe's mother, and we owe her some respect. And I trust you are not serious about attending the funeral, my lord. It would be beyond anything foolish to run the risk of catching a putrid throat, you know."

Roger was amused at the meekness with which Lord Trenton bore Jane's scoldings. His father's health had improved considerably since Jane had taken over the running of the Abbey. She had bullied him, sweetly but firmly, into eating and drinking less heavily and had coaxed the marquess to eat more fruit from the hothouses by peeling and slicing peaches for him with her own hands. It was also thanks to Jane that his father had accepted the fact that he now had an illegitimate granddaughter in the house.

Under Jane's gentle persuasion, Lord Trenton remained behind when the coach left for the village, its lighted lamps swathed in black cloth. Mrs. Watson, Maud's old abigail, had requested permission to attend her former mistress's last rites, and Jane insisted she ride in the coach with them.

They drove in silence through the gloom, and Roger noticed that the trees in the Park were beginning to turn. The beeches and chestnuts that dotted the parish cemetery also showed signs of approaching autumn. An occasional sodden leaf fluttered to the ground as Roger handed his wife down and escorted her into the austere Norman church where most of the local gentry attended Sunday service. The church was nearly empty this morning, and Roger felt a sharp pang of resentment against his neighbours for their lack of Christian charity.

"Never mind them, Roger," Jane murmured, as though she had read his mind. "Remember it *is* a horrid day, and you must admit Lady Horton led rather a shocking life by most standards. Father and Aunt Octavia will be here, of course, and perhaps the Beechams will come, and the Cheswicks. Mrs. Johnson certainly. Some of the villagers are bound to come, out of curiosity if nothing else."

"But not Sir Giles, I gather?" For some reason, the deliberate absence of Maud's husband offended him deeply.

Jane took her accustomed place in the pew at the front of the church that bore the Hastings coat of arms, then turned with a faint smile. "Sir Giles is a sick man, Roger. Oh, here is Papa and Aunt Octavia. I have invited them back to the Abbey for a late nuncheon after the service. Your father will be pleased."

The rain was coming down steadily as the mourners gathered briefly round the freshly dug grave, filling it with water. The paths were as muddy as Roger had anticipated, and as soon as Reverend Johnson concluded his brief and—at least to Roger's ears—meaningless eulogy, he hustled Jane out to the waiting carriage.

Mrs. Watson was waiting for them beside the horses under their weatherproof caparisons, her face blotched with tears. Jane was silent during the drive home, and Roger could only guess at her feelings now that Maud was gone forever. Was she relieved to be rid of a rival? He himself felt nothing but a deep sense of loss. For all her faults, Maud had brought him much joy, and the thought that her spectacular beauty and carefree, fun-loving spirit could be snuffed out so quickly depressed him. Their affair now seemed so ephemeral. Had it not been for the daughter they had made together during their brief, passionate union, it might never have happened at all.

But there was the babe. And thanks to Jane's generosity, Maud would live forever in his memory in the precious presence of his daughter.

The funeral depressed Jane more than she liked to admit. She tuned out the vicar's litany of insincerities and focused on the drops of water that ran down the black umbrella one of the altar boys held over his balding head. The rain had increased since they left the Abbey, and Jane was glad of the protection of Roger's big umbrella. It gave her an excuse to snuggle close to him. She glanced up at his profile. He was truly beautiful, she thought, an ache in her heart.

His attention was fixed on the simple beech-wood coffin that was being lowered jerkily into the gaping hole. Jane followed his gaze and felt a wave of sadness. Something beautiful had been taken from them, and the world would be a sadder place without Maud's laughter. The poignancy of the moment threatened to bring tears to her eyes, but Jane reminded herself that part of Maud lived on in her baby girl, thanks to Roger's generosity. She must focus her energies on the child; there was nothing more she could do for the mother.

The drive home was accomplished in silence, but once her father and Lady Octavia arrived, the front hall was filled with voices as everyone shed damp coats and relinquished dripping umbrellas to the butler.

Lord Trenton awaited them in the newly refurbished drawing room and when Jane saw the hearty welcome the marquess gave his old friend, she was glad she had brought her father back to the Abbey. Lady Octavia immediately demanded to see the baby, whom she had yet to meet.

Jane had to laugh at her aunt's enthusiasm. "She is so delicate I dare not have her brought downstairs, but after nuncheon I shall take you up to the nursery, Aunt. I have brought in my old nurse to take charge of things. You remember Nurse Carter, do you not?"

"Of course I remember Carter. I saw her in the village not ten days ago. She is very spry for her years. I imagine she is delighted to be back with you again."

"Mrs. Watson will help her, of course, but I want Nurse to be in charge. Watson was Lady Horton's abigail," Jane added in answer to her aunt's raised eyebrow, "but Sir Giles dismissed her without a character, the old curmudgeon."

Lady Octavia's face because serious. "I hear that Sir Giles has taken to his bed and is not expected to leave it again," she confided. "Your father heard it from Dr. Graham only yesterday. I suppose the strain of the past week has taken its toll on the old man."

"I am sorry to hear it, Aunt, but perhaps that is his punishment for treating his wife so scurvily. She had a sad ending, poor woman, with no family around her to give her solace."

"I cannot really blame him for not welcoming a cuckoo into his nest," Lady Octavia said with characteristic bluntness.

"Oh, no," Jane exclaimed sarcastically. "He evidently prefers to be known up and down the land as an old cuckold. I cannot see that Sir Giles has gained anything by disputing the paternity of the child. Which only fixes the horns on his head all the more securely, if you ask me. But to brand the poor little mite as illegitimate is a spiteful and vindictive action."

Her aunt gave her a pitying look. "But the child is illegitimate, my love. Nobody seems to dispute the fact."

"Only because the old man was foolish enough to announce it to the world. But actually, that is not quite true, Aunt. The child was born to Sir Giles's wife and would legally be presumed to be his, and still may be, for all I know. What distresses me is that he behaved so despicably, venting his rage on an innocent child. That I shall not easily forgive him."

Lady Octavia sighed audibly. "Are you not forgetting, love, that by giving the child shelter at the Abbey, you are supporting Horton's case?"

Jane shook her head. "It may seem that way, but I will put it about that, with her dying breath, Maud confirmed the babe's paternity, and begged me to be godmother to her child and care for it myself."

"That was your idea, no doubt?"

"Of course." Jane ignored her aunt's skeptical look. "Who will dare to dispute my word?"

"Sir Giles is disputing it vociferously, and I am not at all sure Stephen will be duped by such a story when he comes home."

"Stephen?" Jane sat up with a start. "Is Stephen coming home, Aunt?"

"The housekeeper over at the Hall told our Mrs. Daley that the captain will be back in England by Christmas. I imagine he will want to spend it with his father now that Lady Horton is not here to pester him," Lady Octavia answered enigmatically.

"Pester him?" Jane paused a moment, the implications of her aunt's words sinking in slowly. "Are you saying that Maud and Stephen . . ."

Her aunt patted her arm affectionately. "You always were such an innocent, my dear. When Maud

Barnes first came to Horton Hall she set her sights
firmly on Stephen, fine strapping fellow that he was.
He slipped out of her grasp by joining Wellington's
army, so she wed that Danvers boy and followed him
to the Continent when he bought his colours. Some
say she was still chasing Stephen, and that may have
been true, but she never caught him. When she came
back a widow, he stayed in the army, and our Maud
settled for the old man. At least that is what the gossips say."

"That all happened the year Roger was in Scotland
with his godfather, if I remember correctly," Jane
mused.

Her aunt nodded. "He came back to find that little
orphan chit installed as mistress of Horton Hall. I have
always suspected she did it to thumb her nose at Stephen—"

"Oh, Aunt, do not say so," Jane interrupted, per-
turbed at the direction of their conversation. "You
make poor Maud out to be a scheming hussy."

"Well, she was no saint, my dear. That I can say
with some certainty. And I doubt Stephen, when he
does come home, will take kindly to the news that she
besmirched his father's honour with his best friend."

Jane was appalled at what her aunt implied. "He
would not seek to harm Roger, would he, Aunt?" she
demanded in a hushed voice.

"You can hardly expect him to swallow that cock-
and-bull story about your close friendship with Maud.
He is no fool, is Captain Horton. He will put two and
two together and demand an accounting."

"But if the rumours are correct, Roger was not the
only one to . . ."

Her aunt smiled a little grimly. "That is probably
true, dear, but you cannot deny that Roger was the
most prominent of Lady Horton's lovers. And then
there is the damning presence of the child here at the
Abbey. Yes," she added, nodding her head, "I fear
there will be trouble when the captain comes home."

Jane shot a glance at her husband across the room.

He was deep in a discussion with his father and Lord Penhallow on the merits of certain breeds of sheep over others. He had no inkling of this new threat that loomed in the future.

Jane's heart sank. They had not yet deflected the scandal of introducing Maud's motherless babe into the Trenton household, and much remained to be done to stem the inevitable rumours that must be flying around the neighbourhood. With the support of the marquess and her own family, Jane had been confident of winning that skirmish.

She could brazen it out.

But how would Stephen react to his half-sister's presence under the roof of his stepmother's debaucher?

Jane knew with sudden clarity that, if Captain Horton was like most gentlemen of her acquaintance, he would doubtless plunge her family into chaos again, all in the name of that nebulous thing called honour.

Chapter Fourteen

The Christening

With this new worry hanging over her head, Jane threw herself into the task of restoring Roger's daughter to full health. She knew the babe was in good hands. With Nurse Carter, Mrs. Watson, and the wet-nurse from the village all hovering around her, the child would want for nothing. Except, of course, a mother's love. From the first moment she laid eyes on the tiny, wrinkled creature, Jane made it her special aim to fill this gap in the baby's life. Every free moment she had, she ran up to the nursery to convince herself that all was well. It was the first thing she did in the morning, and the last thing every night.

Dr. Graham was a regular visitor to the Trenton nursery, and by the end of September reported that the child was responding nicely to the care lavished upon her. Jane was pleased but did not relax her vigil.

"I was so very afraid for her," she confessed to Roger one evening as they sat over a glass of sherry in her private sitting room. "But Dr. Graham told me this morning that her chances of survival have improved considerably. She has put on weight, and her colour is better. We must not delay her baptism any longer."

Roger set his empty glass on the mantel and reached for her hand. He pulled her to her feet and slipped an arm about her waist. "It seems to me you are wearing yourself to a frazzle, Jane. I do not want you to make yourself sick. We must keep some of this wonderful enthusiasm for the babes we will have together, my love." He ran his lips down the curve of her neck, and Jane shuddered at the heat this simple act generated in her, from the top of her head to her toes.

Jane realized that she had been talking non-stop about Maud's abandoned baby since Roger had joined her, dressed in his heavy blue silk robe. She knew from experience that her husband was naked under the robe, tied loosely with a matching sash. Now, as he pulled her intimately against him, she could tell that his thoughts were not on babies, but on the making of them. She wished fervently that they might make one together, but her previous hope had turned out to be a false alarm. Her October courses were also late, but Jane refused to put any faith in the fact. She would wait and see.

In the meantime, she thought, conscious of Roger's increasing arousal, she would keep trying. This would be no hardship at all, since Jane had grown irreversibly addicted to the sensual caresses Roger dispensed so expertly in their beddings. She had grown comfortable with, though no less excited by, his tender explorations of her body. His store of new ways of delighting her and bringing her to dizzy heights of ecstasy seemed inexhaustible.

The only shadow that lingered in Jane's heart was the uncertainty of Roger's true feelings for her. Was she still only a wife of convenience, forced upon him by a promise made by his father long ago? Or had she managed to worm her way into his heart without his even noticing it? And if he ever did notice it, would he confess it, or did he consider love a missish affliction fit only for females?

Jane refused to allow this small shadow to affect her cheerfulness, so when towards the end of October Dr. Graham pronounced the baby strong enough to be christened, she threw herself into the preparations. Jane drove into the village to speak to Reverend Johnson. Although that worthy gentleman did not show much enthusiasm, Jane reminded him none too gently that the Marquess of Trenton required his presence at the christening of the child under his protection.

Undaunted by the vicar's reluctance, Jane wrote to invite Elizabeth to the child's christening. A week later she got an enthusiastic reply and, delighted that she would enjoy a second visit from her friend that year, Jane ran into the morning room to tell Lord Trenton. She found him in the company of her husband.

"Oh, excuse me, Father," she said breathlessly. "I did not mean to interrupt you, but I have just received the best possible news."

The marquess rose to his feet and smiled affectionately at her. "I daresay your news is more entertaining than the diseases our sheep seem to have contracted. Sit down and tell us all about it."

Jane took the place next to him on the settee and held up Elizabeth's letter. "I have just received this from Elizabeth. She has agreed to come to the baby's christening, and says that the timing is perfect because she and her family plan to spend the Christmas season here in Torrington with her parents. Since Tony will be here, too, I would like to ask him to be godfather. That is if you have no one else in mind."

After Lord Trenton assured her that she might choose anyone she pleased to be the child's godparents, and Roger had agreed with his father, Jane broached a subject she longed to have resolved.

"Have you had any thoughts about the name you wish to give the child, my lord?" she asked, directing her gaze at Roger. Although she had brought up the subject several times in the past two months, Roger had seemed oddly reluctant to discuss possible names for his daughter. With the christening right around the corner, however, Jane felt it imperative to force the issue.

When Roger made no reply, she glanced helplessly at the marquess. "I suppose the main question is whether or not you wish her to be linked to the Trentons through her name. I am assuming that she should carry one of her mother's names, which include Margaret and Abigail." Jane did not suggest Maud because she had no liking for the name and what it represented.

Lord Trenton cleared his throat. "Abigail was one of your grandmother's names, Roger. Rosamund Abigail. Remember that old dragon who used to make you sit up straight at table and finish every scrap on your plate? Holy terror she was to be sure."

"Perhaps, but with a heart of gold," Roger broke in. "I remember all the sweetmeats she would feed me when I visited her sitting room in the afternoons. I seem to remember spending a lot of my time there," he added with a laugh. "Abigail should do nicely, if you agree, Father."

"Abigail it is," the marquess concluded. "I like Margaret, too, since it was your mother's name, Roger. But that must be reserved for Jane's first daughter. What do you think, my dear?"

Jane blushed. Her father-in-law had fallen into the habit of talking about his future grandchildren as though they were a foregone conclusion. She thought about them, too, but with less confidence as the weeks went by and her body showed no sign of accepting the seeds Roger enthusiastically planted there every night.

"I like Abigail," she murmured, keeping her eyes away from Roger, who would certainly be grinning at his father's remark. "What about Abigail Rose?"

And so it was that during the first week of November, the day following Guy Fawke's Day, Abigail Rose Horton was christened in the Trenton chapel by a stern-faced Reverend Johnson. As Jane stood beside the Baptismal Font with Roger as one of little Abby's godparents, she felt a deep bond growing in her heart for this motherless babe. Abigail Rose was like a real daughter to her, and as she held the warmly bundled baby, her joy was so great, she wanted to cry.

As the vicar's dry voice began to recite the Order of Baptism, Jane felt the blood drain from her face.

Dearly beloved, forasmuch as all men are conceived and born in sin . . .

Was it her imagination, or did Reverend Johnson pronounce the opening lines of the ritual with particular relish? She dared not glance at Roger, who stood like a rock at her side listening to the words that must have cut deeply into his conscience. Although Jane knew they represented one of the basic tenants of Christianity—the concept of original sin—and applied to every babe brought to the Baptismal Font, to her sensitive ears they appeared tailored with particular accuracy to the case of little Abigail Rose.

Jane watched as Aunt Octavia, the second of Abigail's godmothers, took the naked babe from her arms and handed the child to the vicar. In a firm voice, Lady Octavia confirmed the names they had chosen. Jane held her breath as the vicar held little Abby over the Font. Given the fragile health of the child, she was not immersed but received a few drops poured upon her, and the sign of the cross.

As they drove home slowly beside the lake, Jane relaxed against the blue velvet squabs, Abigail dozing in her arms. The air was chilly, but the sun shone brightly, giving the tranquil surface of the lake a peaceful aspect that belied the violence lurking beneath.

Suddenly her terrifying nightmare flashed through her mind, and Jane thought she understood the significance of it. Maud had abandoned her babe and Jane had saved it. All this had come true. Abigail was safe, but what the nebulous ghost had wanted with her was still a mystery.

But then again, perhaps she had imagined the whole incident, Jane thought, clasping the babe more closely to her.

She turned and smiled at Roger. She was glad she had never told him about the nightmare. Especially Maud's viciousness and the close call his daughter had had with death.

Some things were better not spoken about.

*   *   *

Two events occurred in the weeks following Abigail Rose's christening that disturbed the peace and tranquillity that seemed to have descended upon Trenton Abbey.

One morning Roger was called away from his breakfast by an urgent message from Peterson, who requested the viscount to meet him in the sheepfold. When he arrived, he found his agent with a small group of men who greeted him somberly. They were gathered around the carcass of one of his prize rams. Roger could tell at a glance that the animal had had its throat cut.

"Dobbs," Peterson said to one of the shepherds in charge of the flock, "tell his lordship what you told me."

Dobbs stepped forward at Peterson's command, looking apprehensive. "Beggin' yer pardon, milord," the man said, touching his forelock, "the dogs started barkin' around two this mornin' and I thought it was a fox sniffin' around, but there was nothin' there. At least naught that I could see. The flock was restless, and I waited around until they settled down again. Then this mornin', when I came to open the gates, I found this." He made a helpless gesture at the dead ram.

"What caused it, do you know, Dobbs?" Roger asked, bending down to examine the mutilated carcass.

" 'Tweren't no fox, milord, that I can tell ye. Nor any animal I ever seen."

"Dogs?"

"Nay, milord. Looks more like a two-legged beast if ye ask me."

There was nothing to be done except double the watch at night, which Roger ordered. He took one last look at the carcass of the ram so recently purchased in Okehampton. Who would slit an animal's throat and leave it lying in the fold? he asked himself as he made his way back to the house. His father should be informed at once, but Roger hoped to keep news of the ugly incident from Jane.

Two days later, he received another of the letters he had written to Maud at the height of their infatuation with each other. It had been slipped under his bedchamber door, and when Roger made discreet inquiries, none of the servants seemed to know anything about how it got there.

What disturbed him most was the irrefutable evidence that someone was in possession of those letters. Someone who wanted to cause trouble for him. He had no idea where Maud had kept the letters. They must have been carefully hidden, for he could not believe she would wish Sir Giles to find them. Was it a maid, perhaps? Mrs. Watson? He doubted it. The abigail had been devoted to her mistress. During those final days there had been constant confusion at Horton Hall and it was not unlikely that anyone in the household might have had access to her chamber. But why send them to him? A servant would have tried to sell them to him. Why go to the trouble of stealing them if not for profit? And who had slipped it under his door?

And who else might be receiving them? His father? Or Jane? The thought that Jane, his own unsuspecting, innocent Jane, might read the lascivious, frankly erotic nonsense he had written to his *inamorata* caused Roger to feel nauseous.

At first he did not connect the two incidents, but when the bailiff was called in to investigate the slaughter of the ram, one of his questions caused Roger to wonder.

After it was clearly established and agreed upon that the ram was not killed by any animal but by a long, sharp knife, wielded by a strong man, Mr. Coates, the bailiff, cleared his throat nervously, glanced out of Peterson's window, then at his feet, and finally rumbled in his gruff voice, "Can your lordship think of anyone who might wish you harm?"

Roger exchanged a speaking glance with his agent,

who stood beside the desk. Peterson said nothing, although he must know—as did everyone in the neighbourhood, including Coates himself—that there had been bad blood for months between Sir Giles and Lord Summers on account of the rumours, which everyone knew to be well-founded, linking Roger with Lady Horton. There could be no denying it now.

Roger's smile was grim. "I cannot think of anyone, Mr. Coates. Aside from Sir Giles, of course, I am on good terms with all my neighbours."

The bailiff cleared his throat again and looked flustered. "And do you believe Sir Giles capable of having your animals slaughtered, milord?"

"No, I do not," Roger replied firmly. "If it were me and not that ram lying out there, I might have my doubts, but I cannot see Sir Giles involved with anything as senseless as this."

"Quite so, milord," Coates said in a relieved voice. "I agree with your lordship. Yet this has all the signs of a vindictive act. So I must ask you to let me know if you can think of anyone with a grudge against your lordship. A disgruntled servant, perhaps?"

"I doubt that, too. What do you think, Peterson?"

The agent shook his head. "I have had no complaints recently, milord." He paused. "Except for Barnes, of course. Your lordship mentioned that he was impertinent, and the head-groom reported him as lazy and too fond of his ale. I have been meaning to let him go."

Roger looked at him sharply. "I would not be too hasty in dismissing him, Peterson," he said. "At least until we have come to the bottom of this incident. It is as well to keep him close by where we can watch him."

Barnes! Roger thought later, as he trod upstairs to join his wife and Lord Trenton in the morning room. He had forgotten that Barnes was Maud's cousin. Had he not given the man a position in the stables to please her? The surly stable-man looked capable of anything, and certainly had easy access to the sheep. The dogs would know him, too, so might not have barked once they recognized him. It would have been a simple matter to slip down to the sheepfold and do the deed. The only question Roger could not fathom was what had Barnes to gain?

And the letters? It was entirely possible that he had stolen the letters from Maud during a visit to her sickbed. He would have to ask Mrs. Watson. Or perhaps Maud had given her cousin the letters for safekeeping to get them out of Horton Hall. But why would Barnes send them to him?

He would have to find out more about the enigmatic Barnes.

"I saw it plain as day, milady. Plain as day, I did. Floating over the lake it was. And then it came at me, and I run all the way home."

This tearful recitation, punctuated by plentiful hiccups and applications of a damp rag to the girl's blotched face, came pouring out as soon as Jane made the mistake of telling Sally to stop crying and tell her story.

"Stop yer blubbering, gel, and confess to her ladyship that this is all a cock-and-bull story ye be tellin' us."

Sally broke down in a fresh torrent of tears. "Oh, no, Mrs. Collins," she gasped. "I truly did see it. Ever so clear I did, too. The poor wee thing looked at me so sad-like. Nearly broke me 'eart it did."

"Don't ye be tellin' no lies to her ladyship, Sally McBride," the housekeeper snapped, giving the quivering girl a shake that set her mobcap askew on her red curls. "Admit ye be making all this up, ye pesky gel. A good hidin' is what you be askin' for, and no mistake."

The housekeeper looked quite capable of carrying out her threat, and Sally cowered back from her.

"No," the girl said stubbornly. "I seen it, milady. Big black teeth it had, and clammy fingers clutching at me arm." She shuddered dramatically. "I willna sleep a wink for weeks to come," she muttered sullenly.

That did it. Jane realized suddenly that whatever it was the girl had seen had acquired these terrifying characteristics in the retelling of the story.

"Then perhaps Mrs. Collins can find some extra tasks to keep you busy all night if you are not sleeping." She saw the housekeeper nodding in approval. "And you must not invent things, Sally. Ghosts do not have black teeth, my girl. This is nonsense. Neither do they have clammy fingers. All you saw was a swirl of fog off the lake, which your imagination tricked you into thinking was a ghost. And even if it was the Trenton ghost, this particular one is only the soul of that poor boy rumoured to lie at the bottom of the lake. What is there about that to throw you into a fit of the vapours?"

The girl glared stubbornly. "It had feet, milady. It run after me, I swear it. Black feet. Looked like boots. Scared me out of my wits, it did."

"Ghosts do not wear boots, Sally," Lady Jane said with more assurance than she felt. Actually, she knew little about ghosts except what she had seen that night Roger had gone over to the Horton gatehouse to meet Lady Horton.

When she recounted the ghost story to Roger and Lord Trenton that evening after dinner, both poohpoohed the report, blaming it on the overstimulated imagination of a servant girl. Female hysteria, they scoffed. None of their male ancestors in the history of the Abbey had ever witnessed any apparition on or near the lake, Roger insisted. Which only proved that females, even gently-bred ones like his own mother, were plagued with hallucinations and other fanciful quirks of imagination.

"That only proves that gentlemen lack imagination and are not sensitive to such things," Jane said with some heat. "In no way does it prove that females are prone to hallucinations or fanciful quirks, as you call them. I resent the implication that I am addlepated as you seem to suggest.''

"No such thing, my dear," Lord Trenton hastened to assure her, but Jane caught the wink he exchanged with his son. "We gentlemen are overwhelmed by the superiority of the female brain in many areas, my dear. The male mind is concerned with more mundane affairs, I am afraid, so we lack the power of females to connect with the spiritual and emotional side of life.''

Jane stared at him, quite certain that neither Lord Trenton nor his son believed a word of this blather. She chose to ignore it.

"Last night was the full moon, in case you had not noticed," Jane pointed out, unwilling to drop the subject. "The time when the Trenton ghost is said to rise from the lake and visit his mother's grave." Both gentlemen regarded her in amusement. "And what about the boots Sally swore she saw?" Jane demanded. "Begging your pardon, my lord, but I feel there is something more than local superstition here. What respectable ghost would wear boots, I ask you?''

"I was not aware that ghosts were either respectable or otherwise," Roger drawled, a teasing grin on his face. "So I cannot tell what a respectable ghost would do. Particularly since I have never seen one.''

"And you probably never will," Jane snapped, "which does not prevent you from making fun of those who have. Most unkind of you, Roger.''

"And you have, I suppose, my dear?" the marquess murmured, one eyebrow raised quizzically.

"If I had, I would certainly not tell either of you," she retorted, getting crosser by the minute at this male obtuseness. "And if you were not so busy scoffing at Sally's story, you might see that the boots she saw are a discordant note. It might even occur to your practical minds that what Sally saw was not a ghost at all, but a man playing at being a ghost." She smiled sweetly. "You might even be tempted to ask why anyone would wish to frighten the maids. Or this maid in particular.''

"It sounds like a harmless prank to me," Lord Trenton remarked.

"Perhaps it is," Jane agreed. "Then on the other hand, perhaps it is no prank at all but something more sinister. In either case, I believe it could use some looking into. What do you say, Roger?"

Roger looked at her with an odd expression on his face. Lord Trenton glanced at them both in turn. "You may rest assured, my dear Jane, that we shall look into this ghost-who-may-not-be-a-ghost matter first thing in the morning. In the meantime, do not let it affect your dreams, Jane. There is an answer to this mystery somewhere, and we shall find it."

As she went up to the nursery to look in on Abigail Rose, Jane fervently hoped her father-in-law was right. The notion of a masquerading ghost was not conducive to a restful night.

Chapter Fifteen

Masquerading Ghost

The very next morning Jane had further cause to remember her suspicion that something sinister was afoot.

The damp weather had given way to brilliant autumn sunshine that beckoned her outdoors, reminding her that it had been days since she had taken Ginger out for a gallop. Upon entering the stable-yard, she saw Barnes lounging against a stall, a broom held idly in his hand. He straightened up when he saw her, but only after what Jane considered an insolent pause.

"Please saddle Ginger for me, Barnes," she said, determined not to allow the surly groom to spoil her enjoyment of the morning.

He stared at her, mouth agape. "Beggin' yer pardon, milady, but Ginger ain't goin' nowheres today. That pesky mare got 'erself a loose shoe yesterday."

"Why have you not taken her to the farrier's, then?" Jane felt her frustration rising at the lackadaisical reaction of the groom. He grinned at her facetiously, and she noticed with somewhat of a shock that what few teeth remained in his head were stained a dirty brown. Had not Sally reported seeing black teeth on the ghost two nights ago? Black teeth and boots. Instinctively her eyes dropped to the groom's feet. He was wearing boots, scuffed and caked with mud. But then, all the stable-hands wore boots, and bad teeth were not unusual, she reminded herself, feeling a little foolish.

"Dinna 'ave the time, milady. Mr. Riley sent me over to Torrington to pick up the new 'arness for one of the Clydesdales. All broke up it was, the old one. And then in the afternoon—"

"Never mind," Jane interrupted. "You may saddle Misty instead. Where is Mr. Riley?"

Barnes had turned away, but at her question, he glanced at her oddly. "Talkin' to the bailiff, milady. Shall I get 'im for ye?"

Jane shook her head and marched through the wide doors into the dim barn lined with stalls and smelling of hay and horses. The head groom was standing beside the wooden stair that led up to his quarters, talking to a rotund figure she recognized as Mr. Coates, the local bailiff. Both men straightened at her approach, and the bailiff removed his bowler hat to greet her.

"Good morning, Mr. Coates," Jane returned his greeting pleasantly. "I trust Mrs. Coates is recovered from that nasty cold she had last week."

"Oh, yes indeed, milady, and thank ye fer askin'. Mrs. Coates will be most gratified when I tell her ye asked, milady."

"What brings you here, Mr. Coates? Making enquiries about the ghost, are you?" she added with a smile.

The bailiff looked nonplussed. "Oh, no, milady. Although the women in the village are all talking about it, of course. Being a rational man meself, I do not put much stock in those yarns. That Sally McBride always was a fanciful gel, like 'er mother before 'er."

"Then why are you here?"

Jane saw the bailiff glance uneasily at Riley, and sensed that the men were reluctant to answer her. They were unable to escape a direct question, however, and after tugging at his collar and clearing his throat, Mr. Coates told her that he was investigating the strange death of one of his lordship's rams.

"Sheep have never been known to slit their own throats, milady, at least not to my knowledge. So I promised 'is lordship that I would make some enquiries around the estate."

"Oh dear, how terrible," Jane exclaimed, wondering

why neither Roger nor Lord Trenton had mentioned
this matter to her. "And have you discovered the
culprit?"

"No, milady," the bailiff replied. "But it would appear to be someone from the estate, since the dogs
did not make any fuss."

Jane pondered this strange occurrence as she cantered along the lane to the village. She had intended
to pay a visit to the vicarage, but as she passed the
gates to Horton Hall, the thought of Mrs. Johnson's
parsimonious gossip about Maud's untimely end and
the fate of her daughter changed her mind. She felt
the need to discuss the strange events at the Abbey,
but the vicar's wife was not her idea of a cosy confi-
dante. So she turned Misty about and rode over to
Penhallow instead.

Aunt Octavia was delighted to see her, as she always was. After they were settled in the morning room
with a tea-tray, she was more than willing to listen to
Jane's speculations about the latest ghostly sighting at
the Abbey.

"Are you saying that you suspect mischief in this
affair, my dear?"

"I know it sounds peculiar, Aunt, but I cannot rec-
oncile Sally's description of the ghost as having black
teeth and wearing boots. The girl was adamant that
the apparition actually chased her along the lake path.
She claims she *heard* its boots on the muddy bank.
How can one hear a ghost's boots in the mud, I would
like to know?"

"Well, there are plenty of ghosts around who moan
at night and rattle chains in the attic, dear. My dear
friend, the Countess of Strathford, lives in a castle
with two ghosts who appear regularly after midnight
and roam the upstairs halls. She has the greatest difficulty persuading her servants they are in no danger.
But I must admit that your gel's story about a ghost
in boots with black teeth sounds a wee bit melodra-
matic to me."

"I agree, Aunt. It smacks of human mischief rather

than supernatural goings on. And then there is the strange matter of the letters," she added impulsively, remembering Roger's unexpected question two nights ago. He had asked if she had received any strange letters recently. At her insistence, he had confessed to receiving one of his own love letters to Maud mysteriously slipped under his bedchamber door.

"And did you?" Lady Octavia wanted to know.

"Not since that first one I told you about, Aunt. But that was some time ago. And I know it came from Maud herself because she enclosed a note that said so. It was deliberately nasty, as I told you at the time—most unpleasant, actually. She obviously wanted to upset me."

"How did you receive it?"

"Barnes, the stable-boy, gave it to me. Though how he came by it, I do not know."

"Have you told Roger?"

Jane shook her head. "I saw no need to give Maud that satisfaction."

"What will you do with it, then? Surely you have not read the thing?"

"I shall probably burn it. The letter is certainly not the kind of memento I would wish Abigail Rose to have of her mother."

As she rode home later that morning, Jane wondered why she had kept that incriminating love letter written by her husband to another woman. From that brief glance she had stolen at the first few lines, it had been abundantly clear to Jane that Roger had loved his mistress. Maud must have known it, and gloried in the knowledge that, although married to another, Roger's heart had been hers up to the end. Perhaps it still was, Jane thought dejectedly. Even in death, Maud must be gloating that Roger had no love left for his wife. He was still irrevocably tied to the red-haired beauty by his daughter, the living proof of their wild passion for each other.

Passion. Jane shuddered at the thought. She knew nothing of passion. Perhaps it was incongruous for a wife to yearn for passion from her husband. Particularly if he had come to her straight from the arms of the most sensuous female Jane had even known. How could she possibly expect to arouse any but the most dutiful of emotions in such a man?

Somehow that clandestine letter—which Jane suddenly longed to read—revealed a side to Roger that she would never know. How could she when she was only his wife? She must be content with tenderness, with kindness, and the laughter they shared in the intimacy of her bedchamber. Her heart must find fulfillment in carrying his children, in keeping his house in good order, in loving him utterly and without question.

Only a mistress could demand passion, Jane told herself morosely. Only a mistress might drive a gentleman to express himself as immoderately as Roger had in that love letter. What would it feel like to receive such a letter? she wondered, her mind wandering along new and dangerous paths.

What would it be like to be a man's beloved mistress?

The notion startled her.

Brushing it aside, Jane urged Misty into a canter, hoping the autumn wind would blow such nonsensical fantasies from her head.

Ten days before Christmas, with none of the fanfare that characterized him in life, old Sir Giles Horton died in his sleep. Roger heard the news when he strode into the stable-yard early in the morning, his boots crunching the hoar-frost that had collected overnight on the grass.

Riley was using a curry-comb on Jason when Roger arrived, and the bay gelding was moving restlessly, his breath rising in white plumes in the cold air.

The head groom touched his forelock in greeting. "My boy Jamie—the one who is in service over at Horton Hall—just brought word that the old master passed on last night," he said, indicating a gangling youth who appeared to be the spitting image of his father.

Roger glanced at the lad, who confirmed his father's words.

"Aye, milord. Sir Giles is gone. Joined 'is Maker just after midnight, 'e did, and methinks 'e will be missed, leastwise by those as served 'im."

"I am sure he will," Roger agreed, although privately he considered his neighbour an irascible old codger who would be missed in ways the youth had not intended. He felt no animosity towards Sir Giles himself, but rather pitied the baronet for his disastrous marriage to a woman who had no affection for him at all. By comparison, Roger felt blessed that he had Jane. His wife might not be a raving Beauty, but he had discovered that raving Beauties were difficult to live with and well nigh impossible to please.

No, he thought, turning Jason's head towards the cluster of tenant cottages where he had promised to meet Peterson to determine which were in need of new thatching, he had not envied Sir Giles his beautiful wife. He much preferred his own. He smiled at the thought of Jane and her evident delight in his little daughter. He hoped she would soon be a mother herself, for she had a generous heart and a natural way with children that delighted him.

From his agent, Roger learned that the news of Sir Giles's death had already spread throughout the neighbourhood. Being in constant contact with everyone attached to the estate, Peterson was always a ready source of information. Roger also learned that Tony Cheswick had come down from London for the holidays, and that Elizabeth and her family were expected daily. He was quite used to having his own aunts and sisters and their broods descend upon Trenton Abbey at least once a year, but this year Jane had taken over the task of corresponding with both Letitia and Augusta, whom she knew well.

"And of course, Captain Horton will be here for the funeral, I hear," Peterson was saying, interrupting

Roger's musings about the invasion of relatives his
father encouraged every year. "It will be quite like
old times with the captain back home again. What has
it been? Five or six years since he joined the army?"

Roger had mixed feelings about a reunion with his
childhood friend and playmate. They had been an in-
separable threesome—Stephen, Tony, and Roger. Stephen, a year older than Roger, had been the natural
leader, while Tony, the youngest, had followed un-
questioningly into any wild adventure the other two
chose to lead him.

Would Stephen remember those good times? Roger
wondered nostalgically. Or would he feel obligated to
vindicate his father's honour? He must know of Roger's liaison with Maud. Perhaps even the disputed paternity of her daughter. Stephen would also know that
Maud's reputation had never been spotless. Had he
not himself been the object of Maud's flirtations long
before she married his father?

Stephen Horton had never given the orphaned
Beauty more than the most cursory attention, Roger
recalled. He had been surprised at his friend's indifference to Maud, since he himself had already been thoroughly captivated by her saucy ways. He later
suspected that Stephen had a *tendre* for little Lady
Jane, with her fascination for flowers and sketching,
her gentle smile and unassuming manner. Roger had
been amused and perhaps a little sorry for his friend,
who must have known that such an attachment was
impossible. Jane was his. Promised to him from the
cradle.

They had half expected Stephen to make Elizabeth
Cheswick an offer when he and Roger came down
from Oxford together. She had not seemed averse to
the idea. But Maud had still been at Horton Hall,
and threw herself at him shamelessly. Roger had been
jealous then, and spent many sleepless nights wondering why his rank and fortune, his famous charm and
fair good looks failed to impress the tempestuous red-
head when the dark, serious-minded Stephen was

present. Later he figured out that it was marriage the Beauty was after.

Privately, Roger considered Stephen a bit of a dull dog. Oxford seemed to have filled his head with all sorts of rubbishy notions about philosophy and other esoteric topics. Tony Cheswick, who went up a year later, fared better, and came back with a smattering of knowledge that helped him obtain a position in the War Office. As for his own sojourn in that centre of learning, Roger was the first to admit that most subjects passed through his mind like water through a sieve, leaving little but a lingering dampness behind. His only regret was that he had not picked up more Latin and Greek to match Jane's quite unexpected learning. He had returned home to find his promised bride already started on her wildflower manuscript and fully conversant with the classical nomenclature of most plants in Devon.

A disquieting thought struck him. Was it not possible that Stephen, with his penchant for obscure knowledge, would have made a more satisfactory husband for Jane? It had never been Roger's custom to question his own worth, but this doubt, once acknowledged, nagged at him. Was Jane, deep in her heart, dissatisfied with the match that had been thrust upon her? Would she have been happier with a man like Stephen, who had, even back in those early days, shown a genuine interest in Jane's desire to catalogue the wildflowers of Devon?

With a flash of intuition, Roger understood why his friend had never been drawn into Maud's sensual spell. Unlike himself, who had been dazzled by the glitter and glow of her superficial sensuality, Stephen had, even then, seen both girls in their true colours, and known instinctively that Jane's sweetness was a reflection of her true nature, not a mask adopted to dazzle and attract like some gorgeous butterfly.

Roger's mind was so full of this new insight into his relationship with his wife that his heart gave a leap when he encountered Jane in the stable-yard upon his return. She had dismounted from the bay mare Misty, and stood in conversation with Riley, as Barnes busied himself rubbing down her mount.

Her face lit up when she saw him, and Roger knew in his heart that whatever else happened, he would make sure that Jane found as much delight and happiness in their marriage as he was finding himself.

"Have you heard the news about poor Sir Giles?" she demanded as they walked up to the house together. "Riley tells me his passing was peaceful, which is a blessing. Apparently Stephen is already on his way home and expected tomorrow. I wonder . . ."

Her words trailed off, and given his own recent speculations on his friend and neighbour, Roger suspected that Jane was thinking of Stephen.

"What do you wonder?"

She glanced at him and smiled. "I was wondering if the lake will freeze over enough for us all to go skating together on Christmas Day. Remember the fun we used to have? You and I, Stephen, Tony, and Elizabeth."

And Maud, Roger thought nostalgically. Her name hung in the air between them but neither spoke it aloud. Although not a skillful skater, Maud had enjoyed the attention her squeals of fright had garnered from every gentleman present. Except from Stephen, who preferred to skate arm-in-arm with Jane and Elizabeth and leave the lady in distress to other eager swains.

Roger had the uncomfortable feeling that this was what his wife was remembering, but he said nothing.

"There are only ten days left till Christmas, and the lake is nowhere near safe enough for skating yet," was all he said. "I would not count on it if I were you."

"I wonder what that poor little ghost does when there is a full moon and the lake is frozen over," Jane said suddenly. "It must be terrible to look up and see us twirling around above him and not be able to get out."

The wistful note in her voice tugged at his heart,

and Roger impulsively flung an arm about her shoulders and pulled her close. "I forbid you to mope over the ghost of a lad who died four hundred years ago, my sweet," he said bracingly. "And by the way, I think I have solved the mystery of Sally's ghost with black teeth. You were right, love, it was no ghost at all but a disappointed suitor."

Jane turned a radiant smile upon him, and Roger felt his breath catch in his throat. She was truly lovely, in ways that Maud had never been. He marvelled at his blindness, and bent to kiss the tip of her nose.

"Oh, Roger, how can you?" she protested with a giggle. "The servants will see us. Now tell me what you found out about Sally's ghost."

"Peterson tells me there is a love triangle here. Sally forgot to tell you, my love, that she is walking out with your own Tom Jones from Penhallow. Apparently this does not sit too well with Jim Barnes, who has his eye on the lass himself. Our Sally seems to have a weakness for stable-lads."

"So it was Barnes who chased her that night?"

"It seems that way."

"Did he also kill your prize ram?"

Roger looked down at her and wondered who had broken this distressing news to her.

"I wormed it out of Coates this morning. The poor man could not think of a good excuse for his presence at the Abbey."

"I wanted to spare you the ugly details, my love," he said mildly. "And as for Barnes, Coates believes he might well be guilty. But he has yet to discover the knife, which Barnes has had ample time to hide."

"Perhaps it is at the bottom of the lake, where it will never be found. Unless, of course, the ghost—"

"Stop right there," Roger interrupted brusquely. "I have heard quite enough ghost stories for one day. We have more practical things to worry about," he added, leading his wife up the steps and through the front door, held open by a poker-faced Collins.

Jane threw him another radiant smile, and Roger

caught—or imagined he did—a slight softening in his austere butler's granite features. His wife had evidently won over the hearts of his staff as well as his own.

Chapter Sixteen

Surprise Will

The funeral service for Sir Giles Horton, Baronet, was so well attended that chairs had to be brought from the vestry to accommodate the mourners. Jane guessed the entire village was present, and as Roger and Lord Trenton escorted her down the aisle to their family pew, she saw many unfamiliar faces from outlying farms and neighbouring towns.

There had been Hortons at Horton Hall for many generations, and their influence upon the region was evident today. Sir Giles had been at Oxford with the marquess and her own father, and the three of them had gained a reputation for extravagant wagers and the quantity of ale they imbibed.

Now there was only Stephen left, both his younger brothers having been carried off with scarlet fever early in life. If only Maud had produced a son, Jane mused, inclining her head in response to the many greetings she received, the succession would be secure. As it was, Stephen would have to marry and settle down as the new master of Horton Hall.

The thought troubled her. Would it be uncomfortable to have Stephen back amongst them, in view of Maud's liaison with Roger? How would he feel about his little half-sister and his father's disavowal of fatherhood? And perhaps most troubling of all was how Stephen might react to Roger. Would they be at daggers drawn, or would they fall back into the easy camaraderie they has shared as boys?

Jane suspected that neither of these options would satisfactorily bridge the new tension between the two

men, and she could only hope that they would not stir
up another scandal. Stephen had never been a hot-
head, of course; it was Roger she feared. He had settled down considerably since their marriage, but his
attachment to Abigail Rose was genuine, and Jane
hoped Stephen would do nothing foolish.

In any case, there was little she could do to influence either of them. Of the two, it was Stephen who
had been more amenable to reason, and although he
had never breathed a word to her, Jane knew—as only
a woman can know—that he had harboured a *tendre*
for her in those heady days of their youth. She also
remembered his one and only kiss. She had not
thought of it in ages, being lost in her infatuation with
Roger, but now as she approached the Horton pew,
Jane wondered how different her life might have been
had she . . . Abruptly she cut short that perfidious
thought. She must have windmills in her head to be
mooning about passion, love letters, and mistresses as
she had the other day. And now these unwanted fantasies about Stephen.

And there he was. Jane raised her eyes and found
him staring at her. For a moment she felt a surge of
joy sweep away her troubles. Everything would be all
right. He was still the same old Stephen. Then she
noticed his shoulders, much wider now and ramrod
straight; his face, weather-beaten and hardened into
rugged lines she did not recognize; his hair, still raven-
black, but cut shorter with fewer curls about his collar.
Suddenly he seemed like a stranger, and Jane's heart
sank.

It was unfortunate that they had to meet for the
first time in years on such a sad occasion and in front
of the entire local population. Jane was aware of every
eye upon them. There could be no spontaneous welcome. Except for Lord Trenton, whose gruff condo-
lences broke the ice, the meeting with their former
playmate was stiff and awkward.

After the service, they followed the black-draped
carriage carrying the casket back to Horton Hall,

where Sir Giles was to be laid to rest among his ancestors. The autumn sun shone brightly down on the mourners' heads as they gathered by the graveside. How different from poor Maud's last rites, Jane commented briefly to Roger as they stood, side-by-side, listening to the Reverend Johnson's fulsome praise of the departed baronet. Maud had been buried in rain with a grudging tribute by the vicar.

After a moving eulogy by the Marquess of Trenton, Jane fell in beside Elizabeth and her two eldest boys to pay their respects to the captain. She could not think of a single thing to say, and when she found herself before him, she was mortified to feel the dampness in her eyes. She stretched out a hand instinctively, and Stephen took it in both of his. The familiar clasp brought back memories of happier times, and she looked up at him.

"A sad homecoming, Stephen, but I am glad to see you safe and sound," she murmured, comforted by his brief smile. His dark eyes seemed to have softened since that first glance in the church, and suddenly he was no longer a stranger, but the dependable old Stephen of her childhood.

Jane smiled and withdrew her hand, moving on to join Elizabeth and her boys. "We must plan a skating party at the Abbey now that we are all back together again. Another hard freeze like last night, and the lake will be safe for skating. What do you think, Elizabeth?"

Her friend looked skeptical. "It may not be that simple, Jane. Only consider how uncomfortable Stephen might feel knowing that Roger practically stole his half-sister from under his father's nose."

"He did nothing of the sort," Jane protested hotly. "Sir Giles wanted nothing to do with Maud's baby, so what was Roger to do? You cannot have wished him to allow the vicar to send her to the poor house. Abigail is the daughter of a gentleman."

"No, of course not. But it might be prudent to let the gentlemen sort things out among themselves be-

fore we start planning skating parties. You know how
touchy they can be about matters of honour."

Jane had to agree with this sage advice, although
privately she considered that most matters of honour
might be settled with a dash of common sense and
less histrionics.

Next morning she was glad she had not pursued her
plans for a skating party with Roger. Jane and Mrs.
Collins were going through the linen closets, making
sure they had an ample supply of bed linen for the
guests about to descend on the Abbey for the Christmas season, when Collins sent up a message that the
marquess requested her presence in the library.

Alarmed at the formality of the request, Jane hurried downstairs, tucking in stray wisps of hair as she
went. When she burst into the library, she knew instantly that something was terribly amiss, for both
Lord Trenton and his son greeted her with grim faces.

"Whatever is the matter?" she exclaimed before either of the gentlemen uttered a word.

"Sit down, gel," Lord Trenton said gruffly, "and
read this." He thrust a letter into her hands.

Jane sat on the edge of her chair and perused the
letter that carried the name of a London solicitor
across the top. The words swam before her eyes and
refused to make any sense. She read it through again,
more carefully this time, her mind going numb as the
meaning became clear.

"They cannot do this!" she exclaimed angrily, resting the letter in her lap. "I will not allow it. This is
sheer perversity. How can that sick old man disown
his child with his living breath, and then demand her
return from beyond the grave? This must be a mistake." She looked pleadingly from one gentleman to
the other. Neither of them would meet her gaze.

"That is what we are hoping, my dear," Lord Trenton said finally. "But I know this solicitor, a reputable
man, so I would not count on this being a mistake.
Such men do not make errors of this nature. And then
there is Sir Giles's will, which is quite clear on the

point. His daughter—now legally acknowledged, it appears—is to inherit rather a large sum of money."

"And Stephen is to be her guardian?"

"So it would seem," Roger said flatly. "The old man is to have the last laugh after all." His own laughter was anything but amused.

"I will not give her up," Jane declared coldly. "What does Stephen know about babies? Abigail needs special care; she is still so fragile."

"The law is on his side, my dear," Lord Trenton said gently.

"There *must* be something we can do. This is all so unreasonable."

"The law is often unreasonable," Roger muttered.

"Then I will speak to Stephen myself," Jane said defiantly. "He will agree with me that Abigail should remain here."

"I forbid you to go near the Hall," Roger exclaimed harshly, startling her with his ferocity.

"But she is your daughter, Roger."

"Not according to the law."

"The devil fly away with the law," Jane snapped, exasperated at this male obtuseness. "Abigail Rose belongs here with us."

"Watch your language, gel," Lord Trenton said sternly. "Roger and I are invited to hear the reading of the will tomorrow afternoon at four o'clock. Perhaps something can be worked out then."

"I will go with you."

"No." Roger's tone was final, but Jane ignored it.

"And why not? What harm can it do? Abigail belongs to all of us, Roger. We cannot give her up without a fight."

"I will not have you throwing yourself on Horton's mercy, or begging him for favours. Do I make myself clear?"

Jane stared at her husband mulishly. He had never forbidden her anything, and she was not about to stand for it. Before she could protest, Lord Trenton intervened, his calm voice diffusing what threatened to be their first open confrontation.

"I daresay it will do no harm to take Jane with us, Roger." He turned to survey her anxiously. "But you must promise not to turn into a watering-pot if Horton insists upon taking the child back, my dear. Tears are not likely to move him if he is determined to go forward with this."

Jane nodded. But she made no promise. She knew too well that female tears often did move men, and she was prepared to use any means in her power to keep little Abigail safe at Trenton Abbey. Regardless of what the law said.

Roger came down to breakfast the following morning feeling like a bear with a sore head. His life, which had appeared to have settled into a comfortable and satisfying pattern after Abigail Rose had been added to his family, had abruptly been turned upside down. That dratted letter from the Horton solicitor had exploded like a blunderbuss in a nunnery, and its repercussions still rang in his ears.

To top it off, Roger appeared to have lost his appetite.

"If you are not going to eat that ham, Roger, I suggest you let Collins remove your plate," his wife said sharply from across the table. "The sight of it quite upsets my stomach."

Jane sounded miffed, which Roger found totally unreasonable. After all, had she not defied his express wishes yesterday and insisted upon accompanying him to Horton Hall? To what ends he could not imagine. This matter of Sir Giles's sudden acknowledgement of Maud's daughter was between him and Stephen. He did not want Jane involved. Her presence was bound to increase the tension between the two men that Roger had sensed at the funeral.

And furthermore, Roger admitted reluctantly, he did not want his Jane exposed to the company of Captain Stephen Horton. The fellow had become too damned dashing for his own good. He had seen the covetous female glances at the funeral and heard the excited whispers.

But Jane had insisted, and they had argued last night in their private sitting room. As a result, Roger had stormed out, hoping Jane would relent. She had not done so, and he had slept in his own bed last night.

Roger glared at her but swallowed his angry retort when his father walked into the breakfast room. Jane looked particularly lovely this morning in a holly-green wool gown with bright red trimmings, and he could have kicked himself for losing his temper with her last night. He had grown accustomed to spending most of the night in her bed, and his own had seemed cold and lonely when he had finally retired. Nor had sleep come easily. His thoughts had been too full of the cruel joke Sir Giles had played on him and his little Abigail. How the old codger must have chortled at the disarray his surprise will would create at the Abbey. Thinking of it gave Roger indigestion.

The carriage was at the door at half-past the hour that afternoon, and as he assisted Jane up the steps, Roger made one last attempt to dissuade her.

"Are you quite sure you wish to go through with this, my dear? It could turn nasty, you know."

Jane's face relaxed a fraction. "I am prepared for the worst, Roger. But I cannot believe Stephen would go to such lengths to thwart me."

Roger smiled grimly. "I fear it is me he intends to thwart, not you, Jane."

"You cannot be sure of that," Jane replied, moving over to allow Lord Trenton to settle himself beside her. "How do we know that Stephen is not an unwitting pawn in this affair? He cannot be unaware of local rumours about his little half-sister, and it must be hard for him to face the prospect of having to support her legitimacy himself."

"Precisely," cut in Lord Trenton gruffly. "I have given serious thought to this matter, and I fancy you are both losing sight of little Abigail's best interests here. Of course, I have yet to read the will, but I wager Sir Giles's last-minute reversal will erase a heavy stigma from the little lass."

"But she is *not* his daughter; she is mine," Roger said bluntly. "And the old blighter knew it."

Lord Trenton sighed. "You are not listening to me, lad. We all know, or rather we assume because you and Maud say so—no one but the Good Lord knows for certain—that Abigail is a Hastings, not a Horton. But if you insist on claiming her, Roger, she will be branded an illegitimate Hastings. Have you considered this against the possibility of being a legitimate Horton? This is what old Giles's will offers her. Do you wish to deprive your daughter of at least the appearance of respectability?"

Roger stared at his father, unwilling to believe his ears. "Are you saying I should let her go, Father?"

"Abigail needs special care, my lord," Jane broke in. "She is unlikely to get it at Horton Hall."

Lord Trenton shrugged. "I daresay those are the questions that need to be discussed this afternoon, not whether the child is a Hastings or a Horton." He turned to gaze out at the snow-covered Park, and Roger met Jane's troubled gaze.

There was a disturbing logic to his father's words that troubled him, too.

Horton Hall was shrouded in gloom when the party from the Abbey was ushered into the chilly front hall. The mirrors and portraits on the walls were covered with black cloth, and Jane noticed that the butler, never a jolly individual at the best of times, was positively dripping funereal melancholy.

Mouth drooping and eyes downcast, the butler took their coats, scarves, gloves, and other winter accoutrements, then, without a word, ushered them upstairs to the drawing room where a meagre fire strove to chase away the chill in the air.

"When I go to meet my Maker," Lord Trenton muttered, rubbing his hands together vigorously before the hearth, "I insist that you keep the fires burning, Roger. And the spirits flowing," he added, glancing at a sideboard noticeably devoid of bottles. "In fact, I shall include in it my will. Does Horton still imagine he is bivouacking with Wellington on the Peninsular, I wonder?"

"Please do not talk like that, Father," Jane begged. "Besides, I suspect you will outlast us all now that you are eating properly." And drinking less, she could have added, but held her peace.

Lord Trenton snorted. " 'Tis a sad day when a man cannot grow old and stick his spoon in the wall without being stuffed with cabbage and deprived of drink," he muttered belligerently.

Realizing that his lordship's testiness was entirely due to the stress of the moment, Jane smiled and led him to a comfortable chair.

Further conversation was cut short when the door opened and Captain Horton entered, followed by his solicitor.

It was Sir Stephen now, Jane reminded herself, listening to the captain make the introductions. Seated next to Lord Trenton, she had a clear view of all the gentlemen and particularly of Roger, who was unnaturally formal with his old friend. Jane wished there had been time to discuss the marquess's startling insight into the consequences of Sir Giles's will as it affected little Abigail. He had been right, of course. Much as she hated to admit it, Jane realized that the orphaned child's future would be easier if she were officially recognized as Sir Giles's daughter.

Yet she was loath to let her go. In the short weeks Abigail had been at the Abbey, the little girl had become like her own daughter, and Jane loved her. Roger loved her, too, and Jane was not at all sure he would see the surprise will as anything but a conspiracy to steal his daughter. Lord Trenton was right in that, too. They had both been more concerned with their own desires than with Abigail's future. If only Roger had had time to mull over his father's words, perhaps he could muddle through this interview without flying into the boughs.

Mr. Archibald MacIntyre cleared his throat. "I have here a copy of Sir Giles's last will and testament for your perusal, my lord." He picked up a heavy sheet of velum and carried it over to Lord Trenton. "Sir Giles was quite adamant that you and Lord Summers should both attend the reading and receive a copy. It was evident to me that he trusted your good judgement in this delicate matter, my lord." He did not so much as glance at Roger, but Jane clearly perceived that the baronet had not had any such faith in her husband's judgement.

Jane saw Roger's face darken at the implications and prayed that he would not lose his temper and blurt out that Abigail was his and no one else's. She met his eyes across the room, and smiled, wishing they had not argued the night before and slept apart. She had missed his warm body next to hers in the cold bed, and his kisses and teasing lovemaking by the light of the single candle they invariably left burning on the dresser. She should not have chided him at the breakfast table about the ham, either, although it was true that the mutilated heap of meat on his plate had threatened to bring on a fit of nausea.

And that was yet another thing she should have done. She should have told Roger that she was indeed carrying his child. Perhaps in a small way the news that he was to be a father again might mitigate the loss of his first daughter. If indeed they were to lose Abigail Rose, as she was beginning to fear.

"I notice that the child is to receive a sizable legacy," Lord Trenton remarked after reading through the document. "Can you tell me when this will was executed, sir?"

"Sir Giles wrote to me less than a month ago, expressing his urgent desire to change his will," Mr. MacIntyre responded promptly. "I sent down my junior associate, Mr. Hamilton, who rewrote and witnessed the new will, which is, I might add, both legal and binding," he added somewhat pompously.

"After Lady Horton died, then?"

"Yes, my lord."

"And after he had thrown the newborn child out of his house," Roger put in harshly.

"Sir Giles claimed that Lady Horton conspired to deprive him of his legitimate offspring, my lord," the solicitor responded without the slightest inflection in his voice that might tell Jane whether or not he believed this story.

"That is a damned lie," Roger exclaimed. "Ask any of the servants. Or Dr. Graham. They will tell you what really happened." Jane noticed that he did not advise them to ask her, who had spent so much of her time at Lady Horton's bedside during those last days.

"Unless I am much mistaken," Lord Trenton interjected calmly, "how the child came to leave Horton Hall is a moot point. Is that not so, sir?"

"Indeed, you are correct, my lord."

"What concerns us today is who is to have custody of the child."

"Again, you are absolutely in the right of it, my lord. Although, I would do my client a disservice"—he bowed slightly in Stephen's direction—"if I failed to point out that Sir Giles was well within his rights to dispose of his wife's child, legally assumed to be his daughter, any way he saw fit. As he states in his will, Sir Giles has named his son and heir as her guardian."

"The child was not—"

"*Dispose* of her?" Jane interrupted quickly, before Roger could finish his sentence. "How can you refer to an innocent child as you would an unwanted dog?" She glared at the solicitor. "What heartless creatures you are."

Impassive as ever, MacIntyre inclined his head. "It is the law, my lady," he said gently. "And I do not make the laws."

"But—"

"Hush, my dear Jane." She felt Lord Trenton's hand clasp her arm and subsided, close to tears. "I am sure there is no question of harming the child in any way. I would not permit it. 'Tis a mere legal term, no more. Calm yourself."

Jane noted that Stephen was looking at her fixedly, his dark eyes enigmatic. She held his gaze, her own eyes damp with unshed tears. "Stephen," she said huskily, addressing him directly for the first time that afternoon, "you cannot mean to—"

"He means to carry out the vindictive wishes of a jealous old man," Roger snapped, "even if this means dragging the child over here where there is no way she can be cared for properly."

"Roger!" Lord Trenton's roar caused the candelabra on the sideboard to tremble. "You will keep a civil tongue in your head if you please."

"I was merely questioning the sanity of this demand, Father."

"It is not your place to question Captain Horton's duty to his father. I would expect you to do no less for me if the roles were reversed."

"A true father would want what is best for his daughter," Roger continued stubbornly. "And I cannot see that happening here."

"The only thing I see questionable in this will is that Sir Giles did not see fit to inform his wife of his change of heart regarding their daughter. It might have relieved her last days to know that her child would not be thrown out of the house, which effectively she was. Had my daughter-in-law not taken her in, the wee thing would be in the poorhouse at this very moment."

"We can never know that for certain, my lord," the solicitor pointed out patiently. "We are dealing with suppositions here. And even in the event that such an action took place, there is no denying that Sir Giles had the right to—"

"Oh, poppycock!" Jane burst out before she could control her exasperation. "I am tired of all this talk of suppositions, and rights, and what the law does or does not allow."

"Jane, hush!" Roger and his father explained in unison.

"I will not hush." She turned towards Stephen. "All this legal talk is merely a long-winded way of asking a simple question, which you, Stephen, must answer, one way or another."

"And what is that question, Jane?" The captain's voice broke into the silence that followed Jane's impulsive outburst.

She smiled at him, noting with pleasure the gleam of affection in his eyes. "Do you intend to take Abigail away from me and raise her here at the Hall? Or will you consider allowing me to keep her until she is completely healthy again? I love her dearly, you must know, and can give her the family life she needs. And you must admit, Stephen, that you are hardly in a position to care for a baby."

She paused and looked around the room at the four masculine faces. Only Mr. MacIntyre showed signs of approval. Lord Trenton and Roger both looked cross as crabs. While Stephen . . . the slow smile that spread over his face told Jane all she wanted to know.

"You are surprisingly accurate in your assessment of the issue at stake here, Lady Summers," the solicitor began ponderously.

Jane interrupted him with a gesture. "No more legal opinions for the moment, if you please, Mr. MacIntyre. While we wait for Captain Horton to ponder his answer, I suggest you send for the tea-tray, Stephen. I am sure we could all use a cup of tea."

Chapter Seventeen

Nemesis Overcome

"Will you be needing any more holly, milady?" Jane steadied herself on the ladder and looked down at Mrs. Collins. They had been working together all morning, decorating the ballroom with branches of holly and other greenery, while three maids in white mobcaps swept, and dusted, and polished the grand old room that was to be the centre of attraction for the Christmas Day ball.

"I think not, Mrs. Collins. The front hall already looks lovely, and also the breakfast parlour. I am not to touch the library or the billiard room, his lordship says, and we did the drawing room, the dining room, and the morning room yesterday. All that remains is to finish up here and then decorate the banisters. There should be enough left for the servants' quarters, which you can get some of the maids to do."

She surveyed the room critically. It looked festive with all the red berries and dark green leaves, and she wondered how many generations of Hastings had celebrated their Christmases there. The enormous Yule log, brought in by Roger and his men only yesterday, was already in place in one of the huge hearths, while at the other end of the hall, another open hearth was stacked with logs ready to warm the guests as it had for centuries.

"Shall I ask Collins to send out for the mistletoe, then, milady?"

Jane's thoughts returned to the present. "Yes, we should be ready to hang it by this afternoon. And we shall need a few branches of holly for the wreath on the front door."

A discreet cough interrupted her. "What is it, Collins?" she said.

"Captain Sir Stephen Horton to see you, milady."

"Show him into the drawing room, Collins, and tell him I shall be with him directly."

It was a good ten minutes later that Jane swept into the drawing room to find the captain admiring one of her latest watercolours.

"I am glad to see that you have kept up your painting, Jane," he remarked after greeting her. "You were always so talented. Are you still working on your wildflower monograph?"

Jane smiled with pleasure. "How did you remember that after all these years?"

"I helped you search for specimens up on Hogdon Hill that summer before Roger and I went off to Oxford, remember?"

"Indeed I do," she exclaimed, gratified that Stephen remembered that afternoon they had spent on the hill together, collecting summer flowers for her sketching.

"You were looking for lady's-mantle if I remember correctly, which I had never heard of before. We finally found some in that small meadow down near the pond, I believe."

"I am impressed that you can remember the name, Stephen." Jane was more than impressed, she was delighted to find that her childhood friend had not lost interest in wildflowers.

"I suppose Roger is your official specimen collector now," he murmured, regarding her keenly.

"Whenever he can spare a moment, poor dear. Lord Trenton has been in poor health for several months, you know, and Roger has taken over the running of the estate, which takes most of his time." The mention of the viscount threw a pall on the conversation, and there was an awkward pause.

"Marriage appears to agree with you, Jane," the captain said suddenly. "You are even more lovely than

I remember. I trust Roger realizes what a treasure he has."

Flustered by this unexpected praise, Jane blushed. "You flatter me, Stephen. Did you wish to speak to Roger?" she demanded abruptly to change the subject. "He went out with Peterson hours ago and will be sorry to miss you. We have been anxious to know your decision regarding Abigail." She paused and glanced at him. "I trust you do not plan to change her name, Stephen. Your father would not receive us when we went over to consult him, so we decided on Abigail Rose. Abigail is a traditional Hastings name, but it was also Maud's middle name." Realizing that she was chattering aimlessly, Jane stopped abruptly.

The captain smiled. "Ah, Maud. What a beautiful, feckless, willful creature she was, to be sure. I have yet to thank you, Jane, for all the care you lavished upon her in those last days. My housekeeper assures me that you were tireless, and that my father only heaped invective on your head."

"He was a sick man, Stephen. I do not hold it against him."

"You are far too generous for your own good, my dear Jane." He paused for a moment, then sighed and added softly, "I sometimes wish that things had been different between us, but that is fruitless, of course."

Jane dared not ask what things he referred to. With a flash of insight, she realized that she might well be poised upon the brink of a forbidden adventure. She had always wondered how such affairs began. Now she began to understand that the vicar was right, sinful thoughts could indeed lead to sinful acts. Unless one was very very careful.

Mesmerized by the warmth in the captain's dark eyes, she felt herself glow with anticipated pleasure at the thought of a stolen kiss. How easy it would be, she mused, to let herself fall into this man's arms, and from there it would be but a step to a secret rendezvous. Perhaps under the same spreading oak tree by the stream where she had stumbled upon Roger mak-

ing love to Maud. Or by the secret pond where she
had seen him kiss her rival. Would Stephen write her
love letters full of sensuous descriptions and vowing
eternal love?

But did she really wish him to?

The picture of Roger's handsome face rose up in
her mind, and Jane read the answer in her heart. No
other man's love would satisfy her. There could be no
other man but Roger, and she would love him as long
as she could breathe. It was one of life's ironies that
he had married her to pay off his father's gambling
debts and save his estate. Had he not seen that she
had been waiting for him for so very long? But she
must not think of what might have been, she reminded
herself philosophically. She must be thankful for what
she had now—and would have in the near future, if
the Good Lord willed. Of its own accord, her hand
drifted downwards across her flat stomach.

"Jane?" Stephen's voice was warm and caressing.

Abruptly aware that she had been staring at him,
and that the captain's eyes had changed expression,
Jane jerked herself out of her treacherous daydream
and stepped back from the sweet allure of illicit love.
"I do beg your pardon, Captain. I seem to have forgotten myself. Here I am prattling away, and you must
be wondering when I will get around to offering you
some refreshments."

"Perhaps I should not stay," he said with a rueful
smile. "I had wanted to speak to Roger, but will call
another time."

Reluctant to let him go so soon, Jane asked if the
captain would like to meet his sister before he left.

"I was hoping you would ask, but I do not wish to
disturb her."

Recovering her poise, Jane rang for the butler.

"Ask Mrs. Watson if she will bring little Abigail
down to meet her brother, will you Collins? And serve
Captain Horton a glass of sherry."

Before the butler had time to complete his duties,
Jane's description of the daily improvement Dr. Gra-

ham reported in Abigail's health was cut short
abruptly by piercing screams coming from upstairs.
She jumped to her feet and dashed out onto the landing, followed by the captain. The screams had grown
louder and now appeared to come from several voices.
To her horror Jane realized the commotion came from
the nursery. Lifting her skirts, she raced upstairs to
find both Nurse and Mrs. Watson berating the wet-
nurse, Mrs. Jacobs, at the top of their lungs.

"I must 'ave closed me eyes for a sec, and when I
opened them—" the wet-nurse whined, copious tears
flowing down her round cheeks.

"You are not paid to close your eyes, you foolish
woman," Nurse yelled, beside herself with fury. She
had the other woman by the shoulders and appeared
intent on shaking her teeth out of her head.

" 'Er ladiship will 'ave yer liver for this, she will,
and no mistake," Mrs. Watson screeched, wringing her
hands in great distress.

The three women, surrounded by two footmen and
three upstairs maids were gathered in the hall outside
the nursery when Jane arrived. Upon seeing her, the
footmen and maids melted away, and the women burst
out into fresh lamentations.

"Whatever is the matter?" Jane exclaimed, raising
her voice above the clamour of the nursery staff.

" 'Tis the wee babe, milady," the wet-nurse began.

Without waiting for the woman to finish, Jane
rushed into Abigail's room, only to find her crib
empty. Her hands flew to her mouth, and she felt the
room sway sickeningly under her feet.

"W-where is she?" she demanded, her voice edged
with panic.

"Yes, where is the child? Answer her ladyship this
instant." Jane heard Stephen's voice in a fog, but his
presence seemed to spur the women to greater heights
of hysteria.

"Stop this wailing at once," she shouted above the
hubbub. "What happened here?"

" 'E took her, milady," Mrs. Watson blubbered,

throwing her apron over her head so that Jane could barely make out her words.

"*Who* took her?" Jane fairly screamed at the frightened woman.

"A m-man took her, milady. We saw him r-running down the hall," Nurse stammered, her eyes wide with shock.

"When did this happen?" Stephen demanded.

"Just a moment ago, sir,"

"Which way did he go?" He addressed a footman, who had reappeared from somewhere.

"Down the back stairs, sir," he responded nervously. "One of the stable-lads it was, I think. Bumped into 'im when I was coming up with the hot water Nurse asked for. Asked 'im what 'e was doing with the little one, and 'e laughed at me."

"Come with me," the captain ordered and ran down the hall towards the servants' stairs.

Jane ran after them but by the time she reached the back stairs, they were already out of sight. She could clearly hear several pairs of boots clattering on the wooden stairs and Stephen's voice shouting orders. Her heart in her mouth, Jane hesitated, then raced along the hall to the main staircase. Instinct told her that the kidnapper would not risk using the servants' stairs all the way down to the kitchen since it was in constant use with footmen or maids going about their duties. He would be safer on the main stairs with only the old butler in the hall below to stop him.

Standing on the landing of the third floor, Jane leaned over the banister and saw a muffled figure casually walking downstairs as though he owned the house.

"Stop!" she cried out, knowing that her voice alone would not deter him.

The figure paused and looked up at her. A cold weight suddenly materialized in the pit of her stomach. The man was carrying a bundle of clothes under his arm, and Jane knew this must be Abigail.

"Bring that baby back here immediately," she ordered, grasping the banister with fingers that trembled.

From under his slouched hat pulled low over his face, the man suddenly grinned, and Jane recognized the brown teeth and the sly grin.

She felt herself go pale, and her fingers gripped the banister until they hurt. The face looking up at her was one she had long mistrusted. Now she knew her instincts had been correct.

With a shrug, Jimmy Barnes continued his way downstairs.

The cold air felt invigorating against his face as Roger strode down to the sheepfold with Peterson. There had been another hard frost during the night, and his agent had commented that the lake was in a fair way to being solid enough to walk on. Jane would have her skating party on Christmas Eve after all. Roger smiled with satisfaction at the joy this would bring her.

The thought of his wife distracted him, as it always did, and he regretted having to miss meeting Jane at the breakfast table. She was invariably prim and proper in the mornings and conversed with his father as though she had never entertained a naughty thought in that pretty head of hers. Roger delighted in making her blush by dropping casual reminders of the games they played at night in the cosy intimacy of her bed.

Jane had never been coy or prudish as Roger had imagined a wife would be, judging from the depressing reports he had received over the years from friends unfortunate enough to have fallen prey to parson's mousetrap. Jane had enchanted him from the first night with her sweetly wanton eagerness to please him in any way. It had often occurred to Roger that he was supremely blessed with a wife who combined the best qualities of both mistress and wife. He had never told her so, and he had definitely not mentioned his amazing luck to any of his acquaintances. This was his secret, which he intended one day to share with Jane.

"I thought you might want to take a look for yourself, milord." Peterson's voice interrupted Roger's pleasant thoughts and brought him back to the latest attempt on his sheep.

"Yes, of course, Peterson. I want to see this sheep-killer caught as much as you."

"Dobbs noticed the sheep milling about a little after three this morning, and when he went to take a look, there was this chap in the pen as bold as brass."

"Did he recognize the intruder?"

"Claims he looked familiar. Wore a slouch hat, he says. But then so do half the lads in the county. He did raise the alarm, but the chap leaped the fence and made off into the darkness."

With the old shepherd Dobbs as their guide, they examined the snow-covered ground around the sheep-fold. It was easy enough to follow the footprints leaving the scene, but when Roger sent a younger lad to see where they went, he discovered that the prints doubled back to the lake where they were obliterated by the early morning traffic along the lane.

"This seems to confirm what Mr. Coates suggested last time," Peterson said, "that the villain is someone from the estate."

Roger reluctantly agreed, and they spent some time making enquiries among the tenants and hired workers without much success.

The morning was nearly over when Roger walked back to the house alone. He was deep in thought as he trod up the shallow stone steps and pushed open the great oaken door, surprised that Collins was absent from his post. He soon discovered the cause of his butler's dereliction of duty. Collins lay on the black-and-white tiled floor of the hall, one hand to his head, his gaunt countenance deathly pale.

At the far end of the hall, against the backdrop of the blazing fire, two figures were engaged in a noisy fistfight. Once his eyes became accustomed to the dim light, Roger recognized one of the contenders as Stephen Horton, who appeared to be intent upon pounding a burly, ill-dressed fellow into a pulp. The captain had shed his blue superfine coat, and his cravat, splattered with blood, hung in a disordered tangle from his neck.

Roger stared in consternation, which changed to awe as the captain landed a magnificent facer on his opponent with a sickening thud, sending the man reeling back against a table. The table tottered but did not fall. The Chinese vase full of holly branches was not so lucky; it bounced off the table and shattered into a hundred pieces on the tile floor.

A sharp cry of distress from above distracted him from this scene of mayhem. He raised his eyes and saw Jane, clutching Abigail in her arms, standing halfway up the first flight of stairs.

As soon as she caught his eye, she ran down into the hall and threw herself into his arms. Abigail contributed to the pandemonium by letting out a howl worthy of a baby three times her size.

"Oh, Roger," Jane sobbed, evidently as upset as Abigail, "that man tried to steal Abigail from her room, but Stephen saved her." She turned to gaze at the captain, who was directing several footmen in securing the erstwhile kidnapper.

Roger disentangled himself from Jane, who set about trying to pacify Abigail, and strode over to Collins, who was gamely trying to struggle to his feet. After assuring himself that his butler had suffered no lasting injuries, and sending one of the footmen to find Mrs. Collins, Roger went to examine the prisoner.

He stood beside the captain and looked down at the scruffy intruder. The fellow's nose was bleeding copiously all over his grubby shirt, and his left eye was already swollen and turning black. His hair was long and unwashed, falling over his face. Roger gazed at him with distaste.

"Do you know him?" the captain asked, prodding the semi-unconscious man with the tip of his boot.

"Yes, his name is Jimmy Barnes, one of our stable-lads."

"Barnes? There are not many Barneses around these parts. Is he from over on the coast?"

"Yes," Roger said again, then added defensively, "And yes, he *is* related to Maud. Some sort of cousin, I believe."

There was a slight pause during which Roger could hear Mrs. Collins and several maids fussing over the butler. Abigail had ceased crying, and he saw that both Nurse and Mrs. Watson had come down to take charge of her. Jane still looked pale and shaken, and Roger resisted the impulse to take her in his arms and comfort her.

"We had best send for the bailiff and take the wretch before the magistrate," Stephen suggested. "I am sure Jane wants him out of here as quickly as possible."

Roger ordered one of the grooms to ride over to the village to fetch Mr. Coates, who would take the prisoner back to the roundhouse to await the pleasure of the magistrate. Jane had joined them by this time and suggested they all repair to the drawing room for a glass of sherry before nuncheon was served. As soon as they moved away from Barnes, who was now on his feet, supported by two footmen, Mrs. Watson let out a shrill cry.

" 'Twas *you*, was it, ye worthless piece of work?" she called out, advancing towards the hapless Barnes, who glared at her sullenly. "Pestering the poor lady 'alf to death for money was not good enough for ye, I take it. Ye must needs steal from 'er, too—yes, I know all about ye sneaking into 'er room when she was sleeping, poor thing. And now ye steal 'er poor wee babe. Shame on ye, Jimmy Barnes, devil's spawn that ye be. What did ye 'ave a mind to do with 'er, if I may ask? Or did it just to be spiteful, did ye?"

There was a sudden silence in the hall. The servants, including old Collins, stood around agog with curiosity. The unexpected outburst took Roger by surprise, and he turned to look at the object of Mrs. Watson's wrath. Barnes looked uneasy, but he answered with his habitual cockiness.

"Maudie's babe don't belong 'ere with all these bleedin' nobs," he growled, his expression hard. "I wus takin' 'er up to Appledore to 'er grandma's. That's where she belongs."

Mrs. Watson snorted in disbelief. "And I suppose ye'll be telling me next the little mite will be better off in a fishing village than 'ere at the Abbey? Yer wits 'ave gone beggin', ye wicked lad."

Barnes sneered. "She'd do better as a plain fisherman's wife and not a fancy tart like 'er mother," he retorted, ignoring the collective intake of breaths. "Don't ye go denying it, ye old bat. Ye saw what the gentry did to poor Maudie. Laughed at 'er be'ind 'er back then made 'er into a tart, they did." He glared malevolently at Roger, who felt a flicker of sympathy for the uncouth creature. And also guilt. The local gentry had indeed laughed at Maud's attempt to become a lady, a sad but inevitable commentary on the callous rigidity of his class.

"Enough of this ranting," Roger snapped. "Take the man away and keep him under guard until the bailiff comes for him."

Barnes did not go quietly. It took three of the burliest footmen to drag him out of the door and down to the stables.

Roger watched him go with mixed feelings.

Chapter Eighteen

The Skating Party

The party that gathered in the dining room for nuncheon later that morning was well provided with topics of conversation. Jane was relieved to see that Stephen had dropped his stiffness with Roger and that the latter seemed to have regained the easy camaraderie the men had shared as youths. Lord Trenton, who had missed the dust-up with Barnes, plied them with questions, and filled their ears with tales of similar incidents of servant disloyalty in his father's day.

"It was a happy coincidence that Mrs. Watson was present in the hall when Barnes was caught," Jane remarked, signaling to Collins to serve the captain more of the succulent York ham he so enjoyed. "I do believe he might not have confessed so readily had she not challenged him."

"I gather she served over at the Hall," Stephen remarked.

"Yes, she was Maud's abigail, who begged for a post here where she could be near the baby." She thought it wise not to mention that Sir Giles had ordered Mrs. Watson put out of the Hall within hours after Maud's death. Neither did she voice her suspicion that Barnes had been responsible for sneaking Roger's love letters out of Maud's room and sending them. He had certainly handed one of them to her down at the stables.

The footmen were bringing in the fruit and sweetmeats when Collins, still looking somewhat battered by his experience with Barnes, brought in a note for Roger. After a quick perusal, Roger laid it on the table beside him. "Coates reports that Barnes has made a full confession, not merely to abducting Abigail, which we all heard him admit to, but also to killing my ram, stealing Maud's letters, and masquerading as the Trenton ghost." He smiled affectionately at Jane. "I hope that relieves your mind about the black-toothed ghost, my dear."

The captain regarded her curiously, and Jane recounted Sally's tale of being chased by a ghost in boots with black teeth. "Roger assured me that ghosts have no teeth, and I had to agree that it seemed rather strange. Thank goodness that mystery is cleared up."

"And what is this about Maud's letters?" Stephen enquired, accepting another apple tart from Collins.

Jane glanced at Roger, who shrugged. "I was foolish enough to write her some indiscreet letters, which she promised to return and never did."

Stephen grinned suddenly. "You are lucky Maud did not publish them, old man. That is quite the sort of thing I would expect of her."

Jane let out a little cry of dismay, and Roger looked rather alarmed at this suggestion.

"I never thought of that," Jane said a little breathlessly. "That is not amusing, Stephen," she scolded as the captain laughed.

"If one were not involved, it might be," Roger said unexpectedly. "I can even imagine the salacious title the press would use."

"Ah, so can I," Stephen remarked. "What about *Scandalous Missives from an Infatuated Gentleman to a Lady of Dubious Virtue*?"

Roger laughed ruefully, but Jane was hard put not to protest this unseemly levity at Maud's expense.

"No, I am sure our Maud would be more direct," Roger said. "Something like *Indiscreet Letters from Viscount S. to a Lady H. of Devon*. That would invite all the gossips to start rumours about the identities of the letter writers. Provide them with hours of amusement, I daresay."

"You are both being absurd," she said reproachfully. "And unkind. Besides, no respectable press would publish such lascivious material."

There was a sudden silence at the table, and Jane realized her mistake.

"*Lascivious* material?" Roger repeated softly. "And how would you know that, love?"

Jane felt the three gentlemen looking at her with interest. She waved a hand dismissively and poured more cream on her gooseberry pie. "I imagined they would be, of course," she responded airily. "They were not invitations to tea, I gather." She glanced up in time to see Roger and Stephen exchange speaking looks.

Lord Trenton cleared his throat. "These letters you speak of, my dear, were undoubtedly the outpourings of an addled mind." He glared down the table at his son. "The fairer sex often has this effect on us gentlemen. They bring out the worst in us, I fear. Not at all fit for your gentle ears, take it from me."

Jane stared at the marquess in astonishment. "Are you telling me that you have—"

"Indeed, I have been made a fool of by a lovely woman," he interrupted quickly. "But that was long, long ago, before I met Roger's dear mother. And my aberrations ran more to bad sonnets than scurrilous prose."

Roger grinned. "I would give my best horse to read one of those sonnets, Father. Perhaps you would consider entertaining us one evening—"

"Roger, do not tease your father," Jane cut in quickly, noting that the marquess' face had turned a dangerous purple. "Unless of course," she added innocently, "you would be willing to read us some of these infamous missives of yours."

"No!" both Roger and his father replied in unison.

Jane laughed. "You are right. Your sisters might not consider it proper to have your love letters read to them after dinner, Roger. And as for your bad sonnets, my lord, I daresay both Augusta and Leticia would rather not hear those, either."

"No fear of that, my dear. I threw them out thirty years ago," Lord Trenton snorted.

"Well, if we are to be deprived of *literary* entertainment," Jane continued, ignoring the stifled laughter from the two younger gentlemen, "I suppose we must make do with the sporting kind. What does Peterson say about the lake, Roger? Will it be solid enough by next Friday? I am quite determined to hold the annual skating party, let me tell you."

Roger acknowledged that, barring any unforeseen change in weather, the lake would indeed be safe for skating by Christmas Eve, adding that there was no better way to keep all his nieces and nephews happy than with skating and sledding.

"I am counting on you, Captain, to help Roger keep the older boys out of mischief," Jane remarked. "How long has it been since you have skated?"

Any response the captain might have made was drowned out by a sudden commotion in the hall, followed by the familiar sound of children's voices, and trunks and valises being unloaded from three travelling coaches that had pulled up at the front door.

"It seems that our Christmas season has officially begun," Roger said with a grimace.

Lord Trenton had already risen, and Jane experienced a pang of regret that for the next weeks she and Roger would have little time to themselves. Expect in the intimacy of their private apartments. She caught his glance and knew that he was thinking similar thoughts.

With an affectionate grin, he tucked her hand in the crook of his arm, and together they followed Lord Trenton and the captain out into the hubbub of relatives in the hall.

The following week was a busy one for Jane, who spent most of her time flitting between the kitchen—where she supervised the preparation of seasonal delicacies for the adults, and mountains of cakes, tarts, pies, and other sweetmeats that the children consumed avidly—and the drawing room—where she played hostess to Roger's sisters, and the endless stream of callers who came to pay their respects to the marquess and his family.

She was intensely grateful to Aunt Octavia and to Elizabeth, who helped her prepare the Christmas baskets for the tenants, and to the marquess, who insisted upon driving her around the estate himself to deliver the seasonal bounty.

"I am thankful we Cheswicks are not a large family," Elizabeth remarked on the morning of the skating party, as the two ladies stood in the shelter of a clump of rhododendrons surveying the furious snowball battle taking place among the younger guests.

"I hope they do not harm themselves," Jane said anxiously, as a particularly ferocious barrage of snowballs from Lady Augusta's elder boys half buried some of the smaller lads on the opposite side. "Augusta's sons are natural bullies, I have always said."

"They take after their mother," Elizabeth murmured uncharitably under her breath.

Jane laughed. "Augusta *is* rather managing, I must agree, but she has a good heart and can always be depended upon to tell me exactly how to do anything." Jane sighed. She had needed every ounce of patience to deal with both her sisters-in-law. Augusta with her incessant ordering of things to suit herself, and Letitia's constant complaining that things at the Abbey had never been the same since her poor mama passed on.

"You are much too kind, Jane," her friend exclaimed. "Frankly, I do not know how you stand their constant bickering."

They watched the younger boys climb out from beneath heaps of snow and rally for a counterattack. Jane relaxed. She was heartily glad that her own Aunt Honoria and her brood had decided to spend Christmas with Lord Bristol's family in Norfolk instead of descending upon Penhallow. Honoria invariably man-

aged to set Augusta's back up, and the two were
known for their long-standing quarrels.

"Do you think we might leave these little monsters
to slaughter each other for a while and slip away to
lay a wreath on the little ghost's grave?" she asked.
"I had intended to do so yesterday, but little Bertie
broke his finger, and I had to call in Dr. Graham to
set it."

Carrying the holly wreath she had made up some
days ago, Jane led Elizabeth along the lake path and
up the steep incline to the chapel. Surrounded by a
low stone wall, which Roger claimed was built by the
first Baron Trenton, the graves lay deeply embedded
in snow with only the tops of the stones showing
above the drifts.

"How peaceful they look," she said, her breath
forming a visible cloud of steam in the cold air. "I
find it comforting to know that one day Roger and
I will lie here with them, surrounded by family on
all sides."

"How morbid we are this morning," Elizabeth
chided with a laugh. "You have only just set out on
your life together, Jane, and you are already thinking
of dying. There is much to accomplish before that day
comes, my dear. Not the least of which is to present
your lord with a son and heir."

Jane smiled as she led the way towards the small
grave of the unfortunate little boy whose bones still
lay—if local wisdom had any truth to it—at the bottom of the lake.

"I cannot understand how a woman, herself a
mother, could throw a little boy to his death. It is a
hideous crime that, as far as the records show, went
unpunished."

"You are far too fanciful, Jane," Elizabeth replied
bracingly. "And as for retribution for her sins, I can
guarantee that her spirit is not resting peacefully even
to this day. She may have gained the title for her son,
but she certainly lost her soul along the way. You may
be sure of it."

Jane stopped before the small tombstone and bent to place the holly wreath over the worn stone cross. The inscription was barely legible but Jane did not need to read the name or date to know who the boy was. She had seen the chronicle of his birth and death in the estate records room.

"There you are, Gavin," she said softly, resting her hand briefly on the weathered cross. "May your spirit find peace, and please forgive Roger's ancestors for taking what was rightfully yours." She paused for a moment, then turned away to join Elizabeth on the way back to the Abbey.

"Are you not forgetting to remind the little ghost of his traditional duty, Jane? I hear he appears to the lady of the house to confirm her happy state of approaching motherhood," her friend remarked, stopping abruptly and looking back up the hill. "I understand he appeared to Roger's mother every time."

Jane smiled shyly. "Gavin needs no reminding," she murmured. "He has not forgotten."

Elizabeth stared at her for several seconds before the import of Jane's confession sank in. "Are you saying . . . But of course, you are," she cried, throwing her arms about Jane and hugging her fiercely. "You have seen the ghost? Then you are . . . ? Oh, Jane, how wonderful, but why did you not say so sooner? Does Roger know?"

"Not yet, but he will tonight."

They had little time for further confidences, for Jane noticed Roger and Stephen making their way along the lake path towards them. As they approached, Jane saw that Roger appeared to be excessively pleased with himself. The reason for his exuberance was soon apparent.

"Stephen has agreed to leave little Abigail with us, Jane. At least until he gets himself leg-shackled and can make a home for her."

"Which will not be any time soon," the captain assured them quickly.

"Do not count on it, Stephen," Elizabeth said with

a laugh. "You would not believe how quickly the word spreads that there is an eligible bachelor in the vicinity. And if you put it about that you are actively seeking a wife, you will have to beat them off with sticks."

Jane held out both gloved hands to the captain, her smile coming from her heart. "Thank you, oh, thank you, Stephen," she murmured. "We will take good care of her."

The two couples strolled back to the house—the captain and Elizabeth leading the way, and Jane, her hand snugly caught in the crook of Roger's elbow, bringing up the rear. As Jane gazed out over the frozen expanse of lake, she wondered, in a flash of whimsy, whether the ghost of little Gavin was not watching over the motherless Abigail from his watery grave.

Jane was not sure she entirely believed the tales about the ghost, but she suddenly remembered that, long before Abigail was born and Maud died, she had dreamed of saving the baby from drowning in a scene that had eerie parallels to that other scene, which must have played itself out so long ago with tragic consequences.

She was suddenly glad she had remembered to place the holly wreath on little Gavin's empty grave. Perhaps, she thought, glancing up at the handsome profile of her husband, that sense of disaster she had felt hanging over her head since that shocking discovery of Maud in Roger's arms beside the stream that spring afternoon was beginning to dissipate.

When Roger turned and smiled at her with real affection, she was sure of it.

The annual Trenton skating party was a huge success. Roger received the many compliments from his guests with growing pleasure. Lady Summers had outdone herself, Mr. Archibald Cheswick assured him as they met over one of the barrels of coal burning brightly in a colourful display at one end of the lake. Sir Samuel and Lady Beecham insisted that Jane had more than lived up to the traditional hospitality and good cheer dispensed at the Abbey during this annual event. Despite their years, Sir Samuel and his lady never missed a skating party and elicited the admiration of all and the envy of not a few as they glided smoothly around the lake in perfect harmony.

Even Augusta's interference in the arrangement of the refreshment tables did not mar the festivities. Roger heard his wife calmly instruct the footmen to leave the tables where they were, and that if Lady Stanford insisted she was too far from the warmth of the fire barrels, a chair should be set for her next to one of them.

Roger also marvelled at his wife's dexterity in maintaining the peace among their younger guests. When Letitia's youngest, Bertie, holding his broken finger aloft like a trophy, made himself sick eating roast chestnuts, Jane teased him out of feeling sorry for himself. And when his little sister Felicity burned her gloves catching a red-hot chestnut Bertie threw at her, Jane averted a major explosion by getting Captain Horton to show the child how to execute a perfect figure eight without falling down.

As twilight fell and stars began to appear in the night sky, Roger was joined by his father and several gentlemen guests who gathered round the table set up with bottles of more sustaining fare than the hot punch and cider offered with the general refreshments.

"Well, it appears that we made a good match of it all those years ago, Penhallow," Roger heard his father say to their friend and neighbour as he joined them. "Roger could not have found a more perfect wife had he scoured the whole length and breadth of England. What do you say, Roger?" He slapped his son affectionately on the shoulder. "Penhallow here was just saying that his little Jane has turned into a grand lady since her marriage."

"I was telling your father that my gel has settled down better than I expected," the earl said fondly. "No more foolishness about rushing off to London for the Season or traipsing about the countryside collecting flowers for that silly book she wanted to write. I suppose it could have been worse, of course," he added pensively. "She might have written a frippery novel like those females Radcliffe or what is her name . . . Austen, I believe. That kind of notoriety is to be deplored. Luckily Jane's literary dabblings were at least of a serious nature, however misguided. Nothing like marriage to put a gel in her place, I say."

Lord Trenton snorted his agreement. "No time for such foolishness as mistress of the Abbey, I daresay, although I do enjoy her watercolours. Our Jane has a way with flowers."

"From what I see, my daughter is as happy as a lark to have found a useful role in life," her father remarked, with what Roger considered a serious lack of insight into the state of his daughter's emotional life.

"That she has," his father agreed, nodding as though he had made a cogent observation. "And she is most punctilious in seeing to our every need. For instance, thanks to her care, my health is much improved. I think I speak for both Roger and myself in saying that we are very happy to have her here at the Abbey."

As Roger listened to the two older gentlemen discuss his wife with a complacency that bordered on the ludicrous, he realized that neither of them knew the real Jane beneath that serene, composed exterior. Did he know her himself? he wondered, absently sipping on his mug of mulled wine. He knew her as playful and eager in the bedroom, as efficient and frugal in household management, as courteous and warm as a hostess, as kind and generous with the less fortunate; but was there someone he had not yet discovered lurking behind those warm amber eyes of hers?

Lord Trenton moved on to another subject, and it struck Roger that both his father and the earl had for years taken Jane for granted. Had he not done so himself? They had seen her as a young girl to be married off, to be settled with a suitable husband, to be disposed of with the care one might lavish on a brood mare or a particularly valuable hunting dog. They had scoffed at her personal accomplishments, at her ambitions and dreams. As he had himself, Roger thought wryly.

His eyes roved over the skaters and, when he did not find her, he felt his nerves tense with anxiety. When she came into view, gliding over the ice from the farther end of the lake, he relaxed briefly. Then anxiety turned to a hot rush of possessiveness as he recognized her skating partner. Captain Horton had one arm around his wife's slender waist, and with the other held her gloved right hand in his. They skated well together, Roger had to admit, albeit grudgingly. Tall and broad-shouldered, Stephen made an excellent foil for Jane's delicate figure as they glided gracefully down the middle of the lake. The captain's dark head was bent and when Jane laughed up at her partner, Roger felt an unexpected twist of jealousy.

"Well, well," his father's voice spoke at his elbow. "What a pretty pair our Jane makes with the gallant captain. You are dashed lucky to be wed to her yourself, lad, or I warrant you might have encountered some fierce competition in that direction." Lord Trenton laughed loudly at his own witticism, but Roger was not amused. His father had voiced the thought that had plagued him all evening.

Yes, he admitted, abruptly turning away towards the bench the couple was making for, he was a lucky dog to have such a wife. What bothered him was the nagging question newly arisen about Jane's true feelings. Was his father's original betrothal agreement added to the wedding vows they had exchanged last spring all that held them together? Under normal circumstances, this should be more than enough. After all, the authority of the Church of England had sanctioned his father's choice, binding Jane to him until death parted them. But was it Jane's choice, too?

Roger had never considered himself arrogant, but

now he saw that to have assumed Jane might be anything less than delighted to be his wife was the very height of arrogance. She had resisted his offer, but at the time this had seemed mere feminine contrariness. He had given her reluctance little thought. His father had told him it was high time he made his offer; Lord Penhallow had informed his daughter that she was expected to accept it. And Roger himself had treated it as a mere formality.

As any man in his position would, he reminded himself quickly. Why then was he concerned with Jane's happiness? Of course, she was happy. Was she not the Viscountess Summers, and in the course of time would become the Marchioness of Trenton? What more could a female aspire to? Furthermore, his father doted on her, and Roger treated her with every consideration due her rank and station. It was foolishness to imagine that Jane, an intelligent and practical female, would not fully appreciate the advantages marriage to him entailed.

Why then was he suddenly plagued with doubts about—of all incredible things—his ability to make his wife happy?

Roger tried to brush these uncomfortable thoughts aside as he approached the bench where Jane had sat down. Stephen was kneeling before her, checking her skates when Roger paused beside her. Judging from their laughter, they appeared to be sharing a joke, and Jane's amber eyes were still full of merriment when she looked up at him.

"Oh, Roger, you will never guess what Cupid has been up to," she cried, with obvious delight.

"No, I have no idea, my dear. But I trust you are about to tell me."

"He has skewered the most unlikely victim with his arrow. Stephen and I witnessed it with our own eyes, did we not, Stephen?"

"Aye, that we did," the captain agreed good-humoredly. "Never saw an old codger so pleased with himself."

"Who is this unfortunate mortal?" Roger enquired, captivated by the sparkle in his wife's eyes.

"Old Mr. Morse, the owner of the King's Arms in Torrington. He is out there romancing Mrs. Watson. Can you believe it?"

"*Our* Mrs. Watson?"

"Yes, and she looks awfully pleased with herself," Jane replied. "I would not be surprised if we were to lose her if the innkeeper plays his cards right."

"Plays his cards right?" Roger repeated enquiringly. He had trouble imagining the portly old man in the role of Lothario.

"I think Jane means if the old man's courtship wins the lady." Stephen clarified. "They were acting very foolishly just now, so perhaps love is as blind as they say."

"Love? Old Morse must be sixty if he is a day," Roger objected. "He must have lost his wits, poor fellow."

"Do not scoff at love, Roger," Jane admonished. "Age or rank or fortune mean nothing to Cupid, who plants his arrow where he will, regardless of the consequences."

"How is it that you are such an expert on the subject, Jane?" Roger said without pausing to think. He immediately regretted it, for Jane's face clouded, and she looked down at her skates, ignoring his question.

"That is the one that felt a little loose, Stephen," she said, pointing to her left foot. The captain adjusted the strap and held out his hand to Jane.

"Shall we take another turn around the lake?"

Driven by a overwhelming desire to hold his wife in his arms, Roger stepped forward. "I had a fancy to take you for a spin myself, Jane. It has been a long time since we skated together."

For an instant, Roger thought she would refuse him. When she said nothing, the captain graciously offered his skates and went off to join the gentlemen for a glass of mulled wine. Roger quickly strapped them on and stood up. Jane followed suit but kept her eyes lowered.

Roger slipped an arm about her waist, and marvelled at how vibrant she felt, even beneath the thick woollen cape lined with fur. A jaunty fur bonnet covered her ears, and her gloves and scarf hid the rest of her except her unsmiling face, inscrutable under the light of the full moon.

They glided along in silence for a minute or two, then Roger ventured a comment about the amorous innkeeper and his *inamorata.*

"You must not laugh at them, Roger," Jane insisted. "Love does strange things to people . . . or so I hear," she added hastily. "We should rather envy them the happiness of finding love together so late in life."

The notion of envying fat old Mr. Morse and the aging nursemaid was so ludicrous that Roger was momentarily at a loss for words. There were uncomfortable implications to Jane's comment that he did not like to examine too closely.

"Well, I cannot agree with you there, my dear," he said finally. "I have been in love dozens of times, and I do not recall being driven to do anything strange."

Jane laughed mirthlessly, and he caught a note of cynicism in it. "Do not deceive yourself, Roger. You mistake love for lust. Surely you will not tell me it was love you felt for all those milkmaids, kitchen wenches, tenants' daughters, or barmaids at the King's Arms?"

"How do you know about all that?" Roger demanded, thoroughly shocked that his wife dared to speak so frankly about his youthful infatuations.

"How could I *not* know when you took no pains to hide any of it? Your philandering was common knowledge in the whole county."

Roger took a deep breath. He had never expected this plain speaking from his own wife and was at a loss to know how to respond. "That is all in the past, Jane," he explained, making light of it. "Youthful indiscretions, nothing more."

"That is precisely the point. You have just told me

you have been in love dozens of times, when in fact you know less about that tender emotion than our Mr. Morse. I wager you never loved poor Maud, either, though she clearly believed you did. In fact, I *know* you did not."

"Of course I did," Roger blurted out, his temper rising. "I wrote her love letters, so naturally I loved her."

Jane laughed again. "*Love* letters? If you believe those were love letters, Roger, you know less about love than I thought. Those letters were not about love, they were . . . ugh, they were gross and disgusting."

Roger was paralyzed by this speech, and conflicting emotions swept through his mind. They reached the far end of the lake and were halfway back when he regained his voice.

"What makes you think my letters were—as you claim—gross and disgusting?"

"Because I read one of them," she responded calmly, knocking the wind out of him again. "Maud herself sent it to me." She paused for a moment, then added in a different voice, "And if that is what you call *love*, I want none of it. *None* of it," she repeated vehemently, and Roger distinctly heard a catch in her voice.

Nothing more was said as they covered the rest of the way to the seats. Jane did not wait for him to unfasten her skates, and was gone before Roger could think of anything to say to repair the obvious damage those foolhardy letters had created in his life. She was right, he admitted, placing his skates on the bench and following her. The letters he had so thoughtlessly written to Maud were indeed grossly improper, and Roger was distressed that one of them had reached Jane's hands.

How could he have foreseen that? he wondered, looking around for his wife and not finding her. She seemed to have disappeared. He noticed that the rest of the skating party was breaking up. Both his sisters had retired inside and the nursemaids and governesses

were busy rounding up reluctant charges, most of
whom begged for one more circle around the lake.
The smallest ones were more easily persuaded, being
already tired and ready for bed. The older boys were
causing the most trouble and Roger had to intervene
before they reluctantly shed their skates and allowed
themselves to be herded inside.

Most of the adult guests had called for their carriages and were taking their leave of the marquess.
There seemed to be a sudden exodus from the lake
and as Roger glanced up at the huge full moon hanging like some magical lantern in the sky, he realized
why. It must be getting on towards midnight, and none
of the locals wanted to be caught anywhere near the
lake at midnight. Superstition was deeply rooted in
the area, particularly among the tenants, who had all
disappeared an hour ago.

Stephen and Tony Cheswick were the last to go,
shaking Roger's hand and making some passing joke
about the Trenton ghost chasing all the guests away.
The servants, under the watchful eye of the butler,
seemed to race against the clock to get chairs, tables,
bottles, empty dishes, and other items into the kitchen
before the big clock in the Abbey tower struck the
hour of midnight—the hour the ghost was rumoured
to rise from the lake.

Roger saw his friends into their carriages and then
glanced up at the tower, eerie in the moonlight. There
was light in Jane's chamber, he noticed, and strode
indoors, hoping none of his guests would require further entertainment that evening. The drawing room
was mercifully empty when he went upstairs, and Collins informed him that the only ones still up were his
father and the Earl of Penhallow, who had come in
earlier to indulge in a game of billiards.

The house was still and quiet, except for muffled
noises from the kitchen where the servants were settling the house for the night.

Roger sighed with relief. He wanted no distraction
from the task that lay before him. Somehow, some

way, he was going to persuade his wife that the depressing picture she seemed to have of him was not entirely accurate. Careless and philandering he had undoubtedly been. But she was wrong about one important thing. He did know something about love. Perhaps not as much as the portly old innkeeper, he thought with fleeting whimsy, but enough to know when he had been hit by Cupid's arrow.

And Roger was certain he had been hit. He could not imagine when it had happened, for he had not been conscious of the sting. But the pain and anxiety he now felt was uncannily like that of an arrow wedged firmly in his heart.

Chapter Nineteen

Cupid's Dart

From her window high up under the battlements, Jane gazed down on the scene that so recently had resembled a country fair. Gone were the crowds of noisy children, gone the guests who had flocked in record numbers to Jane's first big affair as mistress of Trenton Abbey. Gone also were the bustling servants who had kept the refreshments flowing, and the gaily coloured marquee under which the less energetic guests had sat to watch the antics of the skaters. All that remained were the barrels dotted around the lake still glowing with hot coals.

Jane sighed. The skating party had been an enormous success. She had attended this traditional Trenton Christmas Eve celebration every year of her life for as far back as she could remember. Only after Lady Trenton had succumbed to pneumonia had the skating parties ceased. Now they would begin again, under her auspices, and the Abbey would once more become the centre of social life it had always been. Jane had every reason to feel happy and content, but her heart was oddly heavy.

She did feel a glow of pride at her accomplishment. Her father had been proud, too, and had complimented her warmly, as had Lord Trenton. She had performed the impossible feat of keeping Augusta and Letitia relatively content, and the hordes of children free from any but the most minor mishaps. She had successfully played the hostess with all her guests, both gentry and tenant farmers, making sure they enjoyed the evening.

Jane shivered and drew her woollen robe more closely about her. And what about herself? she wondered, watching the servants carry the last few chairs into the house. Had she enjoyed her first social triumph as Lady of Trenton Abbey?

Her eyes were drawn to the icy expanse of lake. How peaceful it lay under the moonlight. Not a leaf, not a twig stirred in the cold night air. It was a scene frozen in time, and Jane had an eerie sense of being but a fleeting presence among the many skaters who, over the centuries, had left their ephemeral marks on the frozen lake. Her glance moved instinctively to the graveyard on the hill. There they lay, those phantom skaters, as peaceful as the lake upon which they had frolicked. As she and her guests had done tonight.

Had little Gavin been one of them? Her gaze slid back to the lake, and Jane knew in her heart that he had. In her mind's eye she saw him cavorting with other children on a Christmas Eve many many years ago. For some inexplicable reason, the little boy looked like Roger, tawny curls in charming disarray. And then suddenly he was gone. The happy image vanished and only the icy lake remained, a constant reminder of an atrocious deed.

Jane shook her head to clear away these unhappy thoughts. She was being morbid again. Only this afternoon, Elizabeth had accused her of the same thing when they had visited the graveyard to lay the wreath on Gavin's tomb.

She had yet to answer her own question. Had she enjoyed her first skating party? True, she had not done much skating herself, but had been pleasantly entertained in helping some of her younger guests find their feet on the ice. The memory of the children's shrieks of delight brought back Elizabeth's other reminder: She must present Roger with a son and heir.

Instinctively her hand settled on her belly. Was it her overactive imagination again, or did she feel a flutter of life beneath the flat surface? Too early to tell, but the notion filled her with joy.

She had avoided answering the question again, and Jane knew why. She had enjoyed the children, enjoyed the guests, certainly enjoyed skating with Stephen, and wishing—she realized with sudden clarity—that he had been Roger.

"Ah. Roger," she murmured, touching the window-pane with her fingers, and feeling the cold snake up her arm. Roger was the key to her happiness. She had looked forward to skating with him all evening, and when he finally approached her, she suspected he only did so to prevent her skating with Stephen again.

From then on, everything had gone wrong.

Perhaps it had been a mistake to mention Cupid's attack on old Mr. Morse. Stephen had understood instantly what was going on between the innkeeper and Mrs. Watson. He had been amused but not scornful. Stephen had known exactly what she meant when she spoke of the power of love.

Roger had scoffed at the two aging lovers. He had not understood at all, announcing brazenly that he had been in love dozens of times. Jane had felt her heart cringe as she listened to him. Even so, she should not have reacted so immoderately. What had she achieved by telling him he knew nothing of love, and using his letter to Maud as proof? That confession had been unwise, as was her outburst about wanting none of *that* kind of love.

She had made a mull of everything.

Worse yet, she might have made him so angry he would not come to her tonight. And Jane needed Roger to come to her. She wanted him to love her, if not with his heart, at least with his hands, and lips, and body. She yearned for him so intensely, it hurt.

And she wanted to tell him about the baby. Their very own baby. Their first-born. Perhaps the son and heir Elizabeth had reminded Jane that it was her duty to produce. But a little girl would be lovely, too. A sister for Abigail. There would be time for boys later. Lots of them. A dozen or so, she thought, feeling lightheaded and sick with apprehension.

What if Roger did not come?

The clock in the hall downstairs struck twelve, and Jane felt her throat tighten and a tear slide down her cheek. Her eyes fixed on the lake; she wondered how she could possibly bear living with Roger for the rest of her life without love.

She was distracted by a faint swirl of mist that had formed in the hollows of the Park and drifted towards the lake. The heated barrels had kept the fog at bay, but it now crept slowly down from the graveyard and onto the icy surface at the far end. Jane held her breath, enchanted by the sensuous movements of the mist.

Then she saw it, and her heart stood still.

A faint spiral of mist seemed to rise from the centre of the lake and pause, motionless, shimmering in the moonlight. Jane's head told her quite firmly that this was nothing but a wisp of stray mist that had detached itself from the blanket of moisture invading the lake. In her heart, things were not quite so simple. Even as she watched, the spiral grew denser and assumed—at least to her overwrought imagination—a human form. A *small* human form.

So enthralled was she with the apparition on the lake, that when the door opened behind her, Jane nearly jumped out of her skin.

It was Roger, and she noted immediately that he was wearing his robe. She knew what that meant. He was naked underneath and had obviously come to stay.

He hesitated, then closed the door behind him. "I did not mean to alarm you, my love," he said in that caressing tone he used when he had passion on his mind.

"Oh, Roger," Jane exclaimed, suddenly dizzy with the heady sight of him. "I am so glad you came. I have something important to show you. Do come over here." She reached out a hand impatiently and drew him to the window.

"You will catch cold standing here by the window,

Jane. Come to bed with me, and I'll warm these icy fingers for you."

"In a minute," Jane said impatiently. "I want you to see this first."

"What?"

"Over there. In the middle of the lake. Do you see it?" The spiral of mist was less distinct now, but still clearly visible to Jane.

Roger stared out of the window, but his expression told her he saw nothing unusual. "What is it, love?"

"Oh, you must see it, Roger. You *must*." Her voice quavered.

"I am trying, Jane, but all I see is some fog coming in off the lowland."

"There!" Jane repeated, pointing at the swirl of mist that had begun to move slowly off across the ice towards the graveyard.

Roger shook his head. "Sorry, my pet. If this is your ghost you want me to see, remember that it has never appeared to any male in the family. Ever. Only to females. And then only . . ." His voice trailed off and he gripped Jane's arms and turned her against him. "Are you telling me, Jane, that the ghost has appeared to you for a specific reason?"

Jane gurgled with laughter. "Are you referring to the local superstition that the appearance of the Trenton ghost heralds an addition to the family?"

"My mother swore it happened to her every time."

"But your father scoffed at her, did he not, as you are scoffing at me now?"

He gazed down at her, his eyes darkening from cobalt to almost black. "No, love, I do not scoff at your little ghost, and never will again if he has indeed brought good tidings to us tonight." The unspoken question in his voice hung there between them, waiting for her response.

Jane smiled. It felt good to be in his arms again. Cradled against him, she let her body mould itself to his, slowly relaxing into the familiar shape of him, letting his warmth soak into her chilled heart and set it aflame with love.

"Well? Has the cat run off with your tongue, love?"

They were so close that Jane could feel every breath he took, every heartbeat. It was exhilarating. She felt herself grow soft and warm inside; her own breath quickened in anticipation. If only she could confess her love, perhaps he would realize how important it was to her to be loved in return. Perhaps, being a man, he thought passion was enough, and Lord knew he had always been passionate with her. Even now she felt the evidence of his desire for her through the thick wool of their robes. She could not complain that Roger was cold. Perhaps she should not be complaining at all, she told herself wryly, a smile curling her lips.

"So? Is it true, you minx? Is that what that sly smile is all about?"

"Oh, Roger," she murmured, snuggling her face into the opening of his robe and breathing in the intoxicating male smell of him. Jane felt him shudder as she opened her lips and touched his warm skin tentatively with the tip of her tongue.

Against his protests, she raised her head and looked at him steadily. "There is something I must tell you, Roger. I am so sorry I made you angry this evening. I should not have said all the things I did about you."

"Hush, love, there is no need—"

"Oh, please, I need to say this. Perhaps you really have been in love dozens of time. How could I tell? I know so little about love myself. It was presumptuous of me to judge you. I beg you will forgive me."

He stared down at her for several moments and for a dreadful instant Jane thought he was angry again. Then Jane noticed that his eyes revealed an expression she had never seen in them before. It was not passion; she was accustomed to Roger's passion. Neither was it anger. There was an unfamiliar sweetness about her husband's gaze that made her breath catch in her throat. She could not drag her eyes away, and when he slowly bent his head, she raised her eager lips to receive his kiss, soft and gentle, and yes, almost loving in its tenderness.

"I have nothing to forgive, my love," he murmured against her mouth. "You were right on the mark, Jane. I knew nothing about love. Never having been in love before, how could I?"

For a paralyzing moment Jane held her breath. What had he said? Had she heard aright?

"Before?" she queried tentatively, not daring to hope.

"Before *you*, sweetheart." His lips brushed hers gently, unhurriedly, as if to savour a newly discovered sensation.

Jane's heart fluttered wildly. The implication of his words was too tantalizing to ignore.

"Are you telling me that . . ." She broke off, suddenly shy of this man who seemed to be changing before her eyes from passionate husband into tender lover. The longed-for lover of her dreams, she realized, hardly daring to breathe. She felt his smile tremble against her lips.

"I am saying that it is you, my pet, who taught me what love is. You were right, I never did love poor Maud, although I was convinced I did. I even told her I did, but it was not true."

"Hush, Roger, that is no longer important." Jane placed a finger over his lips to halt the flow of words which she knew must be painful to him.

"Oh, but it is, my dearest. This evening when you told me that old Mr. Morse had been slain by Cupid's arrow, I began to see what was before my eyes all this time. I scoffed at him because it all sounded so absurd, but when you said we should envy them for finding happiness, I knew you were right. And I admitted to myself that I did envy this old couple the love they shared."

"So?"

He grinned lopsidedly and planted a kiss on her nose. "Then it dawned on me that I had the same chance for happiness within reach." He drew her closer against him. "Right here in my arms, I should say. I should have seen it long ago, of course, but put it down to male obtuseness, my love. Because you truly are my love, Jane." His voice became husky as he nuzzled her ear and whispered, "I love you, Jane. It is a wonderful feeling. And if you can possibly love me, too, I shall have no reason to envy old Morse, now shall I?"

Jane could hardly contain her happiness. She threw her arms about Roger's neck and sighed. "Particularly since it is highly unlikely that Mrs. Watson can give him a son," she murmured dreamily.

Roger jerked his head up and stared at her. "Are you saying . . . ?"

"The little ghost's appearance only confirms what I already suspected," Jane said, conscious of a certain smugness in her voice. "I am with child, Roger. You are to be a father again."

Her lord's response to this announcement surpassed anything Jane could have wished for, and the clock downstairs struck two in the morning before she finally snuggled up within the circle of her husband's arms and dropped into a contented, well-deserved sleep.